Death of a
Robber Baron

Death of a
Robber Baron

A GILDED AGE MYSTERY

CHARLES O'BRIEN

KENSINGTON BOOKS
www.kensingtonbooks.com

KENSINGTON BOOKS are published by

Kensington Publishing Corp.
119 West 40th Street
New York, NY 10018

All Kensington titles, imprints, and distributed lines are available at special quantity discounts for bulk purchases for sales promotion, premiums, fund-raising, and educational or institutional use.

Special book excerpts or customized printings can also be created to fit specific needs. For details, write or phone the office of the Kensington Special Sales Manager: Kensington Publishing Corp., 119 West 40th Street, New York, NY 10018. Attn. Special Sales Department. Phone: 1-800-221-2647.

Kensington and the K logo Reg. U.S. Pat. & TM Off.

ISBN-13: 978-0-7582-8636-9
ISBN-10: 0-7582-8636-8
First Kensington Trade Paperback Printing: August 2013

eISBN-13: 978-0-7582-8637-6
eISBN-10: 0-7582-8637-6
First Kensington Electronic Edition: August 2013

10 9 8 7 6 5 4 3 2 1

Printed in the United States of America

For Elvy

Acknowledgments

I wish to thank Andy Sheldon for helpful computer services. I am grateful also to Gudveig Baarli for assisting with the maps, and to the professionals at Kensington Publishing who produced this book. My agent, Evan Marshall, and Fronia Simpson read drafts of the novel and contributed much to its improvement. Finally, my wife, Elvy, art historian, deserves special mention for her keen editorial eye and her unflagging support.

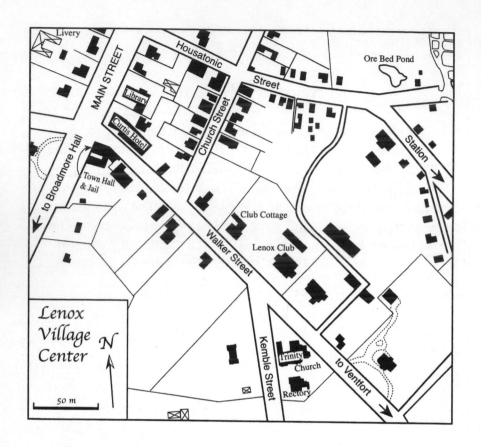

Lenox
Village
Center

N

50 m

Livery

MAIN STREET

Housatonic

Library

Curtis Hotel

Church Street

Street

Ore Bed Pond

Station

to Broadmore Hall

Town Hall
& Jail

Walker Street

Club Cottage

Lenox Club

Kemble Street

Trinity
Church

Rectory

to Ventfort

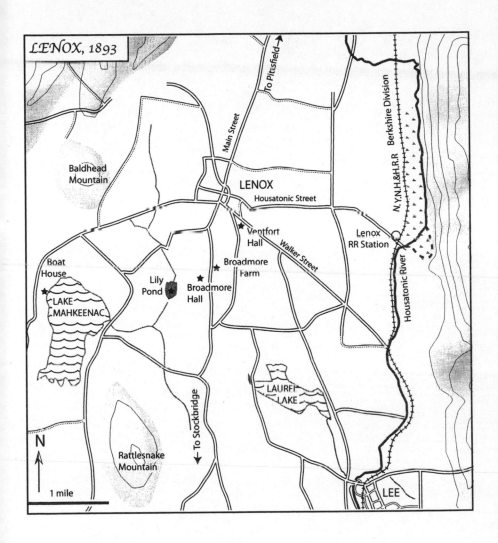

CHAPTER 1

Crisis

New York City, Christmas Eve, 1891

Pamela Thompson sat in the breakfast room of her four-story town house on West Tenth Street, quiet and sad. A clock ticked relentlessly on the wall. She drank the last drop of her morning coffee, gazed out the window, and sighed. Rain was falling steadily, stripping her backyard garden of its soft blanket of snow. The papers predicted a heavy downpour through most of the day, casting a pall over the preparations for Christmas. She had hoped that an infusion of holiday joy would lift her bleak spirit. On this day a year ago, her daughter, Julia, had died.

Her husband sat across the table, hidden behind a page of the *New York Times*. "More coffee, Jack?" she asked, then began to pour.

He replied with a belated, distracted grunt. Breakfast together these days was rare and brief. Jack would usually cool his coffee with cream, gulp it down, and hurry off to his office at the savings bank on Union Square. Today, an item in the paper had caught his interest, and he lingered at the table.

"What's so fascinating, Jack?"

He lowered the paper and stared as if surprised to see her

there. "Yesterday was Henry Jennings's sixtieth birthday. He rented the largest hall in the Union Club and had a huge, glittering party. It must have cost a small fortune. All the top politicians came and so did the cream of the business world. I would have loved to be there."

Pamela had heard that Jennings was greedy and ruthless, as well as rich. But she feigned polite interest. "What's special about him, compared to other successful businessmen?"

"He has an uncanny talent for making money, even where others adept at finance would fail." Eyes glowing, Jack spoke with almost religious awe of Jennings's triumphs, especially in copper mining. "He's called 'The Copper King' for good reason. He's also heavily invested in railroads and banks."

For a few more minutes they discussed plans for the day. She would work on this evening's holiday program at St. Barnabas Mission on Mulberry Street, a refuge for poor, abused women and children. He had meetings and other chores at the bank. They would spend Christmas Eve alone at home. He finished his coffee, gave her a peck on the cheek, and hurried off.

After breakfast Pamela took a tram to St. Barnabas. Caring for its clients gave her the personal satisfaction she lacked at home. In the mission's chapel volunteers were wrapping presents in bright colored paper and loading them onto a large table. A tall Christmas tree decorated with candles stood in one corner. Evergreens hung on the walls. That evening two hundred children and their parents from the poorest families in the city would gather to sing carols, light the Christmas tree, and distribute gifts.

Assisting the volunteers was Brenda Reilly, a fifteen-year-old Irish girl, one of the children served by the mission. Pamela had looked after her since she was a toddler while her mother, Monica, was working ten hours a day, six days a week, in a garment factory. Four years ago, in January, Brenda's father, Dennis Reilly, had killed Monica in a domestic dispute and had been put in prison. Brenda then became Pamela's ward and moved into the Thompson home, where she lived among the servants while attending school.

Brenda finished wrapping a gift and now approached Pamela.

As she hugged the girl, she suddenly felt a profound sense of loss and began to cry.

"What's the matter, ma'am?" The girl handed Pamela a clean handkerchief.

"Thank you, Brenda." Pamela wiped tears from her eyes. "A year ago this very day I lost my daughter, Julia, to influenza."

"I remember her passing, ma'am. She was my age, a beautiful girl. I'm sorry."

In a few moments Pamela regained control of her feelings and returned the handkerchief. "Unfortunately, Brenda, I can't join the party tonight. My husband and I will honor the memory of Julia at home."

Pamela wished that she and Jack could have taken part. But he would be busy all day at the bank—catching up on paperwork. In the evening, he would be frazzled and not in the mood for high-pitched children's voices.

To draw her husband into a holiday spirit, she would persuade him to join her for a festive choral Evensong at the nearby Church of the Ascension on West Tenth Street and Fifth Avenue. Afterward, they would have a quiet holiday dinner at home. Brenda would spend the night with friends.

At noon Pamela left for home. She prepared gifts for the servants, inspected the butler's cleaning and decoration of the main rooms, and checked on the cook's progress with the roast lamb. Pamela set the table for two.

Dining alone tonight should bring her and Jack closer together. Over the past several months they had lived like strangers under the same roof. With that distressing thought on her mind, she went to her room to dress, determined to look her best. Her personal maid joined her, and they set to work. An hour later, the maid announced, "You're beautiful tonight. Mr. Thompson will surely notice."

Pamela stood before a full-length mirror and gazed with approval at her red satin gown, pearl necklace, and diamond ring. Her thick, lustrous black hair, perhaps her chief asset, was set in a chignon. On closer inspection she detected a few thin silver hairs at each temple, but she declared them to be attractive, natural accents. Aside from certain worry lines on her brow, her complexion at the age of thirty-seven was still clear and creamy. Her dark blue eyes gazed back at her with good humor and generous approval, oddly unmarked by the horrors they had witnessed during her work in the tenements. Her figure was still well proportioned and slim enough for her to do without a corset. Finally, she studied her hands and groaned. Despite frequent, generous application of cold cream, they were still red and raw from chores at the mission. A sour thought flitted through her mind: Why bother? Jack probably wouldn't notice anyway.

She gave herself an encouraging smile, turned from the mirror, and thanked the maid.

When all was ready, she and Jack went to the evening service at the church. The music was glorious. While the choir sang passages from the *Messiah,* Jack closed his eyes and seemed transported out of his usual anxious attitude. Pamela felt encouraged. Things were going better than she had anticipated.

Late on Christmas Eve, Pamela and Jack sat down to dinner. The table was covered with fine linen and set with their best china, silver, and crystal. Green garlands and red bows hung on the walls. They went through the motions of holiday celebration with joy on their faces, but they were intensely aware of their daughter's absence. For a year, they had coped with grief in different ways. Pamela had increased her work with poor, battered women and children. Jack had thrown himself into financial investments to the point that they consumed him.

This had led to serious tension between them. Each reproached the other for a lack of understanding. After Monica's murder, Jack had only grudgingly agreed to sign Brenda's guardianship papers and allow her to live in their home. With Julia's death his attitude hardened. "Mind you," he had insisted, "Miss Reilly is to remain in the servants' quarters and in no way take the place of our daughter. The memory of Julia is dear to me. I'll not have a substitute diminish it." He had appeared about to become emotional.

"I understand," Pamela had said, but with a mental reservation. She believed that Brenda would eventually win over Jack and gain an honored place in the family.

To please him tonight Pamela had lighted a candle at a place set for Julia. The meal began, however, with awkward attempts at conversation followed by equally distressing moments of silence while the servants plied them with holiday dishes. When the servants finally withdrew, Jack couldn't hold back his secret.

"I must tell you, Pamela, that I've found an extraordinary investment with Henry Jennings. We will become incredibly rich. You will have a new and grander house on Fifth Avenue, and I'll join the Union Club and consort with the likes of J. P. Morgan."

Pamela tried in vain to conceal her concern. During the past year, Jack had made similar announcements, followed by disappointing results. He gave her a reproachful smile. "You doubt me. Well, you heard me speak this morning of the respect that Jennings enjoys among the wealthy and powerful in this country."

"Yes," she granted. "Most of them share his values."

Missing her irony, he lowered his voice, as if afraid that servants were listening. "I've recently discovered that he's secretly investing in a new company, Copper Mountain. It's going to mine a fantastically rich vein of copper in Michigan's Upper Peninsula. Investors who buy in early, before the price of shares skyrockets, will make fortunes."

Pamela sensed a dangerous enthusiasm in his voice. She asked guardedly, "How is this an attractive opportunity for you?"

His tone turned defensive. "A few months ago, when I was a guest at the Union Club, a lawyer for Jennings took me aside and confided that the new company was initially offering shares to selected buyers, like J. P. Morgan, at a discounted price. I'm one of the chosen few. When the company sells to the public, our shares are bound to double and triple in value. In addition, we can expect annual dividends of twenty cents on the dollar. Most investments yield only three to five percent."

"So did you go ahead and buy shares in this company?" Pamela tried hard to keep her voice level.

"Yes, I bought twenty thousand dollars' worth."

"And where did you find that much money? It's a breathtaking sum, more than you earn in ten years. Was it lying under a rock in our garden?" She was tempted to pound the table and shriek with outrage.

"Don't be sarcastic, Pamela. It's unbecoming. I took fifteen thousand dollars from the trust fund that I administer for you, and I borrowed the rest with this house as security. The shares I purchased and the income from them will go back into your fund."

"Jack! Have you lost your wits! I can't believe you've emptied my trust fund and mortgaged our home. This harebrained scheme rests on the doubtful integrity of Henry Jennings. Granted, he has been successful in business and is very rich, but I've heard that he's a false, predatory rascal. A few years ago I noticed him in the newspapers, railing against his workers' demand for higher wages and safer conditions in his Michigan copper mines. They'd gone on strike, and he'd hired scabs to replace them. Frankly, I wouldn't trust him with a dime."

"You have no head for business, Pamela. When we married, we agreed that you should manage the household; I would take care of our finances. If you were in charge of our money, you'd give it all to the poor. Tonight, we'd be outside in the cold, begging in the streets." He paused to let his remark sink in. "Jennings wouldn't have gained his wealth and respect if he behaved like a larcenous thug. It's in his interest to make this new company successful. He has put his own money into it."

"And I'm sure that he can easily and secretly take it out." She shook her head. "Jack, I'm not a simple, shuttered housewife. I know the value of money much better than you. Honest wealth comes from service to others for the common good. Jennings and his kind strive only to enrich themselves, any way they can. Their wealth is a monstrous sham."

Jack shook his head. "How can you condemn Jennings's wealth out of hand? Your own father was a wealthy man."

She stared at her husband with a mixture of anger and pity. "Unlike Jennings, my father was an honest man, a professional electrical engineer. His inventions literally brought light into the lives of many. He never cheated anyone. The trust fund that you've despoiled is his legacy to me. You were supposed to administer it in my interest." Her voice was becoming shrill. She paused, calmed herself, then spoke slowly and carefully. "Jack, you have grievously insulted my intelligence and betrayed my trust. The very least you could have done was to consult me."

He flinched as if she had hit him. "I see, Pamela, that we can't have a reasonable conversation about this matter. In fact, for some time we've been at odds on almost everything. Perhaps the death of our daughter has distracted you. And I suppose it has affected me as well. I often can't concentrate on business." He met her eye, measured his words. "I've thought this over. It would be best for both of us if I were to move tomorrow into furnished private rooms near the bank. The butler will look after this property, and I'll continue to cover your expenses."

His words came as no surprise, but she grasped them slowly. "I'm sorry, Jack, that our marriage has come to this, and on a blessed Christmas Eve of all days. But so be it. I fear for our future."

"Then good night, Pamela." Slowly, deliberately, he folded his napkin and rose from the table. His chin was rigid, his lips tight. He nodded stiffly and left the room.

For a long moment Pamela sat fixed to her chair, listening to his heavy footsteps in the hall, then lighter on the stairs. Finally his door shut. She stared at his empty chair and began to wonder what to do. At first, nothing came to mind. Minutes passed fruitlessly. She began to feel utterly abandoned. Then she said to herself, "I must seek help. I'll need a lawyer."

CHAPTER 2

Catastrophe

22 March 1892

At home this dull, gray morning, Pamela Thompson kept herself busy with household chores, lest she give in to her worst fears. A few minutes ago, her lawyer, Mr. Jeremiah Prescott, had telephoned that he had crucial information. Could he meet her? She had agreed that he should come at midmorning.

Her husband, Jack, had deceived her about their finances. On Christmas Eve, when she had challenged him, he had grown testy and left her. The next day at church, a friend, Peter Yates, had recommended that she consult his employer, Mr. Prescott. A detective as well as a lawyer, Prescott could investigate the family's financial situation and propose remedies.

A few days after speaking with Yates, Pamela had visited Prescott in his office on Irving Place near Gramercy Park. Dealing with him had seemed risky. He was rumored to be an unpatriotic freethinker. Still, even his detractors granted that he was a capable investigator and would take on domestic conflicts that more respectable lawyers avoided.

While describing her predicament, she had studied him closely. His brown hair was only just beginning to turn gray.

His face was clean-shaven, his body lithe and muscular. He looked ten years younger than his age, fifty-three.

To her pleasant surprise, she had found no outward signs of vice in him. His lively, bluish gray eyes regarded her with respect but otherwise revealed nothing of his inner self. His price was reasonable, so she had hired him.

Now a servant broke into Pamela's recollections. "It's ten o'clock, madam. Your visitor has just arrived."

Pamela hastened to meet him in the parlor. "What do you have to report, Mr. Prescott?" Her voice trembled in spite of herself.

He smiled sympathetically. "As you suspect, madam, your husband lost heavily in shares of a bogus Michigan copper mine."

"Did Henry Jennings truly deceive him?"

"Yes," Prescott replied. "Jennings had paid dearly to open the mine in an area of great promise. But his engineers soon told him that the vein of copper quickly thinned out to nothing. Rather than give up the project and take the loss, Jennings sold the rights to a dummy company, of which he was the hidden owner, and offered shares for sale. His glowing, false prospectus deceived many investors, including your husband. Jennings walked away with a huge profit before the company collapsed. The investors lost everything."

"How much damage has been done to us thus far?"

"Unfortunately, your husband purchased with your home as collateral. To recoup his losses, he has continued to play the stock market—recklessly, in my opinion. Recently, he lost again. I've heard that his job at the savings bank is in jeopardy. As a detective, I must suspect that he embezzled."

"This is terrible!" she exclaimed. "We'll be ruined. Is there any way to punish Jennings and recover the stolen money?"

"None that is legal."

"Then someone among the investors might take it upon

himself to seek justice outside the law." Her voice shook with anxiety. "Jack has recently bought a pistol."

Prescott nodded. "When I learned about the pistol, I had him followed. He stalked Jennings but couldn't find an opportunity to confront him. Jennings is frequently away on trips to his mines and railroads."

"The devil must guard the rogue." Her gaze drifted to a wedding portrait of her husband, a decent, upright man. Sadness mixed with pity nearly overwhelmed her. "How is Jack coping? He must be desperate."

"I'm afraid so," Prescott replied. "He has given up the idea of revenge, but he now seems bent on punishing himself. During the past few days, his movements have become erratic. He frequents a brothel, takes long walks late at night, eats irregularly, and drinks more whiskey than he should. I don't know how he'll survive."

Prescott searched Pamela's face, as if uncertain whether to continue.

"Don't hold anything back. I must know the worst."

"Then I must tell you that he'll soon go bankrupt, thereby threatening the loss of your home and all your other joint assets."

Pamela struggled to take in what Prescott had just told her. She had expected it, but nonetheless it shocked her.

"Are you well, madam?" Prescott gazed at her solicitously.

"I feel distressed that my husband has betrayed me. I should confront him. Do you agree?"

He nodded. "You must immediately get a legal separation to protect your assets from his creditors. I've prepared the documents to begin the legal process. He must sign them."

"I see no other course. Let's go to his office at the bank."

"Do you want me to accompany you?"

"That might be a good idea. He would take you seriously."

* * *

When Pamela and Prescott arrived at the bank, police were blocking the main entrance on Union Square. With Pamela at his side, Prescott approached a uniformed officer whom he recognized and asked what had happened.

"A man has just shot himself." The officer added firmly, "For the time being, we can't let anyone in or out."

Prescott turned to Pamela. "It's probably Jack."

"My God! I pray that it isn't him."

Prescott said to the officer, "The dead man is most likely this woman's husband, the bank cashier. I'm her lawyer. We could be helpful to the investigation."

The officer mulled over this information, then waved them in. They made their way to the office of Mr. Fisher, the bank's president. A private detective from the Pinkerton agency met them at the door. Prescott introduced Pamela and asked, "What happened?"

"Mr. Thompson has shot himself," the Pinkerton replied evenly. "The bank had hired me to investigate him. I discovered that he had embezzled bank funds. Mr. Fisher summoned him to the office with me present. I presented my findings. He offered no defense. Fisher then accused him of stealing money from the bank and ordered me to call in the police. Thompson pulled a pistol from his pocket and shot himself." The Pinkerton turned to Pamela. "Do you wish to see the body?"

"Yes." She felt herself growing numb.

Covered by a sheet, the body still lay on the floor where it had fallen. Prescott asked, "Are you ready? It will be gruesome."

She nodded. The Pinkerton pulled back the sheet.

"It's Jack," she said under her breath. Suddenly, the room began to sway. Her knees gave way. She felt light-headed.

Prescott held her by the shoulder and lowered her into a chair. "Are you well, madam?"

She breathed deeply. Then tears filled her eyes. "Thank you," she managed to say. "I'll be all right in a minute. Poor Jack! What a dreadful end to his life. If I'd come an hour earlier, I might have saved him."

Prescott looked her in the eye. "Don't blame yourself, madam. This was his choice, the last of a series of poor choices. He could have shot himself at any time. You could not have stopped him."

Leaving the building, they were accosted by Mr. Fisher, the bank's president, and the Pinkerton detective. Fisher glowered and said to the detective, loudly enough for Pamela to hear, "Thompson's wife probably got some of the bank's assets from her husband. Investigate her."

The detective fixed Pamela in a cool, inscrutable gaze, then said to the president, "Don't worry, sir. I'll pursue her all the way to hell. She won't get away with a penny."

CHAPTER 3

A Ray of Hope

22 March 1893

In New York's Marble Cemetery on Second Street, Pamela and her lawyer Prescott walked the path to a grave, leaning into a brisk, cold breeze. While Prescott stood nearby, hat in hand, head bowed, Pamela gazed thoughtfully at the site. Last year, she had buried her husband here in the family plot. Next to his name on the gravestone was an empty space for hers. It would remain blank.

Grieving had been mostly dry-eyed. She had refused to wear black. Since he had killed himself before they could be legally separated, he had left her a crushing legacy of debt and financial ruin. For several months, she had also had to defend herself in court and at the bar of public opinion from Mr. Fisher's vindictive accusation that she had connived at her husband's embezzlement.

She emerged a free woman but with a tarnished reputation. Still, the worst was behind her. From now on she would only look forward. As she left the grave, Prescott fell in step beside her.

"What will you do now, madam?"

From her financial wreckage, Prescott had saved a seedy boardinghouse in the Lower East Side of Manhattan. She had moved in as manager and shared a single, top floor room with Brenda. It had two sleeping alcoves, a table, two chairs, and little else.

"I'll continue feeding my boarders and cleaning their rooms. Somehow, I must pay off the rest of Jack's debts. I also feel obliged to pay for Brenda Reilly's books—she's legally my ward and also my best friend and lives with me. She must complete her schooling."

Prescott looked askance.

"You're right," she continued. "I haven't any money, nor should I borrow. I'll have to earn it. I have no idea how. The boardinghouse barely breaks even."

They walked in heavy silence to the cemetery gate. Prescott engaged her eye. "Would you consider working for my agency?"

She stared quizzically at him. He seemed slightly embarrassed, as if thinking she might regard his proposal as inappropriate. Why had he asked to join her at the cemetery? She hardly knew him personally, though he had helped her investigate Jack's secret life and violent death and had defended her interests in court. Since then he had advised her on financial matters, charging her much less than the going rate for New York lawyers.

That bothered her. Was he putting her in debt to him and would he later take advantage of her? Still, her financial situation was so desperate that she had suppressed her fears and accepted his services.

"I'm serious," he went on. "My offer might take you by surprise. But I sense that you're ready to move on." He paused, while he opened the gate for her. "For a start, I need an assistant, preferably female, to guard Macy's jewelry department. You would blend in with the men and women who shop there. You are observant. You also need the money—beginning at fifty dollars a month. We've already worked together and gotten to know each other. Think about it."

"I'm grateful for your offer," she replied. "I'll consider it for a few days, then give you my decision."

He closed the gate behind them. "By the way, I should warn you. Brenda Reilly's father, Dennis, has been paroled from prison."

"Should I be alarmed?" A tremor ran through her body.

"You must be alert. He surely nurses a grudge against you for putting him in prison. Still, he's under a court's supervision, so he might show restraint." Prescott gestured to his coach. "May I take you home? City streets can be dangerous."

"No, thank you," she replied gently. "A brisk walk will clear my mind. Besides, I have a blackjack and a walking stick. My husband insisted that I carry them for protection while I was working at St. Barnabas Mission in such a dangerous part of the city."

"I understand." Prescott tipped his hat and drove off.

On the way to her boardinghouse early that afternoon, Pamela stopped to visit with her friend Peter Yates. Semiretired, he was Jeremiah Prescott's senior clerk and legal reference librarian. In his seventies he remained mentally alert and well-informed.

More than a year ago, when she had needed a lawyer, he had introduced her to Prescott. Initially, Yates had handled most of the details of her case. Later, as it grew more serious, Prescott had played a more active role but had revealed little about himself. Before she could accept his offer of a job, she needed to know him better. She hoped that Yates would offer a cup of hot tea to take the chill out of her bones—and answer a few questions.

His niece, Miss Amy Steele, led her to his study. "He's in good health today," she said brightly, "and will be happy to see you. I'll bring tea." Pamela knocked, and he invited her into his cozy scholar's den. When the tea arrived, he poured for both of them.

"What can you tell me about Mr. Jeremiah Prescott, the man, the person?" Pamela asked. "He has invited me to work for him. I know he was born into a wealthy family, fought in the war, graduated from Columbia, and became a rich, successful lawyer in New York. But he shares those characteristics with dozens of other gentlemen."

Yates nodded and offered her milk and sugar. "I've worked for him for twenty years and know him well. In fact, he joined the Union army at eighteen over his parents' strong objections and was wounded at Gettysburg. He convalesced, stubbornly returned to service, and left the army in 1865 as a captain."

Pamela sniffed. "Am I to conclude that he was a 'patriot' and had a taste for heroics and violence?"

"Yes, at first. But he changed—or, rather, the war changed him. He has since rarely spoken of it and then only with revulsion. Discharged from the army, he spent a year abroad—to recover his sanity, he used to say. After graduating from Columbia in 1870, he studied law and opened a practice in New York. Then he married a young, wealthy society lady, and within a decade he became rich and discontented."

"Discontented? Why?" She tasted the tea and stirred in a little more sugar.

"I'm not privy to his inner life. He doesn't talk about it. Frankly, I don't know what he believes or disbelieves concerning God, the purpose of life, and other big religious issues."

Pamela remarked, "I've heard he's a cynic, believes in nothing, and trusts nobody."

Yates shrugged. "At least, that seems to be his attitude toward politicians and their friends in business. During the war he became aware of their rampant profiteering and other corruption in war contracts. Since the war, he has grown even more critical of social injustice, especially the enormous, growing gap between rich and poor. But he doesn't climb onto a soapbox and denounce abuses as our present-day radicals do. He continues to practice law among the wealthy, while working without compensation for the poor."

"He seems to be an enigma. How does that affect his family life?"

"You are bound to wonder. His wife, Gloria, is fond of high society while Prescott despises its conventions. Over several years, they drifted apart. Finally, in 1890 they agreed to a legal separation. I worked out the details. At that time, their son, Edward, was sixteen and attended a private school. He's now a student, at Williams College in Williamstown, Massachusetts, and keeps in touch. She lives in their New York City house and spends the summer on the coast in Newport, Rhode Island. He moved into a comfortable apartment above his office and built a getaway cabin near Lenox, Massachusetts, in the Berkshire Hills."

"He seems at odds with much of the world around him. Is he a terribly lonely man?"

Yates gazed thoughtfully into his cup. "He smiles readily, but he doesn't let people get close to him. I can't say that he's lonely. He has male sporting friends and also seems to enjoy the company of independent, spirited women from outside high society, including a few actresses and singers."

Pamela met his eye. "And how do you judge him?"

Yates smiled. "He's knowledgeable, considerate of others, and generous of his time and money. I've found him to be a fair-minded and just man to work for."

Pamela finished her tea. "Thank you, Peter. Now I must get home before dark." She paused with a nagging afterthought. "Please forgive my curiosity. If I were to work for Mr. Prescott, is there anything I should know about his wife?"

"I understand your concern," Yates replied. "I believe Gloria is a presence in his life, but he doesn't allow her to influence his business. They meet occasionally and share custody of their son. She's an indifferent mother and a spendthrift. I've been instructed to watch her closely."

"How do they feel toward each other?"

"There's no love between them. Still, she resents having lost him."

"Frankly, I need to know what kind of person she is."

"A rich, beautiful, cultivated woman who demands constant admiration. Be forewarned. Her claws are sharp. She will use them on anyone who challenges her. If you go to work for her husband, you may hear from her."

"You've been helpful, Peter. I'll now go forward with my eyes wide open."

By the time Pamela reached her street, the sun was setting. She quickened her steps. The last hundred yards was a gauntlet of sinister, rude men, clustered in front of decrepit hotels and boardinghouses. The scent of urine and stale alcohol fouled the air. Again and again, men deliberately blocked the sidewalk, forcing her into the filthy street. Their obscene comments and gestures met and followed her. She grew hot with anger but controlled her temper and pressed straight ahead.

Her boardinghouse was soon in sight, and she relaxed. Though in need of repair, it was the most decent building in the block and her only possession. Years ago, when the neighborhood's residents had still been honest working people, Jack had bought the building for her as an investment, claiming that the neighborhood was destined to improve, and that her building would gain in value. In the meantime, he had turned it into a boardinghouse and hired a manager and a cook to run it. His calculations had failed badly. The city's recent wave of immigration had carried many destitute men, women, and children into this neighborhood. Others came from the Five Points slum, where urban renewal had forced out the poor. The value of Pamela's boardinghouse had plummeted.

In September, when the ailing manager had died, Pamela had temporarily taken on the job. She had restored order to the house's finances, evicted a few unruly guests, and brought the rest under control. Brenda's help had reduced some expense. Still, despite Pamela's best efforts, the house's prospects were discouraging.

Suddenly she sensed a movement behind her. Before she could react, a rough hand clamped over her mouth and a strong arm gripped her over the chest and dragged her struggling into a dark, narrow alley. She couldn't see her assailant, but she felt that he was small and wiry. He stank of tobacco and probably hadn't bathed in a month or more.

"Bitch!" he growled. "For years I've waited for this moment. You'll be sorry you ever crossed me. After I finish with you, I'll take back my daughter, Brenda."

Fresh from prison, Dennis Reilly was in a murderous frame of mind. Pamela felt panic coming, but she fought it off. Still, there was little she could do. She couldn't reach her blackjack, and she had dropped her walking stick.

As her assailant dragged her farther into the alley, he loosened his grip over her mouth. She bit hard into one of his fingers. He swore an oath, and his grip loosened more. She could now free an arm and lift it up. She seized a long steel pin from her hair and began stabbing over her shoulder at his face. He leaped back and threw wild punches at her. She ducked beneath them and stabbed him again and again in the groin. He screamed like a wounded wild animal and fled down the alley.

She straightened up, leaned back against the wall, and gulped air. Her legs felt weak. The screaming attracted people to the alley's entrance. A woman ventured in and said with a heavy Irish accent, "May I help you, ma'am?" Pamela nodded and took her arm, and they walked the rest of the way to the boardinghouse.

"He's a mean one," the woman said. "He just got out of jail and moved into the neighborhood. We think he spies for the police. You hurt his pride. So you'd better not walk alone on this street. He'll watch for you and be more cautious the next time."

At the boardinghouse, Pamela thanked the woman and asked if she could offer her something.

"No, ma'am. We help one another as best we can."

Once inside, Pamela breathed a sigh of relief and climbed up to her room in the attic. Brenda was there, reading a book.

"Good God! Where've you been?" She stared at Pamela in disbelief.

Pamela looked in the mirror. Her hair was in disarray, and her upper lip was swelling. There were two dark welts on her face. Her blouse was torn off her shoulder.

"Your father attacked me." Pamela described the incident. "You must take care. He's looking for you."

"The beast! Why isn't he still in prison?" The young woman shook with rage.

Pamela replied in a calming tone, "I'll find out why he's been released." She felt too tired, too discouraged to cry, so she washed with cold water and changed to a fresh blouse. She lay down on her bed, promised herself to watch vigilantly over Brenda, then drove the incident from her mind and rested for a few minutes.

She recalled the visit to the cemetery and Jeremiah Prescott. His offer made her feel uneasy. There must be dozens of women better qualified to be a detective than she. So why had he chosen her? He might have thought she was desperate and in need of charity. How demeaning! Or, had he lusted for her? As his assistant, she might have to submit to his passion. But that seemed farfetched. He hadn't made improper advances to her thus far. To judge from his reputation, he already had a stable of beautiful young women to please him. What could attract him to a poor, nearly forty-year-old bedraggled widow?

These thoughts disturbed her rest, but she couldn't banish them. So she put up her hair, tied on her apron, and went downstairs with Brenda to set the table for the evening meal. Besides managing and cleaning the house, she also served meals.

A dozen boarders soon arrived and took their accustomed places. Many were poor and elderly, and this was their "home." For the third evening, a pair of pale-faced, shifty-eyed young men came to the table. Were they recently released from prison? Pamela wondered. From bits of their conversation she understood that they were "looking into a job." One of them stared at her. "Had a fight with your boyfriend?" he asked with a smirk.

She gave him a gimlet eye. "Yes," she replied. "If you think I look bad, you should see him."

The young man was amused and thereafter treated her with more respect.

When everyone was seated, Pamela ladled a thick pea soup into their bowls. Brenda passed a basket of dark brown bread and poured tea into their tin mugs. The two women then stepped back to the sideboard. They would eat afterward.

Conversation at the table was sparse, but one of the older men—a Mr. Mason—recounted his adventures in the Civil War. Tonight he claimed to have marched with General Sherman through Georgia. On the previous night he had said he was with General Grant in Virginia at the same time. The two young men glanced at each other and loudly snickered.

The older man reddened with embarrassment, his eyes narrowed, and he seized a bread knife from the table. The two young men stiffened and reached into their pockets, ostensibly for knives. Pamela patted Mason on the shoulder and took the knife from his hand. Then she spoke in a friendly way to the two young men. "Mr. Mason actually served under both Grant and Sherman—of course at different times."

With an uneasy peace restored, she brought pudding and ginger cookies to the table. Afterward, the guests drifted away. At the door Pamela confronted a stout, blank-faced woman. "The spoon, Martha." The woman didn't protest, simply pulled a spoon from her blouse and handed it over. "Thank you, Martha." This ritual took place every evening.

After Pamela and Brenda ate their meal, they cleared the table and washed the dishes and tableware. Sour faced, the cook inspected their work and found nothing amiss. The rest of the evening Brenda spent with her book. For an hour Pamela wrote in her journal, then went to bed. The room was cold, so she slept poorly. Prescott's offer surfaced in her mind. In fact, she realized, she was better prepared for guarding Macy's jewelry than she had initially thought. At the boardinghouse, after all, one of her tasks was to keep track of the tableware—cheap stuff by Macy's standard. But it was valuable enough for the cook, the kitchen maid, and the diners at the boardinghouse table to gladly steal it—if they could.

As live-in manager, Pamela had become vigilant and perceptive, often warding off a theft before it could take place. And she had grown more tactful, resolving disputes, allowing a suspected thief to save face. But she also had to retrieve stolen pieces. That had led to distressing encounters with thieves. One of them had threatened her with a knife.

She had found no friends among the guests. Some were wary of her. Others resented her good breeding and her cultivated speech. The food was barely edible, and her room was unheated. If she complained, she received no sympathy from the flint-eyed cook, Mrs. Baker. "It's your house. You can leave or sell it anytime you like."

Then, the neighborhood seemed to become more dangerous

by the day. Her assailant's stench still lingered in her nostrils. He would be watching for her, night after night, and would eventually pounce on her. Brenda was another worry. Her father might take her by surprise on the way to or from school.

As Pamela lay on her cot and weighed these thoughts, Prescott's offer looked more attractive by the minute. She would speak to him tomorrow.

CHAPTER 4

A New Beginning

23 March

The next morning, Pamela awoke to doubts about her decision. But she put them aside. As she left the boardinghouse, a spasm of fear gripped her heart. Dennis Reilly might lie in wait. But after walking a block without an incident, she felt relieved. Perhaps he was nursing his wounds in some miserable hovel and thinking of all the dreadful things he'd do to her later. To be on the safe side, Brenda had gone by cab to her school. A less expensive arrangement would have to be made soon.

Pamela gingerly approached the door to Prescott's law office, screwed up her courage, and knocked. While investigating her husband, she had often come to these rooms that Prescott shared with two associates. A clerk opened the door and showed her into the parlor where she and Prescott usually met. It was the antechamber to his private office, which she had never seen.

While waiting, she studied the familiar hangings on the walls. An engraving of a Raphael *Madonna and Child* showed the taste of a cultivated man. A Columbia College diploma certified his familiarity with science, philosophy, and the liberal arts. But neither the pictures nor the diploma told her much about the man's character.

Over a year ago, when they had been alone together in the parlor, he had begun to call her Pamela. In public, it was always Mrs. Thompson. In private once, she had asked him, "How shall I address you?"

"Just call me Prescott, as others do. My given name, Jeremiah, conjures up the Old Testament and a mighty prophet's dire message to a hard-necked people. That's not at all how I think of myself—nor want to be thought of."

A clerk now interrupted Pamela's recollections. "Mr. Prescott will be with you in a minute."

Shortly afterward, he walked into the parlor, then stopped in his tracks, and stared at her. "What's happened to you?"

"Dennis Reilly attacked me yesterday." She had tried unsuccessfully to conceal the bruises and the swollen lip.

He sat facing her. "Give me the details."

She briefly described the assault, then added, "This morning, I asked neighbors about Reilly. They hadn't seen him since the incident and didn't know where he lived."

"He may lie low for a few days, until his wounds heal." Prescott tilted his head thoughtfully. "What exactly is his grudge against you?"

"How well do you know Brenda Reilly's story?"

"She's the young Irish girl, your ward, who lives with you in the boardinghouse. I gather that Dennis Reilly is her father."

Pamela nodded. "The story is painful to tell. And it isn't over. It also involves more than Brenda, her father, and me. So you should probably hear it."

"I sense as much. Please continue."

"Brenda was a bone of contention between Dennis Reilly and his wife, Monica, poor, illiterate Irish peasants who married in this country. They soon had different aspirations for their only child, Brenda. When she was eleven, her father, a clever but often unemployed man, insisted that she should go to work in a garment factory and bring money home. Herself a garment worker, Monica protested that their daughter needed an education to get a better job with more pay. Dennis also demanded that Monica give him her income. She refused, instead spending much of it on Brenda's schoolbooks and tuition. Finally, Monica objected to him wasting money on drink in a neighborhood tavern.

"One day, while I was working at St. Barnabas Mission, a woman reported that the Reillys were fighting in their room. Could I put a stop to it? I knew them better than anyone else. So I said I'd try.

"With the blackjack in my bag, I ran to the tenement house, collecting a patrolman on the way. I left him waiting on the sidewalk. I said I'd call him if he were needed. The Reilly family lived on the top floor. As I was climbing the stairs to their room, I heard a girl scream. The door was ajar, and I stepped inside. Monica was lying on the floor, her face bruised and bleeding. Her husband appeared drunk and was viciously kicking her.

" 'You sneaky cow!' he bellowed. 'Where've you hidden my money?'

"Brenda was screaming at him and trying to pull him away. I shouted for him to stop. Instead, he threw his daughter across the room, sprawling. He pulled a knife from his pocket, cursed me by all the devils in hell, and charged.

"I stepped aside. As he staggered by, I hit his head with my blackjack. He fell to the floor unconscious. I ran to an open window and called to the patrolman waiting in the street. Within minutes, Dennis was on his way to jail and his wife to a hospital, where she later died."

"Was their quarrel solely about money?" Prescott asked, as if he knew the answer.

"No," Pamela replied hesitantly, "there was more. Before she died, Monica said that her daughter at eleven was tall and strong and quite pretty. Dennis sometimes touched and spoke to her indecently. Brenda had grown afraid of him.

"On the day of the fight, she had been home from school reading a book. Her father came from the neighborhood tavern in an ugly mood. He pulled the book from her hands, threw it out the window, and attacked her. She was fighting him off when Monica returned from work. Enraged, she seized a frying pan and hit her husband again and again. In the end, he rallied and beat her savagely."

Prescott shook his head. "Surely the devil was in that room. How is the girl? Any serious, lasting effects?"

"Possibly," Pamela replied. "At the time, she was stunned and shocked. I took temporary custody of her and moved her into a room in my home. A wise, kindly older servant took care of her. Thanks to the resilience of youth, Brenda's physical and mental health has improved to nearly normal. I notice inner scars, chiefly deep hatred and fear of her father. She also has horrid, recurring nightmares."

"That's unfortunate, but I'm not surprised," Prescott remarked. "Her father richly deserved his years in prison. Nonetheless, he resents that you helped put him there. In fact, how much were you involved?"

"A great deal. With backing from St. Barnabas Mission, I insisted that the police conduct a serious investigation. At first, they wanted to treat it as merely a domestic dispute. But when Monica died, I protested that the beating had caused her death. I also persuaded neighbors to come forward and testify to Reilly's bad character. Finally, the court convicted him of aggravated manslaughter and gave his parental rights to me."

"I mean no offense," said Prescott, "but why should you, rather than someone else, take charge of Brenda? She could have gone into an orphanage."

"That's what my husband thought. As Monica lay dying, she asked me to raise the girl—a reasonable request. I had known Brenda almost from her infancy and loved her. At the time, I also had sufficient financial resources. No one else was as suited for the task. Monica believed orphanages were loveless places and wrong for Brenda. In the end, my husband and the court agreed."

Prescott had listened intently to Pamela's account. Now he remarked, "The fate of the Reilly family is sad and all too common, especially in the poorest neighborhoods. Brenda is fortunate to be under your wing. Still, Dennis Reilly now wants his parental rights restored."

"Surely the court wouldn't change its mind. Reilly may be free from prison, but his character hasn't changed."

"True, but he may have won a powerful patron in the New York Police Department. I checked earlier. He had a ten-year sentence. His early release intrigues me. I suspect that the police intend to make him work for them."

"Then he's a serious threat to me—and to Brenda. What should be done?"

Prescott's brow knotted with concern. "You and Brenda must move to a safer neighborhood. My secretary will help you find a suitable apartment. I'll immediately look into Reilly's situation."

"Thank you. I'm greatly relieved."

Then he said, "I wasn't expecting you so soon, Pamela. May I ask if you've come to a decision yet?" His expression was businesslike. He would not patronize her.

She nervously smoothed her gown, breathed deeply, and nodded. "Since we last met, I've been mulling over your offer. First, I have a trivial question. Would I be the first female private detective in this country? I can't recall ever hearing of one before."

"You would not be the first. A few months ago while visiting the Pinkertons' head office in Chicago, I learned about one of their operatives, the late Mrs. Kate Warne, a young widow like you. The agency's founder, Allan Pinkerton, hired her personally and held her in high regard. He even engaged her in thwarting a plot to assassinate President Lincoln. That led me to think that a female operative might have investigative skills peculiar to her gender, like keener powers of observation and greater attention to detail. I've seen those qualities in you. Hence, my offer."

Embarrassed, she hesitated before continuing. "You said earlier that I should 'blend in' among the shoppers in Macy's jewelry department. Look at me. I would stand out like a scarecrow." She gestured to the patches on her gown, the scuff marks on her shoes.

He waved a dismissive hand. "My agency equips its operatives for their tasks and charges the client. Buy what you need at Macy's. One of my clerks will authorize your purchases. Tell me when you are ready, and we'll begin your training."

With her heart pounding she said, "Then I accept."

"Come into my private office, and we'll go over the details."

He sat down at a cluttered desk, opened a file box, and fingered through documents. Meanwhile, Pamela surveyed the room. On one of the dark oak-paneled walls were shelves bending under the weight of thick legal books. File cabinets and cases of maps stood against another wall. A telephone hung on the wall behind his desk. Finally, a locked cabinet caught her eye.

Prescott noticed her curiosity. "Firearms and other lethal weapons," he remarked dryly, then pulled a document from a file box and read it to her. The brief contract specified her wages—fifty dollars per month—and her responsibilities, such as simple, factual weekly reports. When he finished explaining the contract, Pamela's gaze drifted momentarily to a military sword hanging on the office wall. She glanced a silent question to him.

"It belonged to a Confederate officer at Gettysburg. I saw him fall. He was dead when I reached him. In life he must have looked like a Greek god—handsome and noble. What I saw was a corpse, still expressing that last terrible moment of pain. I meant to return the sword to his family, but the fighting flared up. Soon I was shot. Didn't get his name and couldn't make connections."

The office became very quiet. Prescott seemed to slip into a rare, unguarded mood. He wanted to talk personally. She encouraged him with a smile.

"That day, that dead man, changed my life," he said softly, "No more illusions." His eyes fixed on the sword. "It hangs there to remind me of the madness of war."

He went on to speak of Confederate General Pickett's division charging up a long slope toward the Union army's entrenched position. The Union cannon had suddenly roared. Cut down like grain, Pickett's Virginians gave out a dreadful, collective groan—like a mighty beast in death's agony. "Thirty years later, those sounds are still in my head. I hear them occasionally, especially when I can't sleep at night or when I'm alone and without distractions."

He silently gazed at the sword. Then with a deep sigh he closed this window into his soul, picked up the contract, and offered it to her.

She took it with trembling hands, quickly read and signed it. She felt that her life, too, had just changed—forever.

CHAPTER 5

A Police Spy

29–30 March

At noon, six days later, as Prescott approached a police station in the city's west side Tenderloin district, Pamela's bruised face was still on his mind. He had investigated Dennis Reilly's past, especially his years in prison. The results had led Prescott to Inspector Alexander "Clubber" Williams, NYPD, apparently Reilly's mentor and protector.

For many years Williams had ruled over the district's notorious brothels and saloons and broken up its murderous gangs. He was reputed to be a stern, fearless enemy of criminals and claimed to have a keen understanding of the criminal mind. His nickname came from beating confessions out of suspects who he believed were guilty of a crime or were withholding vital information about it.

From prison records, Prescott had learned that Williams had arranged Reilly's release into his custody. For what reason? Prescott asked himself. Williams must have found some use for him.

While in prison, Reilly had given up drinking, learned useful skills, and been well behaved and cooperative. Prescott suspected that the prisoner had also won favor by spying for the warden and other officers. Perhaps Williams wanted Reilly to spy for him and had even invested money and trust in him. Reilly's recent assault on Pamela could prove embarrassing.

Williams was leaving the station and seemed to be in a hurry. When he saw Prescott, he frowned. "What brings you to the Tenderloin, Prescott? Looking for clients in our stewpots of vice? I might recommend a few rascals you could defend." His eyes were dark, deep-set, and hostile.

Prescott ignored Williams's sarcastic tone. "No, thank you, Inspector. I already have a client who needs my full attention, and her case brings me to you."

The two men knew each other from various court cases, usually as adversaries. Representing lowlife characters accused of serious crimes, Prescott publicly condemned Williams's brutal interrogations. Williams took personal offense at the criticism and had retaliated with attacks on Prescott's alleged loose morals. Williams also charged that Prescott's clever arguments undermined the judicial system and enabled vicious criminals to go free.

Prescott intensely disliked Williams. Still, he asked him politely, "Inspector, may I have a word with you privately?"

Williams stared at Prescott. "You want to speak to me now? I'm on my way to lunch with the boys at Finnegan's Bar. Come along and join us."

Prescott doubted that the invitation was seriously meant. And if it were, it would be like inviting Daniel into the lions' den. "Thanks, some other time. This is serious police business."

Williams looked askance. "Why can't we deal with it later in my office? Make an appointment."

"The matter is urgent. My client's life is in danger. It's to your advantage to deal with her problem here and now." Williams's office was a mare's nest of spies, journalists, and other untrustworthy characters.

For a brief moment, Williams's eyes searched Prescott, trying to detect any hidden or malicious motives. They both were aware of mounting public criticism of high-handed tactics and corruption in the NYPD. Over the course of twenty-three years, Williams had grown rich through bribes and extortion in the Tenderloin district and had acquired a fine house and a yacht on a policeman's meager salary. Reformers in the state legislature would soon launch an official investigation into his affairs and try to drive him and his superior, Superintendent Thomas Byrnes, from office.

Finally, Williams said, "Follow me," and led Prescott back into the police station. "Your business better be interesting. I'm putting off my lunch."

As they faced each other across a table, the inspector's attention became intense. Somehow, he sensed that Prescott would touch on a sensitive spot.

"What's troubling you, Prescott?" he asked.

"Dennis Reilly," replied Prescott. "Late Wednesday afternoon a week ago, he assaulted one of my clients, Mrs. Pamela Thompson."

Williams's tone grew irritated. "Go tell your story to someone at the local precinct station."

Prescott met Williams's eye and measured his words. "The local officers are powerless in this case. You, sir, have custody of Dennis Reilly. I've reason to believe that he also works for you. Order him to stay away from my client."

Williams reacted with deliberate restraint. "It's no secret that Reilly is in my charge. Occasionally, he works for me. But, I would never condone his assaulting a respectable woman. There must be a misunderstanding. Reilly is in the hospital, recovering from several painful wounds. He says Mrs. Thompson attacked him unprovoked with a stiletto. There must have been a dispute. I suppose Reilly defended himself." Williams glared at Prescott. "Why do *you* think he attacked her?"

"In revenge," Prescott replied. "She testified against him in the brutal killing of his wife."

"In fact," Williams countered, "she exaggerated Reilly's part in the dispute. The court recognized that his wife had been lying to him and cheating him of his money. He was provoked, his wife actually assaulted him, and your client put her up to it. Granted, he reacted with more force than he should have."

"Really?" Prescott remarked, his voice dripping with sarcasm.

Williams blinked, then blurted out, "Your client is an arrogant bitch. I can't stand the type. She took the daughter away from her father. Now that Reilly is out of prison, he wants his daughter back and will fight for her, if necessary. I say, good luck. Still, I'll have a word with him."

Williams rose from the table. "Now, if you'll excuse me, I'll go to lunch before I lose my appetite."

As Prescott left the station, he felt disappointed, even though he had had a low expectation of Williams cooperating. The inspector had not clearly promised to bring Reilly under control, much less to punish him for the assault. Reilly could still feel free to harass or intimidate, if not openly attack, his daughter, Brenda, and Pamela. They must be warned. The next time he would be more wary.

The following day, when Prescott arrived at the office, he found a message from Pamela. She had engaged a manager for her boardinghouse and, together with Brenda, had moved into decent furnished rooms on West Fourteenth Street, close to Macy's. He hastened to the address, a boardinghouse for women. A flint-eyed concierge scrutinized him, then showed him into a tiny parlor and fetched Pamela.

"I was about to go shopping at Macy's," she said. "Is something amiss?"

"I'm not sure," he replied. "But I should report what I

learned at my meeting yesterday with Inspector Williams. While Dennis Reilly was in prison, he apparently won a measure of respect from the police. He works for them, most likely as an informer. I'm concerned that the police now seem to have largely accepted his version of the domestic conflict of six years ago. They believe you wronged him, and they support his desire to recover paternal rights over Miss Reilly."

"That's troubling," said Pamela. "How far will the police allow him to pursue us?"

"They have him on a leash. But I don't know how long it is or how tightly they hold it."

She stroked her chin for a moment. "We feel safe in this house and in the neighborhood. Elsewhere, we'll be vigilant."

CHAPTER 6

A New Career

31 March–18 April

At Macy's, Pamela looked for new clothes and shoes. Her taste as well as her new work called for simple dresses free from the excesses of current fashion, such as wasp waists. With an advance on her salary, she also visited a hairdresser and a masseuse. She was surprised by how much this indulgence lifted her spirits.

The next day, when she reported back to Prescott's office, her transformation brought a satisfied smile to his face. "You look like you belong in Macy's," he said. "Now let's begin your apprenticeship." Prescott handed her a thin book from his shelf, *A Handbook for Criminal Investigation*. "This is your bible. I've condensed into simple English the best writing on the subject, chiefly Hans Gross's massive two-volume work on criminology."

She received the book with appropriate gravity, promising to quickly master its contents.

Prescott continued. "Now I'll introduce you to the other detective on my staff, Harry Miller, formerly of the NYPD. I should warn you, he can be difficult to work with. Life has dealt him many bad cards, leaving him soured. But I've hired him because he's the most skillful investigator in the city. He will tutor you in the basics of private investigation and determine your strengths and weaknesses. At the end, he'll report to me, and we'll discuss how best to employ you."

Prescott rang a bell. Into the room shuffled Miller, a small man with thin, sandy hair and sly, searching eyes. He cast a penetrating, unsettling glance at Pamela, as if he thought she was poor material for detecting crime. His greeting to her was curt, almost rude. Instantly, she disliked him. He appeared cynical toward women. Still, she was willing to learn from him.

When Miller left the room, Prescott leaned back in his chair and stared at Pamela, as if he had something distressing to tell her. His words seemed carefully chosen. "You've noticed Harry's bitter attitude toward life in general and women in particular. So, I should explain what I meant by the 'bad cards' in his life. You might understand him better."

"I'm willing to meet him more than halfway," she said. "In my work with the poor, I've often met men like him."

Prescott explained that Harry was about forty years old, born into poverty. "His father was killed early in the war, and his mother became insane. He was raised in an orphanage. At eighteen, he joined the NYPD as a patrolman in the Five Points district, the most crime-ridden and dangerous in the city. He soon showed a talent for investigation. Bright, inquisitive, and fearless, he worked his way up to police detective."

"That speaks well of his character," Pamela remarked.

Prescott nodded. "Now comes the sad part. Several years ago, he was assigned to investigate a murder. It looked like a simple case. An unemployed worker had quarreled with a cab driver over a fare of a few cents. The cab driver pulled a knife. The worker drew his knife, killed the driver, and claimed self-defense. But when Harry looked closely into the circumstances, he discovered that the cab driver had previously chanced upon strong evidence of fraud involving Tammany Hall, the head-quarters of the city's Democratic organization. One of their lawyers had accidentally left a portfolio of incriminating corre-spondence in the cab. The driver had recognized its significance and attempted to extort money from Tammany. The organiza-tion's leader had hired the worker to recover the portfolio and kill the driver in return for a well-paid job in the city's adminis-tration.

"When Harry presented this evidence to his supervisor, Tammany Hall was secretly informed and objected. The super-visor took Harry off the case and suppressed the evidence. Outraged, he protested publicly. His superiors then charged him with fabricating the evidence and trying to extort money from Tammany's lawyer. Harry was wrongly convicted and sentenced to four years in Sing Sing. His wife left him, taking their two children with her."

Pamela remarked, "Having known bitterness and self-pity, I'm beginning to understand Harry. But I wouldn't compare my Lower East Side boardinghouse with his Sing Sing."

Prescott nodded sympathetically. "Bad as it was, Harry made the most of his prison time, studying the mentality of criminals, their characteristic behavior and their skills and tech-niques. Still, he came out of Sing Sing impoverished and dis-graced. No one would hire him. He seriously considered entering a life of crime, where he probably would have ex-celled."

"So, is that when you stepped in?"

"Actually, a year earlier. I had followed his case from a dis-tance and smelled the rank odor of injustice. Shortly after his release, I contacted him and researched his background. I dis-covered a bulldog's tenacity in pursuit of evidence as well as remarkable investigative skills. He knows the criminal mind so well that he can often anticipate a criminal's next move. He also can open any lock ever made by God or man. I hired Harry on probation, and he has proved invaluable."

Pamela remarked, "You've given me a new appreciation of the man. I see why he would distrust almost everyone, including me. I hope to change his attitude."

Despite an awkward beginning, Pamela gamely prepared for training with Miller. She didn't expect it to be easy. Miller disliked and distrusted her. Still, she remained confident since Prescott thought she could cope and would benefit.

They began in Harry's office, a small room with a few wooden chairs and cabinets. A battered table stood against a wall. A large map of the city hung nearby. Otherwise, the walls were bare. Pamela wondered if the office differed much from his prison cell, besides being a little larger. For a week, she sat at the table with Miller at her side and studied the handbook. Finally, he declared it was time for practical exercises at Macy's.

As they explored the vast store, he pointed to its open counters and displays, luring the crowd, mostly females, to buy—or to steal.

"Preventing thievery here must be a nightmare," he said, as they stood on a stairway and surveyed the scene before them.

Pamela added, "The clerks have an impossible task, standing behind counters, needing to be alert for eight or nine hours. To judge from their speech, dress, and manners, most of them are poorly paid young women with little education."

Miller nodded. "Floorwalkers are supposed to enforce strict rules of dress and behavior on the clerks and keep a sharp eye on the customers. But a floorwalker can't be everywhere at once, and some of them are lazy, stupid, or drunk—or all three.

Both clerks and customers find ways to steal. You're learning how to stop them. Now we'll sharpen your powers of observation."

He sent her into the jewelry department for five minutes. When she returned, he asked her to describe specific items that were displayed on a certain counter. Then he had the sales clerks rearrange the items, put a few away, and display a few new ones. Pamela went back into the department for five more minutes. Miller questioned her again to see if she had noticed the changes. In a similar way, she studied visitors to the jewelry department, their mannerisms as well as their physical appearance.

At the end of the day, Miller said, "You've observed well." She thanked him for the compliment but also gave credit to her experience managing the boardinghouse.

During the following days, her instruction focused on shoplifters, especially the upper-class ladies who came a-thieving to department stores, including Macy's. She caught a few of the middling variety stealing inexpensive jewelry and took them to the store's chief detective. He recovered the items and sent the ladies home with the threat that they would go to jail the next time.

Miller asked Pamela, "Why do you think they steal, though they have enough money to purchase whatever they want?"

Pamela replied, "I've known that sort of woman. A few of them are probably mentally ill. An inner, irresistible force compels them to steal. But most are simply bored to tears. Stealing at Macy's adds adventure and thrill to their barren lives."

"I agree," he remarked dryly. "They are pitiful creatures."

One day, Miller called her to his office. "Prescott says you should also be trained in self-defense, including the use of firearms." Like Prescott, Miller kept weapons in his office in a locked cabinet. When he handed her a Colt .44 revolver, she wrinkled her nose in distaste.

He corrected her sharply. "You most likely will never have reason to fire a pistol, but you need to know how one works. Your life or someone else's just might depend on it." He took her uptown to a gun shop's indoor practice range and instructed her in the safe handling of pistols. He warned her, "When you practice indoors, stuff wax into your ears. The noise is deafening."

She had good eyesight and a steady hand. So, despite her reluctance, she managed to hit the bull's-eye often enough to win a grudging smile from her instructor.

On 18 April, the final day of her training, Miller called Pamela to his office. "You may need to defend yourself when you don't have a pistol. That's most of the time. Don't expect to carry one in Macy's. Use your wits instead. Whenever you can, avoid dangerous situations."

She raised an eyebrow. "That should be easy in Macy's jewelry department, don't you think?" His stress on the obvious had irritated her. Did he think she was simple?

Her pert tone annoyed Miller. "True," he replied. "Some places are safer than others, but no place is entirely safe. At Macy's you will be protecting items worth hundreds of dollars. That could be dangerous work. Some thieves would kill for a tiny, exquisite diamond. You've already pointed out that some of the women who steal from Macy's are mentally or emotionally unbalanced. Faced with the prospect of arrest, any one of them—a rich socialite or a poor clerk—could react violently and attack you with a long, steel hatpin."

"I agree," admitted Pamela, grudgingly contrite.

Miller continued. "In the future the two of us might have to work together. I want a partner whom I can depend on." He stared at her with grave doubt in his eyes. "A society lady would faint at the first whiff of danger and be worse than useless."

"Sir!" Pamela exclaimed. "I may speak correct English, but I'm not one of your 'society ladies.' Nor do I faint in the face of danger. Less than a month ago, I fought off a fierce assailant. He fled, screaming."

Miller sniffed. "I'll see for myself how brave you are." He beckoned her to face him in the center of the room. Following his instructions, she was wearing an old, patched dress. "Ready?" he asked. She nodded, without knowing what he intended to do.

Suddenly, his bluish gray eyes filled with menace. He drew a knife from his coat pocket and lunged at her. For a moment she felt that he truly intended to kill her. She grabbed his upraised arm and tried to hold him off. With superior strength, he easily pressed the weapon to within an inch of her throat. A powerful fear surged through her body. But she knew that he wouldn't kill her, so she steeled her nerves and didn't flinch.

"You see," he said as he released his pressure. "A male assailant would almost always have superior strength, and you would lose the contest." He backed away and said, "A female assailant might be no stronger than you, but she would still have the advantage of surprise. Here's a trick that might work initially. If you can, grab your assailant's thumb." He raised the knife and attacked again, this time grinning like a crazed demon.

With a rush of anger that banished her fear, she seized his thumb and pressed back hard.

He flinched with pain. "I see that you get the idea." He put the knife back into his pocket. "You may also try to poke out the assailant's eyes, strike his Adam's apple, and knee him in the groin. These are desperate measures. I'm not going to let you try them on me. But use them if you have to. You've got nothing to lose but your life."

"Have you ever had to use any of these measures?"

His expression grew grim, as if he were under pressure from painful past images. "Do you really want to know?"

She nodded. "Since we might become partners, I'd like to know more about you—as much as you care to tell me."

"As a young patrolman in Five Corners, and a small man, I was frequently in danger of assault. But I had a stout partner, and together we defended ourselves well. In prison I had no trustworthy partner, and the guards were corrupt. It was every man for himself, and the bullies ruled. Worse yet, Tammany hired prisoners to try to kill me."

"How did you survive?"

"I learned to negotiate with other, less dangerous prisoners for mutual protection. We exchanged favors. I taught them to read and write. They identified my enemies, and I tried to avoid them. That wasn't always possible, so I used every trick I've showed you. But they didn't always work. I have scars to prove it. Here's one." He unbuttoned his right sleeve and showed her an ugly scar from elbow to wrist. "I nearly bled to death."

For a moment, Pamela had second thoughts about the career she was entering.

Miller must have sensed her anxiety. "Don't be frightened. Prescott will never put you in Five Corners or Sing Sing. I'm confident you can cope with shoplifters in Macy's."

Shortly after this session, Prescott called Pamela into his private office and offered her a chair facing him. He leaned forward, his arms resting on the desk, his expression professional. "Harry Miller has just reported favorably on your performance, madam. I'm impressed, especially since he's so hard to please. I was already aware of your good judgment, sophistication, and tact. Miller tells me that you also have courage and strong nerves."

"I'm grateful for his instruction and delighted to have earned his compliments."

Prescott smiled. "You may start at Macy's tomorrow."

CHAPTER 7

A Challenging Start

19–28 April

On Pamela's first day as a detective, Macy's was crowded with busy shoppers. By midday, the young female clerks at the jewelry department's counters looked harassed and fatigued. They would be on their feet for another six hours.

Pamela noticed a wealthy lady's maid drift away from her mistress. Pamela walked over to the opposite counter and pretended to admire a tray of gold rings. Looking into a mirror, she secretly observed the scene behind her. The maid took an expensive bracelet carelessly left on a display counter, nonchalantly put it on her arm, and drew her sleeve over it.

Pamela studied the wealthy lady. Slim, tastefully dressed, gracious in her manner, she looked perhaps sixty. Her wrinkled face had an unhealthy pallor and sagging cheeks. She was comparing one bracelet with another, shaking her head in dissatisfaction, and demanding to see yet another. The young clerk complied each time but seemed increasingly rattled and desperate. She struggled to keep her eyes open. Soon, a dozen gem-studded, gold bracelets were spread out across the glass counter.

Eventually, the lady threw up her hands, beckoned the maid, and left the counter without buying anything.

Pamela debated with herself the best way to proceed. The high value of the stolen bracelet seemed to call for an arrest. Indeed the wealthy lady might have deliberately distracted the young clerk and thus worked together with her maid in the theft. An arrest, however, would cause a public and noisy confrontation with unforeseeable consequences for Pamela. She decided to follow the lady and her maid.

Finally, as they were about to leave the store, Pamela approached the lady politely and spoke in a soft voice. "I believe, madam, that your maid has neglected to pay for the bracelet that she's wearing. An oversight, I'm sure."

Irritated and appearing embarrassed, the lady stared at Pamela through watery eyes. Pamela said nothing more but smiled pleasantly and stood her ground. She half expected the lady to dismiss her with a paralyzing gesture of contempt and complain to the store manager. Instead, the lady gazed sternly at her maid. "Is that true, Agnes?"

The maid nodded, an empty expression on her face, confirming Pamela's suspicion that the maid might be "simple."

"Give it to me," said the wealthy lady.

The maid complied without apparent embarrassment. Her mistress handed the bracelet over to Pamela. "My maid is a sweet girl from a family that has served me well for decades. She fails to understand that when the store displays a product, it's not giving it away. If she takes it, she is expected to pay for it. I try to guard against her artless thievery, but unfortunately I was preoccupied and didn't notice her. You behaved with exemplary discretion." She hesitated. "How shall I call you?"

"Pamela Thompson, ma'am, pleased to serve you."

"I'm Mrs. Henry Jennings. I'll commend you to the manager."

These compliments had a patronizing tone. Pamela nonetheless accepted them with a polite smile, though she felt not the least inferior to Mrs. Jennings. When she and her maid finally left the store, Pamela breathed a sigh of relief. She hurried back to the bracelet counter. The clerk had put the bracelets back in their display case and had just realized that one was missing. The floor manager had entered the room. The clerk was watching him and gasping for breath.

"Don't panic," Pamela whispered and discreetly handed her the bracelet.

"Thank God!" the clerk whispered while putting it back in the case. She had turned deathly pale and now began to sway. Pamela grabbed her and eased her into a chair.

By this time, the floor manager, a tall, stern man, had come upon the scene, brow furrowed with irritation and concern.

"She needs a break and some fresh air, sir," said Pamela before he could complain. A few wealthy ladies had gathered at the counter and were looking on sympathetically.

"The poor girl!" said one of the ladies and glanced with reproach at the floor manager.

He yielded grudgingly. "You may take her outside, Mrs. Thompson. I'll find another clerk to fill in."

Pamela lifted the young woman under the arm and led her away. On the way to the street, the name "Henry Jennings" suddenly popped into Pamela's mind. She felt a frisson of concern. A rich, older lady with that name had to be the Copper King's wife. Meeting her was an extraordinary coincidence. Still, it would have consequences. Pamela was sure of that.

During the following week, the image of Mrs. Jennings receded. Pamela was busy, her work uneventful. She encouraged the clerks to be more careful when displaying jewelry. In a demonstration, for example, they were to show only as many pieces as they could keep near and in sight. They realized that she was watching them as well as the customers. Clerks commonly regarded a little pilfering as a fair, even necessary supplement to their pitiful wages. Nonetheless, most clerks grudgingly accepted Pamela's close supervision.

She had a guarded trust in them, but she suspected a new clerk, Sarah Evans, of merely appearing to comply. She was a beautiful, well-mannered young woman with a British accent who had a remarkable familiarity with jewelry and a persuasive way of selling it, qualities most clerks lacked. Her eyes, however, betrayed a cunning intelligence. She appeared to be looking for an opportunity to pilfer.

Pamela grew increasingly uneasy about Sarah's fascination with the more expensive diamonds; she studied them at every free moment. Pamela decided to find out if there were grounds for suspicion. One day at the closing hour, she disguised herself in the old clothes that she kept in an empty closet for a rainy day and followed the clerk through congested streets to Old Bohemia, an inexpensive restaurant, full of clerks and artisans.

A heavily bearded man with a large mustache, sitting alone at a table in the rear of the room, signaled Evans to join him. They shook hands as if they were partners, rather than lovers. On close inspection, he could appear handsome, even distinguished, were it not for that excess of facial hair. To judge from his affected gestures, he should also have been dressed in a fashionable tailored suit. But he wore common clothes as if to blend in with the restaurant's clientele.

Through the meal their conversation grew earnest. Pamela had sat too far away to hear them, but she etched the man's physical appearance and manner in her mind. Afterward, the couple left the restaurant. Pamela tried to follow but lost them in the street crowd.

Then on Wednesday, 26 April, near the closing hour, a well dressed, dignified gentleman wearing a neatly trimmed beard and mustache walked into the jewelry department. Pamela soon recognized him, despite his altered appearance, as the clerk's handsome acquaintance. He briefly browsed at several counters until he came to Sarah's. They pretended not to know each other. To Pamela, that was a sure sign of deception. As the clerk was about to reach for a very expensive diamond ring, Pamela hurried up to her. If the pair were professional thieves, as Pamela suspected, they might attempt to exchange a fake, paste ring for the genuine item.

"Sarah, I'll serve this gentleman. You may help at another counter."

The gentleman and the clerk tried but failed to conceal their frustration and anger. After a tense moment, the clerk left. Pamela said to the man, "What may I show you, sir?"

"Oh, nothing, thank you," he replied testily. "It's late. I'll come another day." He stalked out of the room just as the closing bell sounded.

Pamela released a sigh of relief, believing that she had averted a serious theft. Still, there remained the problem of Sarah. She shouldn't be allowed to work at Macy's, especially in the jewelry department. Without proof, however, it seemed pointless to report her to the store's chief detective. He would simply say to keep a sharp eye on her.

The next day, Sarah served at her counter without apparent resentment or embarrassment. Pamela relaxed her surveillance somewhat, but her uneasiness didn't go away. When Sarah glanced at her, she felt threatened.

In the evening after work, as she walked to her rooms, she found herself looking over her shoulder. At the same time, she reproached herself for giving in to an irrational fear. The suspicious pair would try to rob a different store, she thought, since Macy's jewelry department was on to their game.

She was near the edge of the street when a man coming toward her suddenly leaped forward and pulled her out of the path of an unlighted cab. It had jumped onto the sidewalk and was about to run her over.

"I saw the cab coming," exclaimed the man who had saved her. "You could have been killed."

"Thanks for risking your own life. Did you see the driver?"

"Not clearly. He was bundled up. A thick plaid scarf and a cap concealed much of his face."

As a crowd gathered, Pamela's gaze briefly lighted upon a woman's face. It was Sarah, scowling. For a moment they made eye contact. Then Sarah disappeared into the crowd.

Pamela began to shake uncontrollably. This was no accident. Sarah and her partner had tried to injure or kill her. Had they succeeded, and the jewelry department been left temporarily without strict supervision, they would have again attempted to steal the diamond ring.

"Are you all right?" asked her rescuer.

"Yes, thank you," Pamela croaked.

"By the way, the driver had full control of his horse and seemed to know what he was doing. You aren't safe. May I walk you home?"

She quickly assessed him. He appeared to be an artisan and an honest man. "Yes," she replied. "I'd be much obliged."

The following day, Sarah failed to show up for work. Pamela wondered if she should report what had happened. Would the store's chief detective take her seriously? She was personally convinced of the conspiracy to steal a ring and of the subsequent attempt to assault her, but she lacked demonstrable proof. The detective might simply dismiss her as an excitable, delusional female. She would take the problem to Prescott.

CHAPTER 8

An Opportunity

28 April–5 May

Late that morning, Pamela walked into Prescott's office. He glanced up, smiling. Then he frowned.

"What's happened, Pamela? You look troubled."

"I need your advice." Pamela described Wednesday's attempted theft of jewelry at Macy's by Sarah Evans and her bearded partner.

Prescott brightened when he heard how she had thwarted their scheme. "Well done!"

"Last night," she went on, "they tried to kill me on Fourteenth Street. Should I report this to the store detective or to the police?"

"I think you should warn the store detective, a reasonable man." He paused. "Macy's is pleased with your work, Pamela, and so am I. Thieving in the jewelry department is down. You've succeeded without causing any unpleasantness."

"Thank you." She was very pleased but tried not to blush. "I've trained the clerks to be more observant. Most wealthy would-be thieves are out for a thrill. Their shifty eyes betray them. And they often give off a certain scent. I imagine that professional thieves would be more difficult to detect."

Prescott leaned back in his chair, inclining his head. "I'm truly surprised that they attacked you. If they were planning another attempt to steal jewelry from Macy's, they would make their task riskier by violently removing you from the jewelry department. You might have already reported your suspicions to the store detective. Your injury or death under suspicious circumstances would heighten his concern, and he would have alerted the floorwalker. The thieves would probably have walked into a trap."

"Perhaps," suggested Pamela, "they are amateur thieves, seeking revenge, thrills, or adventure as well as loot."

"You have a point. True professionals would have calculated the risks more prudently. Whether amateur or not, these two may continue to pose a danger to you as well as to others. I'll ask Harry Miller to discover their identity."

She rose to leave and walked to the door. Prescott opened it, gazed at her, then murmured gently, "You dodged death last night. I'm sorry. I didn't think working at Macy's could be so dangerous."

A week later, early in the morning, Pamela went shopping in the market at Union Square. This was a deeply satisfying hour of her day. A variety of flowers and fresh spring vegetables were arranged to delight the eye. Merchants and shoppers nodded and smiled at each other and exchanged friendly remarks about the crops and the weather. Pamela could imagine herself in a charming country village, rather than in the raw, steaming metropolis.

While she was inspecting a bunch of daffodils, she felt the presence of someone close behind her. She glanced over her shoulder. Dennis Reilly stood scarcely a foot away, clean-shaven and groomed. His clothes were cheap and ill fitting but clean. He carried himself like a gentleman. But his eyes burned with hate.

He glared at her, muttering, "Bitch. I've paid my debt to society and reformed my life. So I've gone to court to get my daughter, Brenda, back. Get out of my way. If you try to stop me, you'll be sorry."

For a moment she felt numb and paralyzed. Her body began to tremble. She breathed deeply, struggled to remain calm, and set off for her rooms. Reilly followed her at a distance. She thought of trying to evade him, but he surely knew where she and Brenda lived. Once in her rooms, she locked and bolted the door and hurried to the window. Reilly was across the street, looking up at her. He must have seen her, for he waved, a scowl on his face.

Brenda came out of her room dressed for school. "What's wrong?" she asked, alarmed.

"Your father is across the street, stalking us. I'll take you to school before going to Macy's, and I'll pick you up at the end of the day. He could try to kidnap you. I'll talk to Prescott. His office clerk will know where he is. He has to do something. We can't live like this."

Early in the afternoon, Pamela found Prescott in Gramercy Park, walking briskly up and down the paths. She caught his attention, and he unlocked the gate. She glanced at the key. He smiled and remarked, "A friend who lives here lends it to me. This is the only place in Lower Manhattan where I can find peace and quiet and good air. Please join me. You seem to have something on your mind."

As they walked in the park, she described her encounter with Dennis Reilly in Union Square. "He's applied for custody of Brenda. If I refuse to step aside, he'll do whatever it takes to get me out of the way."

Prescott's brow creased with concern. "Coming from Reilly, a violent man, that's a threat to take seriously. All the more, since Clubber Williams seems likely to stand behind him."

"What can be done about his petition?"

"I'll immediately go to the court and object that it's far too early for Reilly to claim to have reformed. Less than two months ago, scarcely out of prison, he physically assaulted you. Later, the judge will want to consult Brenda. In the meantime, I may have found a way to put you and her out of Reilly's reach."

He pointed to a bench, and they sat down. "The middle-aged, wealthy lady from Macy's, Mrs. Henry Jennings—her given name is Lydia—has asked for your services during the summer. She was much impressed by the judicious way you handled her maid's theft of a bracelet."

Pamela quickly grew attentive.

"Recently," Prescott continued, "an illness of the heart had confined Mrs. Jennings to bed. While she was recovering, she looked more closely into the household management of her country home. It had suffered while the illness had distracted her. Now, she has thought of hiring you to serve as her eyes and ears, ostensibly as a personal companion to read books to her and so on. Your chief task would be to find out if the domestic staff is thieving."

"Where, precisely?"

"Her country home, Broadmore Hall, is in the Berkshire Hills, close to Lenox, Massachusetts, and near my cabin. She didn't offer details, just insisted that something didn't seem right."

"Shouldn't she turn to the police?"

"I asked her. She replied that the police were dull-witted and heavy-handed. Their investigation would seriously disrupt the household and achieve nothing."

Prescott leaned forward and met Pamela's eye. "Are you interested?"

"Summer in the Berkshires, free from Dennis Reilly, sounds lovely. What more can you tell me about her?" The name Jennings had already rung a bell in Pamela's mind during the encounter at Macy's.

"She comes from a wealthy family. Her country home is a wonder of the Berkshires, one of the largest of the 'cottages' and tastefully opulent. Mrs. Jennings's parents died a decade ago, leaving Broadmore to their daughter. When she married Henry Jennings, she retained ownership of the cottage. She's a kindly, cultivated lady, generous to charities—a religious person, I believe."

"And her husband? Is he the Copper King?"

"Yes. He's a big, energetic man, about sixty, and rich as Croesus. Wealthy, respectable people regard him as one of our 'captains of industry.' Critics of his ruthless business methods call him a 'robber baron.' Much of his money comes from investments in railroads and mining—especially Michigan copper. As you recall, he's the trickster who fooled your husband—and many others—with bogus shares in a copper mine."

This reminder of her husband's tragedy was painful. She had always held Henry Jennings personally responsible. The mere mention of his name made her shiver. Jack Thompson was but one among the hundreds, perhaps thousands, of investors he had deceived. He wouldn't know her. How would it be to work for his wife? The prospect was intriguing—and a little frightening.

With some effort, she forced herself back into the present moment. "How shall I meet Lydia Jennings?"

"She invites you to tea and conversation at her Fifth Avenue residence in the city."

"Tell her that I'd be delighted to join her."

As Pamela left Prescott's office, she thought of taking Brenda along. A summer in a great house in the Berkshires might broaden her view of the world and her own possibilities and, incidentally, offer her a safe haven from her father's wiles and wrath.

Pamela marveled that a divine providence appeared likely to send her into the household of Henry Jennings, the man who had ruined her late husband and disrupted her life. For what purpose? she wondered. For personal revenge? No. She had grown beyond that. But was she somehow destined to bring him to justice? Perhaps.

CHAPTER 9

A Companion

14–15 May

Sunday morning was cool and wet. Pamela went as usual to worship at the Church of the Ascension. Located within sight of her former town house on West Tenth Street, the church could have served as a depressing reminder of how much she had lost. Instead, it was a beacon of hope, largely due to Mr. La Farge's magnificent mural painting of Christ's ascension into Heaven.

On this occasion, Brenda joined Pamela. Usually the young woman stayed home on Sundays and studied. Today she had asked to come along. One of her teachers had stirred up in her an interest in La Farge's art.

During the organ prelude, Pamela became aware of someone staring at her. She drew a mirror from her bag and scanned the nearby pews behind her.

The curious person was a woman about fifty, sitting off to the right in a fashionable mauve silk dress with a high neckline and a collar of pearls. The upper sleeves were full, while the lower clung tightly to the arms, making them look like canoe paddles. From Peter Yates's description almost two months ago, Pamela recognized Gloria Prescott's strong chin, long thin nose, and regal posture. Her companion, a bearded, portly gentleman in a dark gray suit, was Mr. Fisher, the president of Jack's bank and Pamela's nemesis.

Neither Gloria nor Fisher had ever attended this church. So Pamela assumed that they had come to observe her. Today, she was wearing a simple, red silk gown from Macy's and had washed her hair. Brenda had put it up into an attractive knot at the nape of the neck. Fisher's spies might have noticed the recent improvement in Pamela's appearance. A sign of suspicious affluence, it probably strengthened his belief that she had hidden away some of the bank's money.

The couple remained for the service without participating in it. After the postlude they conspicuously arranged to confront Pamela in the vestibule.

Fisher tipped his hat. "You look very well today, Mrs. Thompson. Yes, quite chic, as the French would say." He studied her with cold, searching eyes. "I understand that you have found employment at Macy's. I see that they pay very well. When they asked for a recommendation, I was happy to give it to them."

From the ironic tone of his voice Pamela understood that he had told Macy's she was untrustworthy and most likely criminal. How had Prescott managed to defend her? She stared at Fisher unapologetically until he appeared uneasy.

"Mr. Prescott and Macy's seem pleased with my work," she said serenely.

Then she turned toward Gloria. She must be curious about her husband's new female assistant, a novelty that might have attracted the public's notice—and her envy.

The expression on Gloria's face was difficult to read. Her eyes spoke of bitter resentment, of perceived injustice, and possibly of a sad remembrance of a lost husband. Her face was still beautiful, but crow's-feet had begun to appear at her eyes and betrayed her age. Still, she carried herself erect, chin high. It would be folly to trifle with her.

Gloria glanced dismissively at Brenda standing off to the side. "Is this one of the waifs you have rescued?"

Pamela put an arm around the girl's shoulder. "She's Brenda Reilly, my ward and best friend. Now we must be going. Mrs. Henry Jennings is expecting us at her home." Pamela guided Brenda to the door.

Pamela's parting shot seemed to momentarily disconcert Gloria and her banker. They stared wordlessly at each other.

Out on the street, Brenda asked in a whisper, "Do they mean to cause us harm?"

"Yes," replied Pamela. "They're trying to figure out how to do it. But they won't succeed."

The rain had stopped but the sky was still gray as Pamela and Brenda arrived for afternoon tea at the Jenningses' mansion on Fifth Avenue near Fortieth Street. In the early 1880s, Henry Jennings had bought the three-story, mansard-roofed brick house to serve as a symbol of his success. Brenda stared at it wide-eyed.

Pamela had asked Mrs. Jennings if she would hire the young woman for the season as a maid. Mrs. Jennings had agreed to consider the suggestion. "Bring her with you to tea, and I'll take a look at her."

A servant in livery received them. In a corner of the entrance hall a great, stuffed brown bear reared up on his hind legs. Brenda walked past him at a safe distance. The head of a mountain goat and other hunting trophies hung on the wall.

A hint of ironic amusement brushed the servant's lips. "Mr. Jennings is an ardent hunter of wild game. He's fond of saying that hunting is a metaphor for mankind's evolution and its basic law—survival of the fittest." The servant added, "Mrs. Jennings will meet you in her study. Follow me."

He led Pamela and Brenda up the stairs and to the back of the house. He knocked lightly and opened the door. Mrs. Jennings sat at a window overlooking a garden. A low fire burned in the hearth. She rose and welcomed them. "My garden is mostly dormant now. I haven't the time or energy to tend to it. In the past, it would soon have turned into a bright, colorful tapestry, matching anything you have in Macy's."

They moved to a tea table set by the fire. The tea service was silver. Fine linen covered the table. A maid served tea and pastries and withdrew. Mrs. Jennings opened the conversation. "I've played the detective, Mrs. Thompson, and have carefully investigated your background. Macy's has given you a favorable recommendation. I also know about your husband's disgrace and suicide."

Pamela began to feel apprehensive.

"But that shouldn't be a problem," Mrs. Jennings added. "You weren't involved in his business. Indeed, that dreadful experience seems to have strengthened your character." She turned to Brenda. "Your teachers say that you are trustworthy and an excellent pupil. Mrs. Thompson also speaks well of you. As a maid, you will assist her and Broadmore's housekeeper."

The conversation shifted to accommodations at Broadmore. Pamela would have her own rooms adjacent to her mistress and would eat sometimes with her mistress, sometimes with the servants—as appropriate. She would also have free room and board, a generous stipend, and a day off once a week. Brenda would live with Pamela. That business finished, a maid took Brenda on a tour of the house.

When they were alone, Mrs. Jennings said, "You will help me with my medications. I take laudanum and digitalis for a sick heart. At Broadmore, I'll show you where I keep them and how to give them to me."

"I'm familiar with heart problems. My father had them. I should be able to assist you."

Lydia mustered a wan smile. "Last but not least, I'd like you to find out from whom this note came and what it implies." She drew a note from her bag and gave it to Pamela.

An anonymous hand had crudely printed a message on cheap, unlined paper: "Beware, mistress, before it's too late. Someone near you is false."

"Could this be a prank or a joke?" Pamela asked doubtfully.

"Possibly," Mrs. Jennings replied. "But I can't imagine who would send it. In any case, it upsets me. I almost constantly sense evil around me."

"Have you shown it to your husband?"

"No, he's away on business. I don't expect to see him until the beginning of June." She hesitated. "No one but you has seen the note."

So, Pamela thought, the author of the cryptic note could be anyone from the husband to a scullery maid. At the very least, Mrs. Jennings's secrecy about the note showed a lack of trust between her and her spouse. Did they even correspond?

Pamela began to sense that this mission could become more serious than a summer's lark in the Berkshires. She glanced at her companion's hands. Mrs. Jennings was gripping her teacup as if her life depended on it. Pamela's skin tingled with excitement.

"I welcome the challenge and will join you in Lenox," Pamela said. "Be assured, I'll keep you informed and do whatever I can to give you peace of mind."

The next morning, Pamela hastened to Prescott's office. He had asked her to report on the meeting with Mrs. Jennings.

"It went well," Pamela said, and related the arrangements for her and Brenda. "But something unexpected has come up," she added. "Mrs. Jennings showed me an anonymous, threatening note she had received. She wants me to investigate it."

Prescott sat up, alert. "Tell me about it."

"The note declared that someone was betraying her. She's very upset." Pamela described the note in detail down to the paper and ink.

"This may be serious. The note might relate to developments in New York as well as Lenox. Here at the office we'll keep our eyes open."

CHAPTER 10

Broadmore Hall

Lenox, 19 May

The following days passed quickly for Pamela and Brenda. They packed a trunk with clothes, toiletries, Brenda's books, and other necessities, closed their rooms near Macy's, and caught an early morning train to Lenox. Once underway, the two women glanced at each other and breathed a sigh of relief. With every mile they were leaving Dennis Reilly and his threats farther behind.

They soon were enjoying the light green flora of the Berkshire countryside. As they approached Lenox, however, an uneasy feeling seeped into Pamela's mind. That anonymous note seemed to taint virtually everyone at Broadmore Hall. How could she investigate them all? She would need to find someone she could trust.

The train arrived at the station at about noon. They climbed down to the platform and searched for a welcoming face.

"You must be Mrs. Thompson and Miss Reilly," said a burly, ruddy-faced, middle-aged Irishman in a coachman's top hat, long coat, and boots. "I'm Patrick O'Boyle and the one to bring you to the Jenningses' estate." He loaded their trunk onto a cart. "Follow me," he said cheerfully. They edged through the milling crowd to the coach.

O'Boyle gestured to a robust young man. "My son, Peter, home from college." He leaped from his seat and helped his father stow the trunk on the rear rack. A maid was waiting inside the coach and lent Pamela a hand as she climbed in. Brenda managed by herself. The coachman gave a command to the horses, and the coach lurched forward.

"How far do we have to go?" Pamela asked, settling into a comfortable cushioned seat, Brenda at her side. The maid sat facing her.

She was a neat, intelligent-looking woman, approaching thirty. Her face was comely, her eyes bright and observant. Pamela detected a regional accent, perhaps Midwestern. Her speech was better educated than one might expect from a maid. Could she have written the note? Possibly. The woman smiled politely—someone had trained her in good manners.

"In ten minutes," she said, "we'll be in the village. Broadmore Hall lies another few minutes to the southwest."

The coach rolled through a green countryside. The air was fresh, the temperature mild, and the gentle Berkshire Hills welcoming in the distance. "I could live here," Pamela said to herself.

"Shall we exchange names?" she asked the maid. "As you may know, I'm Pamela Thompson."

Her young companion added, "I'm Brenda Reilly."

"And I'm Margaret Rice, the pantry maid. They call me Maggie. The housekeeper told me to point out the sights on our way to Broadmore Hall."

During this exchange, Maggie fixed a searching, skeptical gaze on Pamela as if attempting to figure out why Pamela had come.

They soon entered the village. On Walker Street they drove past a large, handsome brick mansion. The coachman shouted,

"That's Ventfort Hall, built this year. Mr. J. P. Morgan's sister will soon live there."

Pamela admired the building's tall, curved gables and its palatial appearance. It was hard to think of it as merely a summer home.

A minute later, they came to a great stone church, as beautiful as any Pamela had seen in New York. She queried the maid.

"Trinity Church," she replied. "President Chester Arthur dedicated it a few years ago. Mrs. Jennings and many of the rich summer people go there on Sundays."

"And you, Maggie, where do you go?"

"It's also my church," the maid replied. "I live in Broadmore Hall all year long."

An unusually cultivated pantry maid, thought Pamela. The young woman was perhaps being groomed for a higher post in the household.

In the center of the village stood a large inn. "The Curtis Hotel," the maid volunteered. Several expensive coaches were parked in front. Men and women lounged in casual dress on the wide veranda. At the livery stable across the street O'Boyle watered the horses. Then he drove south out of Lenox less than a mile and turned right at a gatehouse. The porter waved him into a shaded avenue of tall elm trees that ended when a large building came into view.

"That's Broadmore Hall," the maid offered. "They call it a cottage."

The stone and shingled residence stood sprawling on top of a high, grassy knoll. From its many porches and the ground floor veranda the view would be breathtaking.

In a low voice the maid remarked confidentially, "Mr. Jennings pays for the upkeep of Broadmore Hall, but Mrs. Jennings built it and still owns it."

At the main entrance, the newcomers met the steward, Mr. Bernard Wilson, a middle-aged man with thinning silver hair and a gracious demeanor. He looked them over with a skeptical eye, then took them upstairs to their apartment on the first floor. The parlor was pleasant, roomy, and tastefully furnished with a desk, chairs, bookshelves, and a table. A fireplace heated the room. The walls were white and left unadorned. There were also two small bedrooms and closets.

A maid unpacked for them while they freshened up. An hour later, Wilson returned with the housekeeper, Mrs. Blake, who addressed Brenda. "Come, my dear. I'll show you around."

The steward led Pamela to Mrs. Jennings's apartment next door. Music could be heard from within. They entered a large drawing room, furnished with early American chairs and a cherrywood table. Landscape paintings and portraits hung on the off-white walls.

Mrs. Jennings sat near a grand piano. A young woman was playing a Mozart piano sonata. Her performance was labored but certainly acceptable from a student. When she finished, she turned around, and Pamela recognized her.

"This is Miss Clara Brown, a neighbor," Mrs. Jennings remarked, then introduced Pamela.

"We know each other from church in New York," Pamela said. "A few years ago, I led a group of young people, including Clara, in an effort to help the homeless." The young woman's parents had disapproved of the program and withdrawn her. They would give money to the poor but not their daughter. She was being groomed for a marriage in high society.

"I'm happy to meet you again, Mrs. Thompson." Clara seemed to mean it.

Mrs. Jennings said, "I'm giving Clara lessons. She'll be an accomplished pianist one of these days."

Miss Brown's cheeks flushed with embarrassment. "I'm really just a beginner. Mrs. Jennings is very patient with me."

For a moment, Pamela studied Miss Brown. She had grown up to become a most attractive young woman. Her auburn hair was thick and lustrous; her green eyes, beguiling. She had a clear, creamy complexion and a shapely body. The best education that money could buy had given her a graceful manner and a melodious, well-trained voice. On closer inspection, Pamela found in her eyes a certain naïveté; in her mouth, a contrary, petulant attitude. She wasn't altogether a happy young woman.

The lesson was soon over. Miss Brown received an assignment for the next session in a week. As she left, she said to Pamela, "I hope to meet you again when we can chat." Her tone was earnest.

When they were alone, Mrs. Jennings said to Pamela, "I noticed that you appreciate Miss Brown's beauty. Men can't keep their eyes off her. That, of course, can be a curse. Her parents are anxiously protective. This summer, they are traveling in Europe, but they've entrusted her to a guardian. These piano lessons are among the few occasions when she can go out on her own."

"She has my sympathy." Pamela wondered how the young woman was coping.

"How was your trip?" Mrs. Jennings asked.

"Warm and uneventful. I especially enjoyed the beauty of the countryside."

"Then let me give you a glimpse of the beauty of our estate." She led Pamela through the apartment onto a balcony, one of many on the house—they were its most remarkable feature. The view was spectacular. Mrs. Jennings lovingly identified its features. A long, grassy lawn sloped down to Lily Pond. In the distance shimmered the surface of Lake Mahkeenac, also called the Stockbridge Bowl. On the horizon gently rose the Taconic Range. Its highest points appeared to be over two thousand feet.

Back in the drawing room, Mrs. Jennings hesitated briefly, then asked, "In private, may I call you Pamela and you call me Lydia?"

"I would be honored." Pamela was pleased that her mistress took a reasonable view of social conventions.

Lydia briefly turned their conversation to the great Columbian Exposition in Chicago. "My husband has gone there for the transportation and mining exhibits. He wants to keep abreast of the latest machines and production methods and find clever men to work for him. 'No grass grows under my feet,' he likes to say." There was a hint of admiration in her voice.

Meanwhile, a maid served tea and sweet biscuits. Mrs. Jennings hardly noticed the servant and didn't touch the food. Pamela was hungry but followed her mistress's lead.

As they finished the tea, Lydia said to Pamela, "I urge you to become familiar with the staff and the estate as soon as possible. You know how anxious I feel. Wilson will assist you."

She rang for him. He received his orders with a compliant bow. As he and Pamela stepped out into the hallway, she asked, "When Mr. Jennings visits Broadmore Hall, where does he reside?"

Wilson nodded toward a door at the far end of the hallway. "His apartment is the mirror image of his wife's, except that it has a separate stairwell and exit in the rear of the house. He can come and go as he pleases, unobserved." For a moment, the steward gazed at Pamela with hooded eyes, concealing whatever he thought of the Jenningses' living arrangements and Pamela's question.

Then he resumed his usual dignified expression. "Please follow me." He led Pamela through the building, introducing her to the domestic staff as the mistress's new secretary and companion. Next, he took her to the chief gardener, who gestured toward a small heated greenhouse in front of a berry patch on the edge of a wooded area. Pamela expressed interest, so the gardener took her inside and pointed out several small palm trees and other exotic plants. "The mistress keeps her favorites here. Across Old Stockbridge Road, near the estate, are more greenhouses for flowers and a modern working farm that sends eggs and milk, fruit and vegetables up to the big house, with some extra to sell in the village. You can see all that on another day."

Wilson handed her over to Patrick O'Boyle, who showed her the coach barn and the stables, both of them designed in the same Shingle Style as the main building. Large, two-story structures, side by side, they were built of rough-cut gray stones at the ground level. Brown shingles covered the upper level. A young coachman had a room upstairs in the barn. Grooms and stable boys lived on the stable's second floor. The coachman, his son Peter, and the stable master had homes in the village.

During this tour, Pamela came to appreciate Lydia's remarkable spirit of enterprise. Twelve years ago, she had designed this vast, complicated estate and had seen to its construction. Thereafter, she had managed it, and it was as dear to her as any child of her own.

At the evening meal, Pamela and Brenda ate in the household servants' dining room, where the steward presided. Pamela quickly sensed trouble. Certain members of the staff averted their eyes or turned their backs. Chief among them were the steward and his clerk, Amos Brewer. Wilson's antipathy probably came from having to yield privileged status to Pamela. He most likely viewed her as a competitor for the mistress's favor. He might also have something to hide.

It was late when Pamela and Brenda returned to their rooms and examined them more closely. A maid had pulled drapes over the windows and had set a low fire against the chilly spring night air. Pamela carefully checked the rooms for peepholes while Brenda tapped the walls in search of hidden doors. They found nothing suspicious, and Brenda retired weary to her room.

Pamela sat at her desk and reflected. For a start, she would aim her investigation at the author of the anonymous note. Wilson was a likely culprit. As steward at Broadmore, he was well placed to know of cheating by members of the family as well as the staff. He could have faked the note's crudity to deflect suspicion away from himself. Even he might fear retaliation if he were to expose the cheater, especially if that were Mr. Jennings.

Facing resistance, Pamela had to find allies on the staff. Brenda could help keep her informed. The coachman appeared friendly. He also seemed to resent the steward's superior airs. The housekeeper had frowned unawares when the steward's name had been mentioned. Maggie Rice, the pantry maid, might also be useful if her trust could be won. But none of these servants would dare to speak critically of the steward. Though perhaps disliked, he was also likely feared, for he had power over those beneath him. Pamela sensed that he would gladly use it to serve his own interests.

CHAPTER 11

Investigation in the City

Lenox and New York, 21–24 May

Over the weekend, Pamela continued to study the estate and its staff. Brenda helped her determine which servants she could trust, Patrick O'Boyle chief among them. Early Sunday morning before church, Pamela visited him in the stable.

"Is there anything unusual about Mr. Wilson's behavior?" she asked.

O'Boyle studied her for a moment and replied cautiously. "Once a week, Wilson takes an early train to New York and returns a day or two later by a late one. He dresses up as if for business in a black suit, bowler hat, and gloves, and carries a fine black leather satchel. No one seems to know what he does."

"Wouldn't his clerk know?"

"If he did, he wouldn't tell you. Brewer is closemouthed and loyal to Wilson."

That afternoon at tea, Pamela asked Lydia if she knew about Wilson's visits to New York.

Lydia grew thoughtful. "I understand that he checks on conditions at our house on Fifth Avenue and runs errands in the city. At least, that's what he tells me. I don't trust him—he's Mr. Jennings's man or, more precisely, his spy." She lowered her voice. "Could you find out what he really does there?"

"I'll try."

On Monday, disguised as a servant, Pamela followed Wilson to the station. She feared that he might recognize her, so she kept a safe distance. Fortunately, his mind seemed preoccupied. He boarded the morning train to the city and took a seat in the parlor car. His formal dress and dignified demeanor made him look like a bank president. Pamela sat in the adjacent coach and opened a cheap novel to conceal her face.

Upon arrival at Grand Central Station four hours later, she followed him to the Jenningses' mansion. She rented a furnished room on an adjacent side street, then hurried back to Fifth Avenue and watched for him from behind a tree. After an hour, he came out, wearing a cap and shabby clothes and carrying a common sack. She followed him across town to a seedy pawnshop in Chelsea and to a nearby tavern called Barney's.

In the afternoon the tavern admitted decent women to a corner table with a view of the room. So Pamela bought a small beer and sat with two female servants who seemed to be regular patrons. From years working at St. Barnabas Mission, she felt comfortable with poor women and could imitate their speech and manners. She pretended to be new to the city, looking for work. "We're all in the same boat," said one of them. "Jobs are hard to find this year."

While keeping an eye on Wilson, she asked them in general about the tavern. Meanwhile, Wilson joined two rough-looking men, their caps and clothes as shabby as his. The three men huddled over a table, unsmiling, clutching drinks in their hands. Wilson listened to his companions and then appeared to give them instructions and to pass money. They soon left.

What had he asked them to do? Pamela wondered. Like Wilson himself, they must work in some way for Henry Jennings. Wilson finished his drink and went into a back room.

Pamela's companions told her that it was a large, well-known gambling den. The police were paid off to ignore it. When Wilson came out after an hour, she asked her companions about him.

"Oh, he's a regular here—a gent down on his luck," said one of them.

The other added, "Gambling will do that to you."

As he went upstairs, they exchanged glances and rolled their eyes. One of them mouthed to Pamela, "A fancy brothel. We don't know where he finds the money to go there."

"How long does he stay?" she asked.

Her companions shrugged. "For hours," one of them replied. "He eats and drinks there, chats with the girls. They say he questions them a lot about other patrons. For a while, we thought he might be a police detective." She hesitated, then asked with a wink, "Do you want to meet him?"

Pamela shook her head. "I'm not in that line of work—yet."

They smiled. "Don't worry," one of them said. "Keep looking. You'll find a job." Pamela thanked them, paid for her beer, and left.

The next day, still dressed as a maid, she followed Wilson again. This time he wore his black suit and bowler hat and visited a law office. Pamela jotted down the name at the entrance: "Allen, Partridge, and Associates." From there he took a tram to Union Square and entered Tiffany's jewelry store—boldly, as if he owned it.

Pamela worried that she wasn't dressed for such a fancy place. She would stand out among the rich, fashionable ladies shopping there. A floorwalker could stop her and uncover her disguise. Wilson might recognize her.

But she saw other maids going into the store, so she took the risk. If challenged, she would pretend to be Mrs. Jennings's maid, sent from Lenox to browse on her behalf for a small but tasteful gift. Still, Pamela got past the doorman without difficulty when an attractive, wealthy lady distracted him.

Once inside, she soon found Wilson hiding behind a pillar, intently watching a clerk showing diamond brooches to a customer. A floorwalker was also observing the clerk. Her back was toward Pamela. When the customer left, the clerk turned to put the brooches back into a display case. Pamela recognized Sarah Evans. Fortunately, the young woman's eyes were focused on the brooches, so she didn't notice Pamela, who now moved quickly to where she could still safely watch Wilson.

Sarah almost certainly was preparing a theft. Wilson apparently suspected as much. But why would he care, unless it would interest Henry Jennings?

Pamela hurried to Prescott's office. It was now evening, but he might still be there.

Lights were on in the office. Pamela found Prescott about to leave. He smiled when he saw her.

"Can I have a minute with you?" she asked.

"Is it something we could discuss over supper?"

"It's business. I don't know how important."

"Then let's go to a quiet place."

He led her to a small, modest French restaurant in the neighborhood, called simply Le Bistro. The clientele was sparse late on a Tuesday, the atmosphere subdued.

"Have you eaten today?" he asked.

"Not since breakfast," she admitted.

"Then I recommend a vegetable soup with a Loire Valley white wine, followed by *crêpes sucrées* and brandy." He paused tentatively and added, "My firm will cover the expense."

"Thank you. I haven't had such a supper in years. But I could quickly regain my taste for it."

While they waited for the food, Pamela described her efforts to uncover what Wilson was up to in New York. "Yesterday, I learned that he frequents a gambling den and usually loses. He also goes to a brothel in the same building. Where does he find the money to support these vices?"

"Possibly from Henry Jennings, one way or another."

"And why would Wilson go to the law offices of Allen, Partridge, and Associates?"

"I'll try to find out. Partridge passed away several years ago, and the associates have moved on to other firms. That leaves George Allen and a clerk, hardly a thriving practice."

"Could Jennings be interested in George Allen and have ordered Wilson to investigate him?"

Prescott smiled wryly. "I have an inkling and may learn more on Thursday afternoon. I have an appointment to meet Allen at the University Athletic Club."

The soup arrived, and conversation changed briefly to the food and wine.

After the soup, Pamela continued. "I followed Wilson to Tiffany's, where he spied on Sarah Evans. Why?"

Prescott thoughtfully sipped his wine. "Perhaps Wilson thinks Allen and Evans are intimate because of his reputation as a lothario."

"If not intimate," Pamela ventured, "perhaps they are at least partners in jewel thievery. By happenstance, while working for Jennings, Wilson has discovered their thievery and hopes to extort money from them in return for not calling in the police." She paused, reflecting. "If our reasoning is correct thus far, George Allen is the bearded man who tried to kill me on Fourteenth Street."

Prescott nodded. "I hadn't thought of George as violent or homicidal, but it's possible. I'll tell Harry Miller to investigate this matter. Go with him to Tiffany's tomorrow morning and point out Sarah. He'll find out if she's involved with George."

A waiter came with the *crêpes sucrées*. Pamela ate a few distracted mouthfuls, then remarked, "Thus far, I haven't mentioned meeting your wife and the banker Fisher after church the Sunday before last. At the time, our encounter seemed brief and unimportant. But now I wonder why they sought me out and tried to pretend that the meeting was coincidental."

Prescott appeared to become annoyed. "Gloria is probably curious why I've hired an attractive and talented female as my assistant. She may fear that I'll slip from her grasp definitively. So she wanted to see you up close and form an opinion."

"How do you expect her to react?"

"We'll know soon enough. She may attack you and me with vile rumors and innuendo. I'm sure you're aware of my notoriety. It's almost entirely due to her."

"So, if she can't have you, no one else shall. Is that her attitude?"

He nodded. "But what's most disturbing is that she tries to turn our son, Edward, against me, fortunately without success."

"What do you make of her relationship with the banker?"

"She's a spendthrift and needs money, so she's turned to this rich, money-grubbing vulgarian, Fisher. He's looking for a sophisticated woman to guide him through the thickets of high society. Gloria can probably help him there."

Pamela remarked, "High society is beginning to look like a poisonous spider's web."

The following morning, Pamela and Harry Miller walked through Tiffany's busy main hall on the ground floor. Miller's eyes rapidly scanned the scene.

She asked, "What do you think?"

"I see opportunities here for a clever, daring jewel thief. Security in such a large, crowded, open building with its riches on display depends on loyal, well-trained clerks. Those I've seen thus far, whether male or female, are poorly paid and disinterested. That deficiency tests even the strictest supervisor."

In the jewelry department Sarah was standing behind a counter of precious stones, showing a diamond to a fashionably dressed woman while other customers looked on. Pamela pointed her out to Miller, who studied her from various angles, committing her features to his retentive memory.

"Her supervisor might tell us more about her," said Miller. "You are more likely to pry information from him than I. Go ask him."

When the floor supervisor seemed free, Pamela approached him. "Sir, your clerk at the diamond counter is remarkably competent."

"I'm pleased to hear that, ma'am. We hire only the best and expect a high level of performance."

"Could you tell me her name and something about her?"

"Sarah Evans. She's been with us almost a month. Came with excellent references." He studied Pamela quizzically. "You're the second person to show interest in her. A gentleman asked the same questions an hour ago."

"Oh, that must have been Mr. Wilson. Was he a distinguished-looking, older gentleman in a black suit and wearing a bowler hat?"

"Yes, that sounds like the man."

Pamela retreated to a quiet corner with Miller. He showed her a remarkable likeness of Sarah that he had drawn in his sketchbook. "My agents and I will follow Miss Evans for a few days. With luck, we'll find out for sure if George Allen is her accomplice."

Late that afternoon at Grand Central Station, Pamela boarded a train to Lenox. An hour earlier, Prescott had informed her that Dennis Reilly had been at police headquarters on Mulberry Street that morning. No one would say why he was there. He looked hale and hearty.

Prescott had remarked, "I think the police will put him to work. If so, he might have less time to harass you and Brenda. Nonetheless, he remains dangerous. Fortunately, you are returning today to the safety of Broadmore."

Pamela took a seat by a window and looked forward to trees leafing and daffodils blooming, early signs of New England's spring. She had also brought along a copy of Mark Twain's latest book, *The American Claimant*. The young noble hero's experiences in an American boardinghouse were so reminiscent of her own. The hours passed pleasantly. The sun dipped behind the Taconic Range. Finally, the conductor announced, "We're approaching Lenox Station."

At that moment, Pamela looked up and saw a familiar face at the far end of the car. The man rose from his seat and pulled down a brown satchel from the overhead rack. As he stepped into the aisle, he gazed over the heads of fellow passengers. He and Pamela locked eyes. "Dennis Reilly," she murmured, then instantly feared he would attack her. Instead, he turned away and left the train. She lost sight of him in the crowd on the station platform.

His appearance had greatly changed. Clean-shaven, well groomed, dressed neatly in a cheap suit, he could pass for an honest artisan on holiday. Why was he in Lenox? Pamela asked herself. Had the New York police sent him on a secret mission? Or was he here on his own initiative, mainly to harass her and Brenda?

"Pamela!" cried Brenda out of the crowd. She and Patrick O'Boyle had come to the station to pick her up. "You won't believe who I just saw." She was trembling, eyes wide with terror.

"Your father, Brenda. He was on the train." Pamela hugged the girl and calmed her down and drew her to a bench in the station. O'Boyle stood guard.

Pamela asked her, "What happened?"

Brenda drew a deep breath. "As my father was passing by, he stopped and stared at me. His eyes burned with desperate desire or fierce hatred—I don't know which, maybe both. He didn't say a word. I thought he was about to attack me. But Mr. O'Boyle was near and frightened him off."

They climbed into the coach and drove away. Pamela said, "Tomorrow, I'll telegraph Prescott. He'll tell us what to do. In the meantime, we'll keep a safe distance from your father."

CHAPTER 12

A Commission

New York, 25–28 May

Early in the afternoon, Prescott waited in an empty lounge in the University Athletic Club on West Twenty-Sixth Street near Madison Square. A clock ticked relentlessly in the heavy quiet of the room. He was worried. This morning, Pamela had telegraphed that Dennis Reilly had arrived unexpectedly in Lenox. She and Brenda had felt threatened.

Prescott had advised her to be cautious. He would try to find out why the NYPD had apparently sent Reilly to Lenox.

A waiter entered the lounge. "Mr. George Allen is here to see you, sir."

Prescott brightened. "Send him in." This visit would be challenging. According to a recent rumor, Mr. Henry Jennings was pursuing Allen's wife, Helen. A fetching, dark-haired beauty and highly regarded singer, she had married Allen ten years ago. At the time, he had showed promise of becoming a rich and famous lawyer, but his career had stalled. The practice of law bored him. He was a charming trifler, who excelled chiefly in tennis. His wife might have lost interest in him and turned her attention to the older, but still vigorous and far more successful, Henry Jennings.

Prescott hadn't seen Allen since his return from several weeks of sunshine, golf, and tennis at the exclusive Jekyll Island Club off the Georgia coast. He went there often. Fit at fifty, Allen had aged little since their college days at Columbia. His clean-shaven, smiling face had a healthy tan and few wrinkles. His pepper-gray hair was thick and wavy. In college he had been notorious for chasing pretty women and gambling. To judge from recent gossip, he hadn't changed much. He and Prescott ordered drinks.

"Is it true that Jack Thompson's widow is working for you?" Allen settled comfortably into an upholstered chair.

Prescott nodded. "Her mind is sharp, and she's got pluck. Her experience working in the tenements has toughened her. With training she has become a good detective."

"Really? That doesn't sound like women's work. What do you detectives do?"

"We gather information for clients that they cannot or will not get for themselves."

"Any information? How about evidence of adultery?" Allen's tone turned serious.

"Detective agencies, such as Pinkerton's, avoid divorce cases as too scandalous to touch. Within the law, I choose investigations, depending on whether the issues are interesting and will yield a profit."

Allen chewed on his lower lip, then blurted out, "You may have heard the rumor that my wife and old Henry Jennings are sleeping together. It's probably just malicious nonsense. People envy his wealth and prominence, or Helen's beauty, charm, and voice. She says that Jennings pays no more attention to her than to any other young woman. I would be a silly goose to believe otherwise. Still, the rumor itches, and I scratch it constantly." He emptied his glass and signaled a waiter.

He filled their glasses. The two men toasted each other. Prescott asked, "Have you any evidence of a romance?"

Allen stared into his glass before responding, then pulled a piece of paper from his coat pocket. "When I recently returned from Jekyll Island, I received this note. At the time, I ignored it. Now the rumor makes me wonder." He handed the note to Prescott.

The anonymous author had crudely printed on cheap unlined paper, "Your wife is a cheating whore. Old goat Jennings has found a way into your bed." The message's form was strikingly similar to that of the one sent to Mrs. Jennings.

"Have you shown it to your wife?"

"No. You are the only person to have seen it."

"Can you think of anyone who holds a grudge against you or your wife?"

"No."

"So, what do you want me to do?"

Allen's eyes narrowed, darkened. "Find out the truth."

"Come what may?"

"Yes!" His voice was hard as flint.

The two men agreed on the terms of the investigation, and Allen left. Before going any further, Prescott needed to learn more about him. Since their college days at Columbia, they had seldom met, but Allen's self-indulgent and vain character appeared unchanged.

He would be unfaithful to his wife. Still, he might kill the man who cuckolded him, assuming that a wife must be true even if her husband was not. Furthermore, Allen could be greedy and might seize this opportunity to extort money from the rich Henry Jennings. If adultery were proved, Allen could sue for damages as well as divorce. The threat of scandal might force Jennings to settle privately on Allen's terms —or, resort to more desperate measures.

For well-informed, discreet advice, Prescott approached the club's steward. The two men had developed a mutually helpful relationship. The steward sometimes paid Prescott to investigate certain candidates for club membership.

The steward was alone at his desk and gestured his visitor to a chair. "What can I do for you, Prescott?"

"George Allen has asked me to investigate his wife. He thinks she's cheating, and he's angry. Can you tell me more about him?"

The steward smiled wryly. "He gambles, lives far beyond his means, and is deep in debt. But that's not what you want to know, is it?"

Prescott shook his head. "Is he faithful to his wife?"

"Not at all." The steward lowered his voice. "Most of Allen's affairs are brief and lighthearted. He chases after good-looking and spirited shop girls. He brought one of them to a large, private party here last night—a young British woman, Sarah Evans."

"Interesting! Tell me more."

The steward frowned. "I strongly suspect she's a light-fingered lady. At the party a guest lost an expensive diamond-studded gold ring. She and Miss Evans were near each other in the ladies' lounge. It was crowded and bustling. Our guest removed the ring and unwisely laid it aside on the counter. While she was washing her hands, someone engaged her in conversation and distracted her. Moments later, she reached for the ring, but it was gone.

"Miss Evans had already left the room. When I finally found her, she agreed under protest to be searched. To no one's surprise, we didn't find the ring. An accomplished thief, she must have immediately passed it on to a partner. We could do nothing."

"Did you search Allen?"

"During the incident he was conversing with the host. I

couldn't see how he would have received the ring. So I refrained from challenging him. Since then, I've wondered."

Prescott nodded slowly, deliberately. "Miss Evans could conceivably have duped Allen, used him to gain access to the party. Or he could have picked up the ring later in a vase or other previously agreed upon drop-off place." Prescott thanked the steward. "I'll pursue the matter further."

Later that afternoon, Prescott called Harry Miller into his office and described the theft of the ring at the University Athletic Club. "Have you discovered any other connection between George Allen and Sarah Evans? Or has Wilson led us down the wrong path?"

"Today I investigated her furnished apartment in a house off Gramercy Park. It's larger and has finer furnishings than you'd expect a shop girl to have. Elegant silk gowns hung in her dressing room closet; on the floor were shoes to match. On a shelf were expensive wigs, gloves, kerchiefs, hats, and other articles only a rich woman would have. But I couldn't find any evidence of Allen's presence or any stolen goods. They might be cleverly hidden. While looking around, I noticed a rear stairway with an exit to the outside."

"Your report confirms our suspicion that Miss Evans is a thief. Your agents should keep track of her movements and search her background for a criminal record. Meanwhile, you and I shall investigate George Allen. We need a better grasp of his character. I'd guess that Wilson is an experienced, clever spy. His interest in Allen and Evans assures me that we're on the right track. I want to find out who attempted to kill Mrs. Thompson last month."

Sunday morning, Prescott and Miller went to Allen's house on Gramercy Park, a handsome three-story brick building in the Federal style. He had inherited it, together with a small fortune, from his father, a wealthy businessman. Allen was often away in Newport or most recently Jekyll Island, but he was in the city now until July, when the season in the Berkshires would begin in earnest.

Miller explained, "His house is only a few blocks away from Sarah Evans's. Like Sarah, he can come and go unobserved. The cook has a small room off the kitchen. Mrs. Allen's maid lives in a second-story room adjacent to her mistress. Allen's manservant has a room on the ground floor, and he doubles as a steward. For cleaning and other chores Allen hires servants, as needed."

"I'll take a look inside," said Prescott.

Miller led Prescott through an alley to Allen's back door. "This is a good time. Helen Allen and her maid are away at a weekend party on Long Island. The other servants have the day off and left the house after breakfast." He glanced at the sky. "The weather is perfect for an outing: cloudless, warm, and breezy. The cook won't be back until dusk."

"And Allen?"

"He left early to play golf. He'll eat a light lunch at the University Athletic Club and spend the rest of the afternoon on the tennis court."

"How did you get this information?"

"Allen's manservant, Frederick. He hasn't been paid in months. So I gave him ten dollars, promised him more, and told him to go bowling."

"I'll charge Allen for that bribe. Now let's go inside."

In a minute, Miller opened the door, and they walked up a stairway to the first floor parlor. Paintings hung slightly askew on the walls, a thin layer of dust covered a coffee table, and the air was stale. The dining room appeared equally unused. A search of the two rooms for stolen goods proved unfruitful.

"As you can see, the Allens do not entertain," Miller remarked as they climbed to the second floor. "In fact they rarely sit down together."

Helen Allen's apartment consisted of a bedroom, a study, and a large parlor with a dining area. A dumbwaiter brought food up from the kitchen. The rooms were clean and tastefully furnished. In the bedroom Miller picked open a small, locked chest filled with elegant, expensive rings, bracelets, necklaces, and other jewelry. "These are gifts from Henry Jennings, not stolen goods. Look." Miller picked up a bundle of note cards with affectionate messages from Jennings to Helen on various occasions.

The third floor was George Allen's apartment, organized on a plan similar to his wife's, but lacking order. Clothes were strewn over the furniture. Piles of old magazines lay helter-skelter on the floor. Remnants of breakfast were left on the dining table. "Allen just camps here, apparently," said Prescott. "Still, we should search his rooms."

An hour later, Miller shouted from Allen's study, "Look here!" He held up a handful of papers that he had retrieved from a drawer in the desk, initialed copies of messages between Allen and Sarah Evans. Prescott sat at the desk to read them. At first, their lack of affection surprised him. He had expected evidence of an illicit romance. Instead, he found a cryptic business correspondence, mostly concerning the dates, times, and places of meetings at various stores, public buildings, and homes.

Prescott called out to Miller in the next room. "Here's the University Athletic Club and the date Sarah Evans stole the ring. Somehow she must have passed it to George."

Several messages exchanged in late March caught his eye—skimpy references to Macy's and the Old Bohemia restaurant and a livery stable. Still, they weren't enough to convict Allen and Evans in court.

Miller appeared at the door and beckoned. "For more evidence, follow me." He led Prescott to Allen's dressing room and opened a large cabinet filled with a wide assortment of gentlemen's clothes. From a drawer Miller pulled out various false beards and mustaches. On shelves behind the clothing were several realistic wigs.

He remarked, "Allen must be Sarah's bearded partner."

"Correct," said Prescott. "The only reasonable, yet incredible, conclusion is that George Allen is a jewel thief." He paused and reflected. "I wonder how much of this evidence Wilson has discovered. If he knows as much as we do, will he report it to Henry Jennings or to the police?"

"Who knows?" Miller added, "Wilson might join the thieves and share the spoils. He needs the money. Jennings pays him poorly."

As they walked back to the office, Miller asked Prescott, "How far shall we pursue George Allen?"

"He should be punished for trying to injure or kill Mrs. Thompson, as well as for thieving. There isn't enough evidence yet to prosecute him. We need to find stolen goods. So, keep looking. I'll go to Lenox tomorrow morning to deal with Reilly."

Chapter 13

A Dangerous Complication

Lenox, 2 June

Pamela put on her most comfortable shoes for an afternoon walk, one of her cherished pleasures on the Jennings estate. It offered such a variety of beauty in its pond and gardens, woods and meadows, as well as charming views of the surrounding hills. There was a knock on her door. A maid handed her a small, plain envelope. Pamela opened it and read: "I need to speak to you in secret. Come to my cabin this afternoon. Directions are included. Prescott."

She felt a surge of anxiety. What could this possibly mean? He must have come to Lenox by an early train. In the course of her service with Lydia, she expected to contact him, and he might need to contact her. But why couldn't they meet in a parlor at Broadmore Hall? This short message's secrecy was also unnerving.

With strong misgivings, she finished dressing and set out for the cabin, a half mile away on the far side of the neighboring woods. He met her at the door.

"Welcome to my cabin." He led her inside and pulled up a chair for her at the table.

The main room was small and rustic with a large fireplace and an open loft. Against one wall was a sleeping alcove. On another wall hung snowshoes, skis, and ice skates. Off the main room was the kitchen with a modern iron stove, a table, cabinets, and a pantry.

"It's Spartan but charming," she said.

"I built it to be as different from the great cottages as possible and still comfortable. An outside well supplies water. The walls and ceiling are insulated. With heat from the fireplace the cabin is warm as toast in the winter."

Her gaze fixed on a photograph of a handsome, smiling young man. She moved up close for a better look.

Prescott joined her. "My son, Edward, hopes to become a lawyer like his father. As a boy, he used to spend the summers here and learned to swim and boat at Lake Mahkeenac. This summer he's living with his mother in Newport and working on a yacht."

"He resembles his father," Pamela observed, then turned and asked, "Why are we meeting here in secret?"

"I'm sorry to be so mysterious," he said. "For a private investigator to appear at Broadmore uninvited and ask for you might arouse unwanted curiosity. It could also alarm Wilson and his allies. Still, I need to warn you of a serious complication in your work for Mrs. Jennings. Her husband is apparently romantically involved with Mrs. Helen Allen. Her husband, George, is paying me to investigate that relationship. He may be thinking of divorce, extortion, or even deadly measures."

"Is this problem urgent?"

"The two men are likely to clash soon. Jennings is combative and ruthless and accustomed to getting what he wants. Allen is unstable but passionate and clever. He also may be inclined to violence—he's most likely the jewel thief who tried to kill you."

"Indeed! I look forward to meeting him again! What's likely to happen in the near future?"

"I foresee a major legal battle. My best guess is that Jennings has ordered Wilson to spy on Allen and gather ammunition to use against him in a court of law or public opinion. Jennings can afford to hire the most cunning, aggressive, and experienced society lawyer."

Pamela frowned. "Could the scandal of a legal battle be avoided? It would distress Lydia Jennings."

Prescott nodded sheepishly. "At first, I thought that I might function as a mediator. Now, since getting to know each man better, I doubt that a peaceful solution is possible. To deal with this situation I need your assistance."

"I'm willing to help."

"Look at this." He handed her the anonymous message to George Allen.

She studied it carefully before reading aloud, "Your wife is a cheating whore. Old goat Jennings has found a way into your bed." She returned the message to Prescott, adding, "This note resembles the one sent to Mrs. Jennings—similar warning, paper, and hand printing. What should I do?"

"Determine the author of the notes and look for evidence of the alleged romantic relationship between Mr. Jennings and Mrs. Allen. Report to me here at the cabin within the next two weeks."

"We're expecting Jennings in a week. I should see him then and draw a first impression." Pamela rose from the table, and Prescott showed her to the door.

"And what has become of Dennis Reilly?" he asked.

"He has taken a room at one of the better boardinghouses in the village. We see him on Main Street. He has found summer work at the casino in Stockbridge. His employer told me that Reilly is skillful at all kinds of card games. He also gambles privately in Lenox with reckless young men from the cottages. To judge from his new clothes, he's winning a lot of money. His transformation seems remarkable. When I first met him, he was an illiterate, unemployed Irish immigrant."

Prescott nodded. "In prison he learned to read and write and found his talent for playing cards. When he was released, he went to work in a gambling den, Barney's, in New York, where he played for the house."

"Barney's?" she asked. "That must be the same den that Wilson frequents. They may know each other."

"We must keep that in mind," noted Prescott. "How has Reilly behaved toward you?"

"Thus far, he hasn't physically or verbally threatened either Brenda or me, but he stares at us with a menacing expression. The very sight of him upsets Brenda. Why is he here?"

"My contacts in the NYPD say that Inspector Williams is personally grooming Reilly for undercover work and has sent him here to ferret out swindlers who prey upon rich, elderly summer visitors. The inspector has perhaps encouraged Reilly to contact his daughter, hoping that her attitude toward him might improve."

Pamela felt her temper rising. "How has Reilly been instructed to deal with me?"

"My contacts couldn't say. But the mention of your name and mine caused the inspector to rant that we were enemies of the police and thorns in his side. He has hinted that someone should push us out of the way. Therefore, I assume he has given Reilly virtually a free hand in dealing with us."

CHAPTER 14

The Only Son

3 June

When Pamela rose the next morning, Dennis Reilly's threat had given way to a new concern. At breakfast, she received an invitation to Lydia's study to meet John Jennings, the family's black sheep. He had arrived at Broadmore Hall late the night before. She needed to know more about him. He might be a source of Lydia's anxiety.

While eating, she recalled what she knew about John. This much was fact. He was thirty years old, the only child from Henry Jennings's first marriage. Lydia got on well with him and was his chief financial support. By all accounts, he was handsome, charming, and an outstanding sportsman.

Over the past few days Pamela had gathered other impressions of the young man. Servants and townspeople often dismissed him as a playboy. She had also picked up a few veiled references to Jennings's displeasure with his son's perverse sexual inclination. If true, it could cause serious tension in the family. Henry Jennings was apparently neither an understanding nor a forgiving parent.

Now, before the meeting with Lydia, Pamela felt she needed

advice from a detached observer. Patrick O'Boyle was a fair-minded, perceptive judge of men and knew the family well. She would talk to him.

She finished breakfast and walked to the exercise track. Patrick was leaning on the fence, watching a pair of pure black coach horses at play. He smiled as she approached.

"Want a ride, ma'am?"

"I'd love it, Patrick, another time. Is this a good place for a few questions . . . about John Jennings?"

His eyes grew a bit cautious. "Sure, fire away. I trust the horses to mind their own business."

Pamela lowered her voice. "I've heard there's bad blood between John and his father. Is sex at the root of it?"

"You're frank, ma'am. So I'll be the same. In a nutshell, John Jennings has what's called an unnatural inclination toward young men. As long as he doesn't hurt anyone, I say that's his own business. But his father hates him for it."

"Could you be more specific?"

He grimaced with distaste. For a moment he focused on the horses. Then with a nod he explained that the issue had surfaced in John's adolescence. When Henry Jennings had first heard of his son's "sick" behavior with other boys, he had beaten him. As John grew up, he became too big and strong to be beaten. So instead, his father had showered him with verbal abuse, calling him a sneaky sodomite. A year or two ago, Henry Jennings had disowned John and struck him from his will.

"How does Mrs. Jennings deal with this conflict in the family?"

"It's a big bone of contention between her and her husband. She welcomes John to Broadmore and puts him up in an apartment next to hers. They enjoy playing the piano together. He comes often, usually when his father is away."

"But if they should meet, what happens?"

"They ignore each other. Mrs. Jennings tries in vain to reconcile them."

As Pamela entered Lydia's study, John was lounging at a side table with his stepmother, drinking coffee. For a moment, his expression was critical, then it quickly turned friendly.

"Pamela, I want you to meet my stepson, John," said Lydia with obvious pleasure.

He was a smiling man with wavy blond hair, a trim mustache, and bright blue eyes. His features were almost too perfect, and he had an athlete's splendid body. His conversation was cultivated and good-humored. Within minutes, Pamela felt comfortable with him.

"Have you been to the lake yet?" he asked her.

Pamela admitted that she had not.

"Then, may I take you out in my boat?"

She thought for a moment, while searching his eyes. John seemed to have more in mind than a boat ride. It probably wasn't about sex. But he might want to unburden himself. That could throw light on relationships in the Jennings family.

"A morning hour on the lake would be delightful," she replied.

During the short coach ride to Lake Mahkeenac, she learned that John's hobby was building small boats. "My father claims it's a waste of time. I say it's more meaningful than anything he does. He just moves money around and takes a generous cut for himself. That doesn't make him a better man."

"Is your hobby rewarding?" Pamela asked.

"I enjoy transforming raw wood into beautifully shaped objects. No two of my boats are alike. One of them, a canoe, is in the Mahkeenac boathouse."

The brown shingled, two-story rustic building was built on rocky ground that sloped steeply down to the lake. From the road Pamela and John entered the upper story. Inside was a spacious, rustic hall with wooden chairs and tables. They walked out onto a long porch for a magnificent view over the lake to October Mountain in the distance.

The boat room was down a flight of stairs. The custodian couldn't be found, so Pamela helped John lift his canoe off a rack and into the water. Long and sleek, it was artfully constructed in an alternating pattern of light and dark wood. They set out into the lake, she on a seat facing him. He paddled effortlessly to the middle and let the canoe drift.

The air was fresh, cool, and nearly still, the water limpid. For a few minutes they silently enjoyed the gentle, green-crested hills to the east and to the west. Across the lake on a knoll stood Broadmore Hall. Pamela pulled field glasses from her bag and scanned the building. On one of the lakeside porches was a tiny figure waving at her and John. Mrs. Jennings, no doubt.

After a few minutes, Pamela sensed that John was eager to speak. She encouraged him with a tilt of her head and an expectant smile.

He began hesitantly. "You may have heard that my father and I have been estranged this year. I've come to Broadmore only for my stepmother's sake." He paused. "Well, not solely. I enjoy the swimming and boating in this place. It's really only my father that I cannot bear. Of course, the feeling is mutual." His expression had turned bitter.

"Is this too hard for you to discuss?" she asked. "We could speak about less painful things."

He shook his head. "I need to talk to an intelligent, empathetic stranger, someone who is not caught up in our family's conflicts. Lydia recommended you."

"I'm willing to listen. Tell me about your father."

For a long moment, he studied her. Then he began to speak in a lighthearted tone as if the conflict with his father pained him too much to treat seriously.

"My father has never cared for me. As a child, my health was delicate. I found pleasure in reading history and fiction, in drawing and music. Father was too absorbed in his business career to pay much attention to me. At age ten, when my mother died, I was developing into a shy, retiring, and dreamy child.

"Displeased that the heir to his fortune was becoming a good-for-nothing, Father tried to 'make a man' out of me. He dragged me to sporting events and on hunting and fishing trips and forced me to shoot and to box. When I failed or protested, he cursed and occasionally beat me. My physical health improved, and I grew to be rather sturdy. He couldn't beat me anymore.

"When it came time for college, Father insisted that I go to Yale. 'That's where a young man must make useful connections for business,' he claimed. I knew that he hadn't gone to Yale. He began as an orphan in the Berkshires, worked his way up from clerk to partner in a mining company, made a small fortune in the war, and has since enriched himself many times over. His career in business certainly hasn't suffered from lack of connections.

"I spent an unhappy year at Yale, then transferred to Williams College, where I was only an hour from Lenox and Lydia by train. I did well in things I liked—literature, art, and music—but I failed science and mathematics. Didn't join a Greek society, lived alone, and had few friends. Father was very angry and called me a lazy coward.

"After a year, I dropped out and spent much time at Broadmore with Lydia. Kind and understanding, she has been my best friend since childhood. We enjoy the piano and play duets. When she married my father, she became my stepmother and my strongest support.

"Father insisted that I do something useful with my life, like go into business. I tried a few jobs in New York without success. That has moved Father to disown and disinherit me. Well, now you know my story. You might wish it were happier. Perhaps better days lie ahead."

He gave her a wry smile and added, "The family will gather at Broadmore over the Independence Day holiday. That should be jolly." His smile faded. His lips quivered. He seemed on the verge of tears.

She felt an urge to hug him, but thought better of it. He had left unsaid the most painful issue, his sexual inclination. Couldn't he bear to bring it up?

On the way back to the boathouse, they met a small sailboat coming slowly toward them. Clara Brown was at the helm in a trim white dress and a jaunty sailor's cap. A portly, middle-aged woman accompanied her. Pamela and John waved. Clara returned the greeting. The companion frowned.

"Poor Clara!" exclaimed John. "Her companion's frown is perpetual."

Pamela asked, "Must Clara have a guardian?"

"Yes," John replied. "Her parents are grooming her for a marriage to a rich man and a place in high society. She detests the idea and has said so. Therefore, her parents have shackled her to this woman while they travel abroad."

"How has she reacted to this parental tyranny?"

"In public she seems to conform to her parents' rules."

"Does she behave differently when her minder isn't watching?"

"Would she be human if she didn't?"

Pamela asked John to explain, but he replied, "You'll find out soon enough."

CHAPTER 15

Church

4 June

Early Sunday morning, Pamela called out to Brenda, "Your coach is ready, princess." The young woman promptly appeared in a simple, light blue muslin gown. Her smile was radiant. Life was good, Pamela thought, and waved her off, marveling at how far Monica's poor little Irish girl had come.

The day before, Brenda had expressed a wish to attend St. Ann's Roman Catholic Church on Main Street, a wooden frame building in the Gothic style, a modest church compared to Trinity. The O'Boyle family had invited her to attend Mass with them, followed by dinner at their home. Brenda was finding friends among the servants and feeling more secure outside the estate. Still, to her distress, her father often appeared in the distance, staring at her.

Though Brenda had been baptized, she rarely attended church. Her father wouldn't allow it in the family. Brenda's new interest in religion had surprised Pamela, but she didn't probe. The coachman's warm, generous nature might have filled the young woman's need for a father she could respect.

She was also attracted to his son Peter, a wholesome as well as handsome young man.

After Brenda's departure, Pamela met Lydia in the breakfast room. It offered a splendid view toward Lily Pond and Lake Mahkeenac. Lydia had invited her stepson, John, to join them, but he had declined without offering a reason. Lydia was obviously disappointed. After breakfast the two women set off in a coach for Trinity Church. During the ride, Pamela asked about John's refusal to attend.

"It pains me to think about it," Lydia replied. "He used to enjoy the worship at Trinity. It's such a beautiful and uplifting experience. But recently it's been whispered about that he has 'unnatural' inclinations. He feels that the church doesn't welcome him anymore. I don't think that's the case, but there you are."

Lydia fell into a profound silence. When she roused herself, she commented on the imposing stone church in the distance, remarkable for the high quality of its design. "Romanesque," she noted, as they approached the building. Behind it stood the new stone and shingle rectory. "It's a gift from Mr. John Parsons, a lawyer from New York." She added, "He's one of the most generous of the summer residents."

As the service got underway, Pamela noticed that many of the congregants were fashionably dressed, cultivated residents who lived year-round or, like Lydia, most of the year in Lenox. They greeted her with the fond respect owed to a pillar of the church. Other members of the congregation appeared to be common folk, like Maggie Rice, who worked on the great estates.

After the service, there was tea in the rectory. Lydia introduced Pamela to a few friends as her new companion. They gazed at her with a mixture of curiosity and apprehension. Pamela wondered if her role as a private investigator might no longer be secret.

From Prescott's earlier description, Pamela had recognized Helen Allen in the church. She was tall and shapely, with a graceful bearing and a youthful appearance. Her hair was thick and black; her eyes black, tinted with gold; her complexion, smooth and creamy. She wore a fashionable, light golden silk gown. At thirty, she was half Henry Jennings's age.

During the tea, Pamela stood apart, observing the crowd. Mrs. Allen walked up to her. "Mrs. Thompson? You must be Mrs. Jennings's new companion. I'm so pleased to meet you. Your arrival has set Lenox society abuzz with curiosity."

"And I presume you are Mrs. Allen. I've admired your gown," Pamela said honestly. "Have you come to Lenox for the season?"

"I think so," she replied, acknowledging the compliment with a smile. "For now, I'm at the Curtis Hotel. My husband will soon arrive to search for a house to rent in Lenox. If he's successful, we'll stay until autumn." She went on about the beauty of the Berkshires and the grandeur of the cottages, gradually warming up to Pamela. After a few minutes, she asked, "Would you mind if we used our Christian names? I'm Helen."

"And I'm called Pamela."

"If you're free later this afternoon, Pamela, we could walk to Ventfort Hall, the new Morgan mansion. It's virtually finished. The family will move in this month."

Pamela showed interest. "I caught a glimpse of it as I rode into Lenox. I've heard that it's the grandest cottage in the Berkshires."

Helen agreed and then added, "It's private, of course, so we can't go inside. But we could admire the exterior. The weather is perfect. We could become better acquainted."

Pamela noted that Helen had taken the initiative in their meeting. Was she scouting a potential obstacle to her pursuit of Henry Jennings? Her present proposal was intriguing. Yet, one should deal with her cautiously. She had intelligence and determination of a very high order. Pamela could imagine how Jennings might fall helplessly into her clutches.

Still, knowing her better could prove useful in protecting Lydia's interests. A walk together would incur no obligations.

Pamela nodded. "Shall we meet at four o'clock on the hotel veranda?"

"Agreed," Helen replied with a smile, perhaps more cunning than sincere.

At that moment, Lydia came by, giving Helen a polite nod. Pamela wondered how much Lydia knew about her husband's affair. For her part, Helen appeared unembarrassed.

Promptly at four, Pamela climbed the steps to the hotel's veranda. At the same moment, Helen walked out the front entrance. For a few minutes they stood on the veranda planning their walk.

Finally, Helen sighed, then asked doubtfully, "I'd love to see Ventfort from the inside. Do you think the porter would let us in?"

"I believe he would," Pamela replied, "thanks to Mrs. Jennings. She knows him well from Trinity Church. Her friend, Mrs. Morgan, has invited her to observe the building's progress." Pamela pulled a note from her bag. "Mrs. Jennings has requested that the porter show us through the ground floor and gave me money to pay him. She would have joined us, but she's indisposed. I'm supposed to give her a full report." Helen seemed relieved.

On the way to Ventfort, Helen spoke with mounting enthusiasm about her visits to the great houses of rich families in New York and in their favorite resorts—Bar Harbor, Newport, and Lenox. To vacation in such places, Pamela surmised, Helen and her husband must have a great deal of money or large debts.

After a ten-minute walk, the imposing brick mass of Ventfort Hall loomed up before them. They stopped to take in its
grand three-story exterior, especially the tall, curved gables and
the elegant porte-cochere at the entrance.

They moved on to Ventfort's Walker Street gatehouse, a
charming brick building in an early seventeenth-century style.
A porter appeared at the door. When they asked to visit the
mansion, he frowned and shook his head vigorously. But after
reading Lydia's note, he agreed. "Please don't tell the world that
Ventfort is open to the public. I would lose my position here."

He led them into an enclosure of greenhouses, fruit trees,
and gardens, protected from the cool wind by a high brick wall.
Helen looked around, eyes wide, like a child in a candy store.

"Who takes care of all this, as well as the trees and the
lawn?" She waved a hand at the greenhouses.

The porter smiled. "Mr. Huss, a Swiss master gardener, di-
rects dozens of skilled men."

A few steps farther on, they reached the mansion's entrance
under the porte-cochere. The porter unlocked the door and led
them into the great central hall that extended through the
building's width. Helen's lips parted in awe.

"The hall's paneling and ceiling beams are made of carved
oak," he remarked and then called their attention to a minstrel's
gallery overlooking the hall. Next, he gestured to the right.
"There you have a library and a salon." Both rooms had richly
ornamented plaster ceilings.

"And to the left," he continued, "is the dining room. The
ceiling and wainscoting are of Cuban mahogany. We expect to
have sumptuous dinners here. Mrs. Morgan is known to entertain in grand style. Ventfort Hall has fifteen bedrooms and can
accommodate many guests."

The porter next led them through a long gallery extending
from the central hall to a huge billiards room at the far end of

the building. Off the gallery were a writing room and a morning room.

He remarked with a touch of pride, "Ventfort has gas and electric lights, an elevator, and central heating. And Mrs. Morgan installed a bowling alley under the long, covered back porch."

They entered the empty billiards room. "It spans the width of the house," the porter pointed out. "There will soon be several billiards tables here for Mr. Morgan and his guests."

"What grandeur!" Helen exclaimed, waving her arms dramatically. "This is truly a palace, hardly a cottage."

"I hope you've enjoyed the tour," said the porter and bowed to the two ladies. "I must get back to my duties."

As they retreated to the front entrance, Pamela discreetly handed him an envelope with a stipend for his services.

He pocketed the money and softly thanked her. "Before you leave, you should visit the flower beds. The Morgans also have Japanese evergreens and many other exotic trees. Mr. Morgan is an avid horticulturist. His flowers have won prizes." Tipping his cap, he left them under the porte cochere.

Pamela and Helen had the entire estate to themselves on this Sunday afternoon. The gardener and his crew were off for the day. The two women strolled on paths through blooming spring flowers. Helen knew many of their Latin botanical names. A brisk wind was blowing, but the tall brick wall shielded the two women as well as the plants. They found a bench facing the flower beds and silently enjoyed the view.

Finally, Pamela asked, "When did you acquire your taste for great houses like Ventfort?"

"For as far back as I can remember, I've always enjoyed large, well-designed mansions and gardens. I grew up in the porter's house of one of the Newport mansions."

Pamela gently asked, "Would you like to own a great house and garden?"

Her companion's eyes grew hooded. She hesitated, then spoke brightly. "I hope that one day a great fortune might fall into my lap. I would then build a mansion even grander than Ventfort. That's unlikely to happen anytime soon."

"Why not?" Helen only needed to snare Henry Jennings.

"At present, my husband can barely find the money for our train fare to Lenox." She chuckled. "I jest, of course. Still, in the world as it is, only a privileged few can afford anything comparable to Ventfort."

Helen tilted her head in a probing gesture. "And what are your hopes and dreams, beyond helping a rich, sick old lady?"

Pamela felt a brief, sharp pang of sorrow. "It's been a while since I've had any grand hopes or dreams. For the moment, I'm happy to assist Mrs. Jennings. I don't know if she's truly rich. She's not really old, certainly not in spirit. But she's unwell and needs a companion."

"How do you assist her, precisely?" Helen's tone was becoming sharply inquisitive. "Rumors are flying about that you've worked at Macy's as a private detective, a remarkable occupation for a woman, especially one of your standing. Does Mrs. Jennings need protection from theft or violence?"

Pamela grew cautious. She shouldn't admit that her chief duty was to investigate wrongdoing at Broadmore Hall. In fact, theft was likely and violence was possible. She didn't trust Helen and couldn't confide in her. So she evaded the question. "I read to Mrs. Jennings, deal with her correspondence and appointments, and help her look after the estate. I tell her if I notice anything that she should attend to."

Helen wrinkled her brow. "Have you discovered anything out of order?"

"Nothing that I may discuss publicly."

"Well, to judge from the authority that you've received from Mrs. Jennings, you must enjoy her trust and use it prudently."

"Of course, we all want the estate to function well."

With that, the conversation returned to Ventfort's remarkable flowers and trees. Helen's true purpose for this visit remained obscure and worrisome.

CHAPTER 16

Testing

5 June

Early Monday morning, Pamela drove a light coach to Prescott's cabin. He had business in New York. Last night his message had asked her to arrange for a coach to take him to the railroad station. She should ride along and report on her afternoon visit with Helen Allen.

Driving the coach herself, Pamela arrived at the cabin a few minutes early and knocked on the door. Prescott opened it, portfolio in hand, ready to go. As they approached the coach, he looked surprised. "Where's the coachman?"

She replied with a teasing smile. "Why, he's cleaning out the coach barn back at Broadmore."

They climbed into the coach. She took the reins, smartly cracked the whip, and they set off.

He turned to her with feigned amazement. "I didn't know you could drive. I'm impressed! Now tell me about yesterday with Helen Allen."

Pamela gave him a quick sidewise glance. "Helen tried to test me. I'm in her way. She intends to push Lydia aside and marry Henry Jennings. Late last night, he arrived at the station in his private car. I believe she joined him there. She didn't return to the Curtis until dawn. I checked at the desk."

He looked alarmed. "Helen Allen is bolder, and more dangerous, than I had imagined."

"Sometime today, I'll meet her lover Jennings and perhaps learn if he's really caught in her net."

Late that afternoon, Lydia called Pamela aside. "We'll go to my husband's study now. I'll introduce you to him. Be warned. He may play the gentleman, or he may not. I can't predict his behavior with any degree of confidence. Unpredictability is a strategy that has thus far worked well for him." Lydia took Pamela's arm and rose laboriously from her chair.

They walked slowly to the study. Pamela shuddered at the prospect of meeting Jennings. After all, his brazen deception in selling shares of a worthless copper mine had led to her late husband's financial and personal ruin. Jennings wouldn't know about Jack Thompson or his loss, nor would he care. From his point of view, gullible investors like Thompson were doomed to fall by the wayside in the struggle for survival.

Lydia knocked. A gruff bass voice invited them in. Jennings sat at his desk, pen in hand, an account book opened before him. "Make yourselves comfortable," he said and gestured toward a group of upholstered chairs by a large, empty fireplace. "I'll be with you in just a minute."

Pamela used the time to study Jennings. At sixty, he looked twenty years younger and had a commanding presence. His hair was pepper-gray and curly, his body muscular, his manner brusque. A great hawk nose reminded Pamela of his predatory instincts. It was hard to imagine that Helen or any other woman could seduce him.

He was sitting upright in a straight wooden chair. A pillow supported his back. As he rose from the desk, he winced and took the pillow with him to a straight chair by the fireplace. "Sorry to act like an invalid, but I've recently sprained my back."

Lydia remarked, "I'm pleased that the pillow I gave you is being put to good use." She turned to Pamela. "I embroidered it ten years ago. A handsome piece, if I may say so myself."

Jennings handed it to Pamela. "Take a look, madam."

A large, finely woven red rose was embroidered on white linen. "It's beautiful," she remarked, "one of a kind, a priceless gift." She ran her fingers lightly over the soft fabric and gave it back to Jennings.

A tender feeling briefly seemed to grip him. He arranged the pillow in his chair, settled in, then fixed Pamela with a searching gaze. "So this is the new companion." With a hint of skepticism in his voice, he asked his wife, "And what are her qualifications?" He idly fondled a diamond-studded pin in his lapel.

Lydia replied, "Intelligence, honesty, and trustworthiness. She's also well educated and has a wealth of experience that has already proved useful to me."

During his wife's remarks, Jennings's gaze remained fixed on Pamela. She steeled her nerves and held a polite smile on her face, quietly defeating his attempt to intimidate her. His expression then took on a friendly aspect. "And what do you have to say for yourself?" he asked.

"I enjoy your wife's company and the opportunity to live in such a splendid house. Broadmore Hall reminds me of the great manor houses of Britain that I visited years ago after college." She glanced at a collection of weapons that occupied an entire wall of the study. There were swords and daggers of all sizes, their handles studded with precious stones, and many pistols and muskets, some of them antique. The most dreadful-looking weapon was a mace or war club, its rounded metal head covered with short spikes.

"I see that Broadmore is armed to defend itself," said Pamela. Jennings left his chair and lifted a pistol from a rack on the wall. "A Colt .44. My favorite." He handed it to Pamela. Mrs. Jennings protested.

"I'm familiar with firearms," Pamela explained. She studied the weapon and returned it to Jennings. "It's beautiful in its own way, efficient as well."

"Then you should enter our target-shooting contest on the Fourth of July. Women take part."

"I regard that as an invitation. If Mrs. Jennings will allow me, I'll play the good sport and join you."

Lydia approved with an unenthusiastic nod.

Jennings addressed Pamela. "You express yourself well, madam. I look forward to further conversations. Now I'll excuse myself and prepare for dinner."

"Before we go, sir, may I ask a personal question?"

He looked surprised but not displeased. "Why, yes, you may."

"I've a serious interest in fine jewelry. Would you allow me a closer look at your unusually attractive lapel pin?" She couched her request in a deferential tone.

He nodded, unclasped the pin, and handed it to her. It was a simple, round piece, consisting of a large, multifaceted, pure diamond mounted on 14-karat gold.

"Exquisite," she said. "And the artist?"

"A jeweler at Tiffany's. It's a charm and brings me good luck."

She thanked him and returned the pin. He gave her a warm parting smile, and the two women left the room.

Out in the hallway, Lydia clasped Pamela's hand and whispered, "Well done, my dear. You showed spirit. That pleases him. He likes challenges. Life's a struggle, he says, and only the strong and clever can thrive."

Pamela felt that she could cope with him. Earlier, she had hoped that someone, other than she, would punish his evil deeds. Now she wondered if hubris so profoundly afflicted him that he was likely to bring on his own destruction. His lucky pin would not save him.

Late that afternoon, her chores finished for the day, Brenda Reilly rode with Mr. O'Boyle into the village. As often before during the past few weeks, she accompanied him as far as the town library on Main Street. He drove on to his home for supper and would pick her up on his return to Broadmore in the evening. Meanwhile, she would browse among the books.

She had become great friends with the librarian, Miss Jenny Krouse, even looking after the desk when she left early to run errands. "Stay as long as you like," she said. "Just turn out the lights and lock up when you leave."

Brenda was alone in the library, lost in Mark Twain's *Adventures of Tom Sawyer,* and barely heard the front door open. Someone approached the desk. When Brenda finally looked up, her father stood before her and said softly, "Brenda, I have much to tell you. I've locked and barred the door. We won't be disturbed. Come, follow me."

He started toward a storage room in the back. She remained at the desk, acting as if she hadn't heard him. Fear paralyzed her. He returned, stood behind her, and put his hands on her shoulders, at first gently, then with more pressure. "I said, come." This time there was ice in his voice.

She still refused to move. "No, I'll not leave this desk. I'm on duty here." Her voice trembled. She could hardly speak. "If you have no library business, you must leave."

"I'll not leave until you've heard me out." He dragged a chair over to the desk and sat facing her. His deep-set, dark eyes seemed to smolder. "Brenda, I'm a free man again, a Christian, and I'm fit. I've taught myself how to read and write. I've given up drink. I do honest work. Therefore, I intend to recover my rights as your father. Mrs. Thompson has poisoned your mind against me. But I'll not allow her to stand in my way. Like a dutiful daughter, you must repudiate her and submit to my authority."

"Never. She's my best friend," cried Brenda. "You killed mother. You're no longer my father. Now leave."

"You're a rebellious daughter and that proud woman's slave. Unfortunately, you will remain under her control until she is destroyed. If you truly care about her, then submit to me, and she will be spared."

Brenda could think of nothing to say—the man seemed mad. Yet he spoke clearly and cogently. And he obviously meant to kill Pamela.

At this moment, there was a loud banging on the front door. "Open up, Reilly," shouted O'Boyle. "I know you're in there. If you harm Miss Brenda, I'll break your neck."

For a moment, Reilly seemed stunned. Then he rallied, stared at Brenda, and spoke in a high-pitched, nervous voice, "Remember what I said." He hesitated and added, "Come with me to the front door and show yourself to O'Boyle. I haven't hurt you."

She went with him to the door. Reilly opened and was about to step out, but O'Boyle stood in the way. He glanced at Brenda, then moved aside. As Reilly passed, O'Boyle clenched his fists, as if about to strike, and growled, "Let her be. I mean it."

Reilly looked straight ahead and walked on.

Feeling faint, Brenda leaned on O'Boyle.

He patted her shoulder and said, "Don't worry, miss. From now on, I'll keep a closer watch on him."

Brenda nodded thankfully but added, "I fear for Mrs. Thompson."

Late that night, Pamela was at her table, writing in her journal. The door opened and Brenda brought in a tea tray. There was a worried expression on her face. "This evening at the library, my father threatened to kill you." Her voice trembled as she described the incident. "He scared the wits out of me. Are you watchful?"

Pamela nodded. "I take his threats seriously and often look over my shoulder when I'm outside Broadmore. I wish the town would make him feel unwelcome and he would leave. Unfortunately, he has won over his landlady. She thinks he has been misunderstood and treated unjustly. Others agree with her. Still, he may find it difficult to carry out his threat against me. He lacks access to Broadmore. I feel safe here. We've also warned certain people in the village that he's dangerous. They help keep an eye on him."

Brenda seemed skeptical. "He could hire a stranger, or someone else you wouldn't suspect." She left the room, shaking her head.

CHAPTER 17

Family Discord

6 June

In the morning, Pamela arose, still not rested. Dennis Reilly's snarling face had troubled her sleep. She fretted about Brenda, who wasn't safe even in the library. What would Reilly's next move be? He seemed impossible to anticipate.

Soon, Pamela was so busy that Brenda's warning and Reilly's threats slipped out of her mind. Preparations for the Fourth of July celebration were becoming intense. At a desk in her study, Lydia involved Pamela in discussing the guest list and writing invitations. A hundred carefully selected men, women, and children, plus servants, were expected to attend. Most lived in the village or the great cottages; a few would come from New York City. They would be treated to food and drink, music and dancing, sports and games. The celebration would conclude in the evening with spectacular fireworks.

Pamela asked, "What moves Mr. Jennings to produce such a lavish celebration?"

"It's his answer to the Lenox Club for denying him membership. When he was nominated ten years ago, someone in the club blackballed him."

Pamela expressed surprise.

Lydia sighed. "My husband's rough, ruthless manner earns him enemies as well as wealth. He makes light of the club's insult, but he has never forgotten or forgiven. He seizes every opportunity to get even. On the Fourth of July, the club has an elaborate, exclusive, and deadly dull luncheon. All the members are expected to attend. So Jennings has organized his own, much grander and exciting celebration. It's said that many members of the club would prefer to go to his festivities rather than to their own."

Pamela pointed to the guest list and remarked in a neutral tone, "I notice that Helen and George Allen have been omitted. A few days ago, I believe you mentioned that Mr. Jennings was expecting them to come."

"Yes, he will be disappointed," said Lydia with a note of satisfaction. "I am not sending them an invitation. We can't invite everybody. Mr. Jennings has asked to see the list before he leaves tomorrow for business in New York City. Please take it to him."

Pamela was troubled but didn't show it. Jennings would surely realize that his wife's snub to his mistress was an affront to him. Would he react in anger? With growing apprehension she walked to Jennings's study. He was at his desk, a newspaper spread out before him. His diamond lapel pin was lying to the side on a green velvet pad in a small opened case.

He glanced at the list, frowned, and penciled in the Allens. "I invited them weeks ago," he growled. "They will be here." Next, he struck his son, John, from the list. "You may take the list back to my wife." In a high-pitched, strident voice he exclaimed, "Tell her that I do not recognize John Jennings as my son. If he comes to the celebration, I'll ignore him."

His outburst shocked Pamela.

Jennings glowered at her. "You should know that my self-indulgent son refuses to marry and have children. He doesn't try to get ahead in the world but prefers to live on his step-mother's largesse. And he refuses to assume any responsibility for the business that I've spent the best years of my life building. What will happen to it when I'm gone?"

Pamela acknowledged his remarks with a slight nod of her head. This family was beginning to resemble a pit of vipers. She returned to Lydia with the altered list and related her husband's remarks.

She sniffed. "I'll not quarrel about the Allens. He can have them—he has his reasons, I'm sure. But I shall welcome my stepson, John, regardless of his father's opposing views. On second thought, I'll add Jeremiah Prescott to the list—though Henry dislikes him. I may need his skills."

Late in the afternoon, the guest list was finished and the invitations were ready for the mail. They would go out the next day.

"Now let's have tea," said Lydia and rang for Brenda Reilly. With the tea Brenda brought the *Berkshire Eagle*, a Pittsfield newspaper. Lydia spooned sugar into her cup and nodded to Pamela.

"Tell me the news."

Pamela read aloud the headline: " 'Lizzie Borden on trial. Selecting a jury commenced today in New Bedford.' " Lydia put down her cup and listened intently. Pamela went on to describe the tense scene in the courtroom and Miss Borden's somber appearance, and then summarized the heart of the case: "The prosecution will try to prove that no one but she could have killed her parents. The defense will argue that an unknown assassin could have done it."

Lydia and Pamela had both followed the case since August of last year when Lizzie's father and stepmother were found hacked to death in their Fall River home in southeastern Massachusetts. The case drew national attention. The crime had been gruesome. The victims were wealthy, prominent citizens.

No eyewitnesses or convincing evidence could be found. Still, within a week, the police had arrested Lizzie, a thirty-two-year-old spinster, chiefly because at the time of the crime she had been in a nearby barn and was alleged to hate her stepmother over the distribution of an inheritance.

Lydia shook her head. "I just can't imagine Miss Borden, a proper, well-mannered woman, attacking her parents with an ax. There are other, more likely suspects, such as the Irish maid, Bridget Sullivan, who was actually in the house at the time."

"She claims to have been resting and says that she didn't hear anything," Pamela countered.

"That's hard to credit," argued Lydia. "The victims' screams should have awakened her. If it wasn't she, then the Bordens must have surprised a burglar or a shiftless tramp, and he killed them to escape detection. These days, it could happen anywhere, even in the Berkshires."

Pamela thought that Lizzie—her gentility notwithstanding—could have swung the ax at her parents if she were mentally ill at the time and sufficiently provoked. In any case, murder among the wealthy and socially prominent was rare. Lydia had no reason to be concerned. Nonetheless, her chin was rigid; her mind was set. So Pamela said merely, "The trial will hopefully shed more light on what really happened."

That evening as Pamela walked by the stables, O'Boyle joined her. "You should know, ma'am, that Maggie the pantry maid has been seen with one of the tramps infesting the neighborhood." He explained that they generally had a bad reputation. At the least they were troublesome nuisances who should be driven away.

"How should we deal with them here at Broadmore Hall?"

"Mr. Jennings calls them 'thieving pests' and has ordered us to report them to the police, who will arrest them as vagrants."

Pamela had already heard that tramps were increasing locally in number and criminal activity since the severe nationwide economic depression began early in the year. Their huts could be found on the outskirts of the village along the railroad tracks near the Housatonic River, a mile east of the estate.

Pamela thanked O'Boyle, then spoke to the housekeeper and the cook and learned that food and supplies were missing. She suspected tramps were pilfering, possibly with inside help. Lydia would want her to investigate.

CHAPTER 18

Tramps

7 June

At daybreak, Pamela hid behind a bush near the back entrance to the kitchen. A few minutes later, Maggie Rice, the pantry maid, sneaked out, glanced furtively left and right, and beckoned. From a nearby grove a tramp dashed up to her. She handed him a large sack, waved good-bye, and scurried back into the kitchen.

As soon as the tramp disappeared into the grove, Pamela went to the pantry and discreetly confronted the maid. She was better educated and more experienced than most of the female servants and enjoyed their respect. Lydia was thinking of her for a higher position in the household, perhaps to replace the housekeeper when she retired in a few years.

Pamela addressed her politely. "Let's go to your room, Maggie. We have to talk."

The woman drew back a step, about to object. But she recognized determination in Pamela's eyes. "Yes, ma'am," she said sourly and led Pamela to her room.

On one wall hung a photograph of her, together with an

older, cultivated gentleman in rather shabby clothes. Pamela detected a strong resemblance.

"Your father?"

Maggie nodded. "He was a schoolmaster and taught the older children. Mother taught the younger ones."

In the background was a substantial brick building. "That's the company school in Calumet, Michigan," Maggie added.

Also on the wall was a shelf of well-used books, including a Bible, a history of the United States, and a few novels by Twain, evidence of a lively mind.

The two women sat at a table, and Pamela came directly to the point. "Maggie, what did you give to the tramp at the back door a few minutes ago?"

For a moment, she was speechless, but she reluctantly yielded to Pamela's insistent gaze. "I gave him bread, cheese, and fruit left over from last night's supper. The man said he hadn't eaten since early yesterday and had no money and no prospect of earning any today. He looked hungry. Feeding him seemed the Christian thing to do."

"I'm sure you know that Mr. Jennings has strictly forbidden tramps on the estate. You should have reported the man to the police, or at least called the steward."

"I understand, ma'am. It won't happen again." The promise seemed too quick and thoughtless to be sincere.

Pamela glared at the woman. "This wasn't the first time, was it?"

The maid averted her eyes and didn't reply.

The question hung in the air. It was clear that the maid had been feeding tramps for some time. Why? Pamela asked herself. This maid was neither gullible nor sentimental. She could see the sense in discouraging the tramps. Otherwise, they would infest the estate. So what was in her mind? Was this particular tramp her lover or a relative? Or was she secretly defying Mr. Jennings for political, religious, or personal reasons? Could she be the person, the enemy, whom the anonymous messages referred to?

"Your silence speaks loudly enough, Maggie. I should simply report your behavior to Mrs. Jennings and let her bring the matter to her husband's attention."

A terrified expression came over the maid's face. "Please don't. These are hard times. I'd lose my position and be put out on the street, destitute, with no prospect of work."

"Then tell me why you are consorting with this tramp or with tramps in general."

"He's Tom, an acquaintance who used to work here. Got into a terrible row with Mr. Jennings and was thrown out. Worked for five years in Chicago. A few months ago, he lost his job and came back to Lenox. Can't find work here, either."

Pamela decided that she needed to include Tom in her investigation. "What's his full name, Maggie? Show me where he lives."

"Tom Parker is his name." The maid frowned. "He doesn't want anyone to know where he's hiding. If the police were to find out, they would arrest him for vagrancy."

"You must cooperate with me, Maggie. Unless you take me to Tom, I'll report you to Mrs. Jennings."

The maid chewed nervously on her lower lip. Finally, she gave a deep sigh. "I'll do it, but he'll be angry."

Pamela nodded. "Nonetheless, we'll meet in the pantry in a half hour."

Pamela put on sturdy shoes for a walk in the woods. She and O'Boyle agreed on a backup plan. Then she went to the pantry. Maggie arrived a minute later, unsmiling. For thirty minutes, Pamela followed her on a narrow trail to the railroad tracks; then they walked a few more minutes along the tracks.

Pamela inquired about Tom. "Why did he quarrel with Mr. Jennings?"

"Tom was a handyman on the estate's farm. A clever fellow, he could repair almost anything and worked ten hours a day, six days a week. But Jennings gave him only a bed above the stables, food in the servants' dining room, and a dollar per week. The other farm workers and the common servants in the cottage weren't paid much better. Tom tried to organize a protest among them for more money. Jennings took it as a grievous personal insult and threatened to fire the lot of them. Tom called him a greedy bastard to his face. Jennings fired him on the spot and said he'd never again find work in Berkshire County. An outcast, he moved to Chicago."

At a thick grove of trees about thirty yards from the tracks Maggie stopped and whispered, "He's in there."

Pamela couldn't see any sign of a human presence. But Maggie led her through tall, dense brush to the grove. A few minutes farther on was a small clearing. Off to one side was a wooden shed, cleverly built of logs and bark to blend into its surroundings.

Outside the shed a man stood by a crude bench, a knife in one hand, a piece of wood in the other. He had heard the women coming. His deep-set, dark, hostile eyes focused on Pamela. He was thinner and shabbier than she had earlier imagined him. His face was gaunt and unshaven. Lydia might be moved to feed the man, but Mr. Jennings would violently object that such charity was misguided and undeserved and would simply attract more tramps to the area.

"Why in God's name did you bring her here, Maggie?" exclaimed the tramp.

"She insisted, Tom, and threatened to turn me in."

"I'm at the end of my rope and don't have the energy to hike any farther." He glared at Pamela. "What do you want?" He pointed the knife at her in a menacing gesture.

"I'm working for Mrs. Jennings. I'd like to ask you some questions."

"I'll have nothing to do with the Jennings family. They can't touch me. My shed isn't on their property."

"But your food and other supplies come from their kitchen. That has to stop. Too much suspicion has already been aroused. This morning Maggie was observed handing you a sack. If she continues to steal for you, she'll soon be caught. Jennings will charge her with theft, and she'll go to prison. Then what will you do?"

"I'll lie down and starve, silly woman. But not before I settle with that old devil Jennings." His grip tightened on his knife.

To calm the man's anger Pamela asked in a soft voice, "What do you do for a living here?"

"I carve children's toys. My partner tries to sell them door-to-door in the town." He showed Pamela the toy he was working on, a big, fat sow sitting straight up with a jolly smile on her face.

Pamela liked it and said so. "May I see your tools?" She wondered if they had been taken from the Jenningses' farm.

"I didn't steal them, if that's what you think." He beckoned her into the shed. Hanging on the wall above a workbench was a variety of tools. None of them had a Jennings mark. "I brought some of them with me from Chicago; others I picked up along the way."

"That may be true. But your blankets and coat come from Broadmore."

At that moment, Tom's partner returned to the shed. "What's she doing here, Tom?" he asked in an angry tone. He was a large man with a mop of curly gray hair and a wide, toothless mouth.

"Asking a lot of questions, Ben."

"She already knows too much," Maggie added, nodding to Tom. His eyes narrowed. He took a step toward Pamela.

Pamela raised a warning hand. "Before you do something you would surely regret, I must tell you that the coachman and his stable hands have followed us to this place. They are armed.

I'll leave you with this advice: Stop pilfering from the Jennings estate. The blankets and the coat look worn. You may keep them. I'll do what I can to promote the sale of your toys in Pittsfield and in New York City. Let's keep Mr. Jennings and the police out of this affair."

"Are you all right, ma'am?" came the coachman's big Irish voice from outside.

"What do you say, Tom?" Pamela asked.

He huffed, "I've no choice. Jennings wins again. He's got millions to burn. I've nothing. What's wrong with taking a loaf of bread and a hunk of cheese from him?" He turned to Maggie. In a voice steeped in sarcasm he exclaimed, "You heard what she said, 'Stop pilfering.' "

Pamela left the grove with O'Boyle and his men. She felt that she had won a battle but not yet the war. The tramp was Mr. Jennings's implacable enemy. A clever, determined man, he could cause a great deal of mischief.

CHAPTER 19

An Attack in the Woods

12–13 June

A few days passed. Pamela went about her routine work for Lydia. She also unobtrusively inspected the household. Everything appeared in good order. Maggie was complying with the estate's rules, and no tramps were in sight.

Then late in the afternoon on Monday, 12 June, Pamela took her usual walk through the garden. Since Prescott was away in New York, she also ventured into the woods, intending to go to his cabin. She would weed his vegetable patch and water his wilted plants. On the way, she left the path at the bridge over a creek flowing from high ground down to Lily Pond. She had discovered a rocky outcrop overlooking the creek.

There she sat listening to the gurgling water beneath her and let her mind wander where it willed. Then she brought forth her journal and began to write an entry for the day. Afterward, she would pick a small bouquet of wildflowers to place on Lydia's table at the evening meal. Lydia always looked so pleased when she saw it.

Today was windy. The trees creaked and rustled. The creek seemed to gurgle louder than ever. Pamela was so absorbed in her journal that she didn't hear the men's stealthy approach until they were upon her. Then she glimpsed a man raising a club. A second later, she felt a sharp, painful blow to her head and lost consciousness.

Brenda Reilly saw Pamela disappear on the path into the woods and thought nothing of it. She usually walked there at this time of day. But a few minutes later, Brenda noticed two men put down their tools, glance at each other, and follow Pamela. They had been trimming grass around the pistol range at the edge of the woods. Brenda didn't recognize them. As summer approached, seasonal workers were being hired. Still, her suspicions were aroused, and she looked for help. No one was close enough. Then Peter O'Boyle came with a large mallet for pounding fence posts. Brenda signaled desperately, and he came running.

"What's the matter?" he asked.

Brenda explained that two strange men had followed Pamela. "I fear they are working for my father," she added.

"Then she's in grave danger. We have to save her." They dashed to the path into the woods.

At the bridge, Brenda whispered, "She often leaves the path here and goes to the rocky outcrop in the clearing above the creek. We must go quietly."

They made their way to within sight of the outcrop. Pamela was lying on her side. One of the men stood above her with a large rock in his hands. He appeared about to drop it on her head.

"Stop!" shouted the two young people together. Peter charged into the clearing, shaking his mallet. Brenda screamed for help. For a moment, the rogues stared at each other. Then the man with the rock threw it at Peter, who dodged it easily. Peter struck him on the head, and he fell to the ground senseless. His companion had drawn a knife. But now he thought better of using it and fled into the woods. Peter followed him to the far edge of the clearing. Brenda knelt next to Pamela. She was unconscious, her face scratched and bruised. Blood was seeping from a wound on the back of her head.

Peter came back. "I lost sight of the other rogue. We can't stay here; he might return. I'll carry Mrs. Thompson out of the woods. Run ahead for help."

As Brenda hurried toward Broadmore, anger nearly blinded her. Her father had carried out his threat. At this moment, she would have killed him if she could.

When Pamela awoke, she was in her own bed. Her head felt twice its normal size. She was drowsy and suffered a low, dull pain. Brenda was at her side, pale and apprehensive.

"What time is it?" Pamela asked.

"It's near six. You've been unconscious for at least fifteen minutes. A doctor was already in the house on a sick call and looked at you. Apparently you've suffered no lasting damage. Mrs. Jennings is asking about you. I've sent for her."

Lydia arrived shortly. "How are you, Pamela?" she asked, her eyes searching the patient anxiously.

Pamela replied, "I'm fortunate. The blow could have been fatal. I'll be well soon." She went on to describe the incident.

Lydia wrung her hands. "The tramps are likely to attack any of us. The police must drive them out of the area."

Pamela tried to ease her anxiety. "I'm sure that the police are looking into the problem."

Lydia left unconvinced.

A couple of hours later, while Pamela was resting, Patrick O'Boyle arrived at the door in his coachman's coat and boots. Brenda asked her, "Could you speak to him?"

"Show him in."

Brenda led O'Boyle into the room. His face was flushed with exertion and triumph. He glanced at Pamela. "Hope you'll heal soon, ma'am. Sorry for the beating you took, but we've caught the two rogues who did it."

"Who are they?" she asked. "I didn't get a good look at them."

"They're a couple of tramps, new to the area, desperate men."

Brenda asked, "How'd you catch the one who got away?"

"You and my son Peter gave me a full description. I passed it on to all the other coachmen in Lenox—we're a kind of fraternity, you see—and we mounted a search. We found the rogue near the railroad tracks, bound him hand and foot, and locked him in the basement. His comrade is also there, still unconscious. We've called the police to take them away."

"Why did they attack me?" Pamela asked.

"With a little persuasion, the conscious tramp confessed fully. He and his comrade were former prison mates of Dennis Reilly. He gave himself an alibi and hired them for a pittance to kill you. Your death was to look like you slipped from the outcrop, fell to the creek below, and struck your head on a rock."

Pamela asked, "What can be done about Dennis Reilly? He will try again."

O'Boyle replied, "Of that I'm sure. Mrs. Jennings told me to telegraph Mr. Prescott. When he arrives tomorrow, we'll discuss the question."

The following day, Pamela was beginning to feel better but remained in bed. In the afternoon, Prescott and O'Boyle came to her room. Prescott studied her with concern. "I'm happy that you've suffered no major injury. But you still must feel pain. So, we'll be brief. We're watching Reilly, but that's only a temporary solution. We need to build a stronger case against him. He put nothing in writing and could deny that he hired the tramps. In a courtroom, it would be his word against theirs."

O'Boyle added, "We think that another person must be involved in the plot. The two tramps were unfamiliar with the estate and with your movements. Reilly must have paid someone to admit them to the grounds. Someone also must have told them about your custom of walking in the woods."

Prescott asked her, "Can you think of anyone in the household who hates you and would cooperate in Reilly's scheme?"

Pamela immediately thought of Maggie, but she didn't sense malice in the maid. She should have the benefit of the doubt. "No," Pamela replied, then mentioned Wilson. "He and Reilly are likely acquainted through gambling at Barney's in New York. Still, I'm not aware that he hates me."

"Whether Wilson or someone else, the accomplice might not have realized what the tramps were up to," suggested O'Boyle.

"I can't imagine such a person," Pamela said. "He or she would have to be unusually naïve, even simple-minded. That would exclude Wilson." Then she had an afterthought. "Agnes Jones, the simple maid I caught stealing a bracelet at Macy's, is often in the village. Reilly might have contacted her. She certainly knows the path through the woods. I've occasionally taken her along on my walks. I doubt that she holds any malice toward me. But Reilly could easily have deceived her about his plan and bribed her with a few dollars or a trinket to cooperate."

"You should question her," said Prescott. "We will have the cook send her with your supper tray. O'Boyle and I will listen in the parlor."

Agnes Jones entered the room with an awkward gait, her eyes glued to the tray, as if she feared dropping it. She placed it carefully on the bedside table and withdrew shyly toward the door. Pamela beckoned her back. "Sit down, Agnes. I'm bored to death lying here. Keep me company."

"I hope you feel better tomorrow," the maid remarked.

Pamela began to eat and turned the conversation toward seasonal visitors to Lenox. "Have you met any of them, Agnes? Mr. Reilly, for instance?"

"Oh yes, ma'am," the maid replied, smoothing her apron over her knees. "A kind and proper gentleman, he's been good to me. Treats me to ice cream in the village shop."

"What do you talk about?" Pamela asked casually, and buttered a piece of bread.

"Mostly about Broadmore Hall, such a grand place. He says I'm lucky to work here. He also speaks well of you. I've told him about our walks in the woods and the rocky place by the creek where we rest and listen to the birds sing. Once he asked, 'Could I take a walk there with you?' I said I'd like that. So he arranged things with Mr. Wilson—they know each other. Mr. Reilly and I spent an hour in the woods and rested by the creek. It was a lovely time."

"Did Mr. Reilly tell you not to mention that you were seeing him?" She laid a slice of cheese on the bread and took a bite, glancing sidewise at the maid, who seemed fully absorbed in her story.

"Yes, he did. He knew that my mother would be upset. She says I shouldn't speak to men unless I'm with a chaperone. I speak to men anyway, but I don't tell her. With Mr. Reilly I needn't worry. He's polite and respectful. He wouldn't hurt me."

Pamela had heard enough. "You needn't wait any longer, Agnes. I'll continue eating. You can pick up the tray later."

The maid bowed smartly and left the room. Prescott and O'Boyle entered.

"We heard it all," said Prescott to Pamela. "At Reilly's request, Wilson probably hired the two villains without realizing that they were supposed to kill you. Likewise, Agnes probably didn't know what Reilly intended to do with the information she gave him. But her mind is more complicated than I thought. She apparently still doesn't understand that Reilly took advantage of her gullibility. Nonetheless, her testimony, together with that of the two tramps, should convince a jury that Reilly conspired to murder you. A judge will send him to a Massachusetts prison for a long time. You and Brenda can now rest easy."

Pamela hoped that was true.

CHAPTER 20

A Thief Uncovered

19–22 June

Over the next six days, while Reilly and his two confederates sat in the Pittsfield jail, Prescott made arrangements for their trial. Freed from her father's threats, Brenda grew calmer, less fearful. And as summer approached in all its Berkshire glory, Pamela's bruised head rapidly healed. She looked forward to preparing Broadmore for a magnificent celebration of the Fourth of July.

So she was startled on Monday evening, the nineteenth of June, when Brenda brought her a sealed note from Prescott: "Come to the cabin. I have important news."

She again felt uneasy meeting him in the cabin. However, she would attract less attention than if he were to come uninvited to Broadmore. It was dusk, and he was outside chopping wood. As she approached, he laid down the ax and showed her into the cabin.

"I apologize for such short notice," he said. "But I wanted to tell you that Harry Miller sent me a report on Wilson. It confirms your observations back in April and offers credible estimates of his large gambling losses and other expenses. He also has no income in New York and no inheritance. His only income, legal or illegal, is from Broadmore Hall."

"Have you found a way to audit his accounts?"

"Not yet. I assume that he keeps a secret register of his illicit earnings and his expenditures. Inform me the next time he goes to New York and his clerk takes his lunch at home in the village. Then with Lydia's permission we could search Wilson's rooms and find that register. What have you learned thus far?"

"He usually keeps both his office and his own room locked. Recently, however, he left the key in the door when he was called out of the office. Brenda seized the opportunity to make a wax impression. I've had a metal copy made. We'll see if it fits."

"If it doesn't," Prescott said, "I could try to pick the lock. What else do you have to report?"

"My encounter with Maggie and Tom the tramp twelve days ago continues to occupy my mind. I hope they will heed the warning I gave them. Since then, I've wondered whether they had more serious mischief in mind than pilfering from the pantry. Tom appears to nurse a passionate grievance toward Mr. Jennings and might do him harm."

Prescott's brow furrowed. "What would he do?"

"Nothing public or foolish. He's too cunning to put himself at any great risk of getting caught. But I can imagine him stealing something of great value to Jennings, or, less likely, even killing him."

Prescott nodded. "Your suspicion seems reasonable. He might have help from Maggie Rice. Her connection to Calumet, Michigan piques my curiosity. I'll have Harry Miller gather more information. As we know from your husband's failed investment, much of Henry Jennings's fortune was made there in the copper mines of the Upper Peninsula."

"At great cost to others," added Pamela, fighting back a surge of bitter feelings.

* * *

The next day, Lydia asked Pamela to join her for a late afternoon walk through the garden. Earlier, the sun's heat had kept her indoors. They sat on a shaded bench and silently gazed at a colorful carpet of flowers.

"Is there any word yet on the Lizzie Borden case?" Lydia asked. "This morning, the jury was supposed to give its verdict. I imagine the entire world is eagerly waiting. I'm on pins and needles."

"We'll soon know," Pamela replied. "The *Berkshire Eagle* should have arrived by the time we return to the cottage."

For two weeks, she had conscientiously reported to Lydia on the progress of the trial. In the discussions between them, Pamela marveled at Lydia's rapt interest. Even now she seemed more engaged with the trial than with the lush flower beds around her.

"After considering all the arguments," she said, "I'm more convinced than ever of Miss Borden's innocence."

"Then who is guilty?" Pamela asked.

"That's what's so frustrating," Lydia replied. "The police haven't identified a credible suspect. William Borden, Mr. Borden's illegitimate son, had quarreled with his father over money. But so had many others. He was greedy and insensitive, a difficult man to deal with."

Pamela reflected that Lydia's own husband had much in common with the murdered man.

"Can you imagine," Lydia continued, "how Lizzie must have felt when she found her pigeons lying slaughtered in the backyard and realized that her father had acted maliciously and without consulting her?" Lydia's voice shuddered as she spoke.

Pamela recalled the incident. Mr. Borden had claimed the birds were a nuisance, so he had cut off their heads. At that moment Lizzie could almost be excused if she had thought of murder.

When the two women returned to the cottage, Brenda Reilly

met them at the door. "Lizzie Borden is acquitted!" she exclaimed, and handed Lydia the newspaper.

"I'm so relieved! I knew she was innocent," exclaimed Lydia, glancing at the headline. "Thank God, justice prevailed." She paused, lines of anxiety gathering on her brow. "Still, it was a heinous crime. The nameless killer is free to strike again." She raised a warning finger. "Pamela, we must be alert or risk suffering the Bordens' fate. Tell the servants to keep tramps from sneaking onto the estate. Report them immediately to the police."

The next day, Pamela duly reminded the servants of the rule on tramps, though she personally believed that Broadmore Hall, or at least its master, Henry Jennings, faced threats to his life and property from within the household. She and Brenda kept looking for an opportunity to search Wilson's office.

Finally, early on Thursday morning, Brenda reported that the steward had left for New York on the early morning train. His clerk was at home, and the office closed until the afternoon.

Pamela went immediately to Prescott's cabin and told him, "Now is the time."

"You must help me," he said. "Four hands are better than two. We'll be in and out of the rooms quicker." He hesitated. "Has Lydia approved of this search?"

"Yes," Pamela replied. "I asked her before coming here. Now I'll contact Brenda. She'll stand guard and warn us if need be."

Wilson's office and his private room were in the basement at a safe distance from the servants' dining room and prying eyes. At ten in the morning, Prescott entered the basement, unobserved. Pamela came down from her room at the same time. Brenda was alert, watching in the hallway.

Prescott tried the copied key to the office. It fit snugly. Pamela followed him inside. She knew the room from previous visits with Wilson. Two high window wells faced east, allowing the morning sun to cast a strong light into the room. Carefully organized file boxes lined its whitewashed walls. The papers on his desk were neatly stacked.

"Any secret accounts should be close to his desk," she said. Prescott checked the floorboards. They were secure. He couldn't find any other hiding place.

Meanwhile, Pamela searched through file boxes on shelves behind the desk. One of the boxes was labeled "old accounts." On a hunch, she fingered through several account books filed by dates. On the outside they looked alike, except for one that had no dates on the cover. She checked it closely. "Eureka," she cried and handed it to Prescott, who quickly scanned it. "I see gambling losses and brothel visits." He smiled broadly. "We'll take the book with us, examine it carefully, then decide what to do with it."

While searching these rooms, Pamela also hoped to find evidence of the anonymous messages that had upset Lydia Jennings and George Allen. Wilson was chief among the suspects in Pamela's mind. She searched the drawer of his table. Among his writing materials were sheets of the cheap paper and the same color of ink used in the messages. That wouldn't be enough to convict him, but it increased the likelihood of his guilt. A few minutes later, in a file of his correspondence, she found a dated copy of each letter, identical to the originals, even down to their crude script and barely literate grammar. Lydia should be pleased.

"How much should we show to Mrs. Jennings?" Pamela asked her companion. They had retreated to her parlor. Even a hurried examination of the secret accounts yielded evidence of embezzlement.

"Everything, including Wilson's financial crime," he replied. "She asked you to find the source of her anonymous message and any other problems afflicting Broadmore. You've completed your mission. She can decide how to present the results to her husband."

"Henry Jennings should be grateful to us for saving his money," Pamela said firmly.

"But he might also resent that we, rather than he, discovered the crime. His peers might think he was a poor judge of men for leaving the management of his money in the hands of a person who was an addicted gambler, a whoremonger, and a thief."

Later in the morning, Pamela and Prescott visited Lydia's apartment. Still in her morning robe and reading by an open window, she met them with an unfocused expression. A moment later, she put down the book and took off her reading glasses. "Pardon my distraction," she said. "Henry James's *Portrait of a Lady* has transported me to a distant place. I fancied myself Isabel Archer in Britain beset by rascals after my money, or at least my cottage."

She studied their faces. "Do you two have something to report? Your expressions give you away."

Pamela spoke first. "We have solved the mystery of that threatening message you showed me back in April." Pamela had decided to hold back the one sent to Mr. Allen.

Lydia grew instantly alert. "And who was responsible for it?"

"Mr. Wilson. Here's the evidence." Pamela handed over the copy that she had taken from his correspondence as well as the cheap paper he had used. "The ink also matches."

Lydia studied the materials closely, shaking her head as she read. Finally, she looked up and asked incredulously, "Did you find these things in Wilson's office?"

Pamela replied, "Yes, with your permission we searched after he left early this morning for New York." She went on to describe getting the key and finding the message hidden among other correspondence.

Lydia breathed a sigh of relief. "I'm pleased to know who did it. I suppose he simply wanted to vex me. He seems more pathetic than evil or malicious."

"In our search," Prescott added, "we discovered other evidence of Wilson's malfeasance."

She frowned. "What might that be?"

Prescott described the secret account book. "Mrs. Thompson's earlier discovery of his addiction to gambling and other vices made me suspect financial skullduggery. My agent in New York learned that Wilson has only the modest income he receives here. To cover his expenses he has apparently been embezzling funds from Broadmore Hall."

Lydia sighed. "That presents a more serious problem. My husband passionately dislikes being cheated, though he takes pleasure in cheating others. He'll be severe with Wilson. Nonetheless, we'll present the facts." She paused thoughtfully. "Jennings apparently trusts Wilson with more responsibilities than he should."

Prescott asked, "Will you confront Jennings yourself or do you need us to come along? He seems to dislike me. Wouldn't he resent my investigation of his steward?"

"And wouldn't he think me presumptuous in searching the steward's office?" asked Pamela.

Lydia replied, "I really don't know how he'll react, and I don't care. He'll be in New York for several days. When he returns to Broadmore, I want both of you to go with me to his study."

CHAPTER 21

Business in the City

New York, 22–24 June

That afternoon, Prescott left Lenox to tend to business in New York for a few days. His secretary had arranged a late supper for him with Harry Miller at a tavern close to the office. Over beer and shepherd's pie, Miller reported recent gossip, concluding with the remark, "They say that Henry Jennings is involved in a new, intimate relationship with a young woman. What do you make of that, sir?"

"If true, Harry, it's another insult to Lydia Jennings. And it means Helen Allen might lose Henry Jennings and the riches she coveted. Check the facts and give me a report tomorrow morning."

Prescott returned to his office and phoned George Allen. They agreed to meet the next day at the club for lunch. By that time, the gossip might be confirmed and presented to Allen. Would he still want to investigate his wife's infidelity?

Allen arrived a half hour late from a tennis match. "Sorry, my opponent put up a better fight than I anticipated. Now I'm thirsty." He ordered an expensive bottle of French white wine and a plate of steamed oysters.

Prescott led the conversation toward mutual acquaintances, male and female, then asked, "How is Mrs. Allen?"

"She's well, thank you, and preparing for the festive celebration of the Fourth at Broadmore. She has been in Lenox almost three weeks, at the Curtis Hotel." His voice began to crack even while he strained to be calm. "She'll be alone at the hotel for several more days. The press of business will keep me here until late on the third." He took a long drink from his glass. "Henry Jennings will soon return to Broadmore Hall. Helen will not lack for companionship."

"Jennings might prove to be distracted company," remarked Prescott. "This morning, my agent in New York told me that a beautiful young opera singer has caught Jennings's eye. Late last night, they dined together at Delmonico's, then retired to Jennings's house on Fifth Avenue. After breakfast, a cab took her to a fashionable address on Fifth Avenue near Columbus Circle, leased by Jennings."

"Helen will be furious," Allen blurted out. "But then Jennings and she are kindred spirits, both of them treacherous."

Prescott shrugged. "Tomorrow, I'll return to Lenox. Henry Jennings is expected at Broadmore this weekend. I'll study his behavior toward your wife, especially in light of the recent rumors."

His nonchalance appeared to irritate Allen. "Remember, Prescott, I've hired you to catch them in the act. I'm certain that they were fornicating behind my back, and will do so again, but I need proof."

"I won't fabricate evidence, but if I find it, I'll pass it on to you. What purpose would it serve?"

"I'll keep that to myself," Allen replied.

Prescott tried to puzzle out Allen's attitude: Was he personally offended or angered that Jennings had seduced Helen, then apparently cast her aside? Would he claim alienation of affection and demand compensation? That could be a dangerous game to play with a man as powerful as Jennings.

Prescott left Allen at the club and took a cab to the courthouse in lower Manhattan. A judge was considering Dennis Reilly's petition to recover custody of his daughter Brenda. When Reilly had been arrested for conspiring to murder Pamela, Prescott had written to the court, requesting this hearing.

Inspector Williams, who had initially supported Reilly's petition, arrived at the courthouse shortly after Prescott. The two men met outside the judge's chambers. Prescott politely greeted the inspector, who responded with a cool, perfunctory nod. Fortunately, they didn't have to wait in stiff, hostile silence. The judge's clerk soon called them in.

The procedure was brief and simple. At the judge's request, Prescott spoke first. He argued that, since Reilly was in jail on a serious felony charge, his petition for custody should be held in abeyance, until the conclusion of his trial.

Williams agreed in principle with Prescott—he could hardly do otherwise. Still, he insisted that Reilly's arrest shouldn't in any way prejudice his petition.

For a few minutes the judge seemed to ponder the arguments, then he ruled sensibly that he would withhold his decision until Reilly's trial was complete. Prescott had no doubt as to what the final determination ought to be. Reilly would surely be convicted, and the judge should reject his petition.

Still, Prescott felt an irrational stirring of anxiety: The judge owed his position on the bench to the powerful influence of Tammany Hall, the political organization loosely allied with Inspector Williams. The judge could reasonably be expected to help the inspector who had invested his reputation in Reilly's rehabilitation and now needed to save face. As a favor to Williams, the judge might find an arcane way to interminably delay his decision, thereby causing unnecessary pain to Brenda and to Pamela.

As they left the judge's chambers together, Prescott glanced sidewise at Williams. The inspector appeared confident. "It's not over yet," he said, with the hint of a sneer in his voice.

The next day, Prescott dispatched routine business in his office. Yesterday's judicial hearing on Reilly was still on his mind. He had hoped to bring more encouraging news to Pamela and Brenda.

Late in the afternoon, he took a cab to Grand Central Station. As the train left for Lenox, he noticed Broadmore's steward, Bernard Wilson, sitting at the far end of the coach. The seat next to his was empty. Prescott sat down before Wilson could object. In the coming hours on board, Prescott hoped to better understand the man at the heart of this investigation.

After the introductions he asked Wilson, "Have you enjoyed a few days in the city?"

"Yes," he replied deferentially. He seemed to realize that Prescott was a man who commanded respect but was also congenial.

From his portfolio Prescott pulled a small silver flask of whiskey and two silver cups. He poured a cupful and offered it to the steward. Wilson declined, but he seemed tempted. Prescott smiled gently and insisted that they honor the finest drink that man and God had ever created. Wilson yielded and accepted first one cupful, then another. He was soon speaking about the wonders of New York City and its fast pace of change. New buildings sprouted like weeds. He enjoyed the excitement.

"Where do you stay?" Prescott asked, though Pamela had told him.

"I have rooms in the basement of the Jennings's residence and my own exit to the outside. After I've met with the housekeeper and her maids, I check the house from top to bottom. When I feel that everything is in order, I run a few errands. For the most part, I can come and go as I please."

"I'm told that Mr. Henry Jennings was at home while you were there. Were you called to serve him?"

"He asked me twice to deliver flowers to an address on Columbus Circle—orchids, no less, very expensive and simply gorgeous. A special friend needed to be consoled, he said." Wilson gave no indication that he might disapprove of Jennings's "special friend."

With Prescott's prompting, Wilson went on to describe how much he enjoyed serving the Jennings family. "They live like royalty," he said, his voice quivering with admiration.

Prescott filled the cups again and asked tentatively, "Have you ever had a family?"

"Oh, no," the steward replied. "The Jenningses are family enough for me. I'll serve them until I'm pensioned many years from now."

As the train pulled into Lenox Station, Prescott said, "I wish you well, Wilson. Shall we share a cab to Broadmore Hall? I vacation in a cabin nearby."

"Yes, indeed. That would be most kind of you." They continued their conversation until they reached Broadmore. Prescott paid the driver and bid Wilson good night. As Prescott walked to his cabin, he reflected that beneath the steward's show of integrity beat a thieving heart. Still, he inspired pity. All his assumptions and aspirations for a good life would soon be shattered.

CHAPTER 22

A Reckoning

Lenox, 25 June–1 July

On Sunday, Lydia and Pamela went to Trinity Church. To their surprise, they met Prescott at the door. He sat with them through the service, respectful though apparently not inwardly engaged. Afterward at lunch in the Curtis Hotel he described Jennings's latest romance in New York with a young opera singer, speaking hesitantly out of concern for Lydia.

She waved a dismissive hand. "Your report hurts but it doesn't surprise me, Prescott. I'd much rather hear it from you than from a gossipmonger." She hesitated, then asked, "Would you come to the cottage with us? I may need you."

He nodded. "Your servant, madam."

At Broadmore they discovered Jennings had arrived an hour earlier in his private railway car. After lunch and a short nap, he had gone to his study. Lydia sent a note asking to see him there.

He agreed in a curt reply.

As they entered the study, he was at his desk wearing his signature diamond lapel pin. He seemed to be in pain; the embroidered pillow supported his back. Lydia had announced her coming "on a serious matter." He glared at Pamela and Prescott, then turned to his wife.

"Why did you bring your companion and your lawyer?"

"They'll add to what I have to say, Henry. May we sit down?"

"If you must," he replied irritably.

Prescott pulled chairs up to the desk for himself and the two women. They acknowledged his courteous gesture and sat down, Pamela and Prescott to Lydia's right side.

"So what's on your mind?" Jennings's voice was cool and unfriendly. He irritably fingered the diamond.

"Your steward Wilson is a rascal and a thief," Lydia replied. "Here's the evidence." She handed him the secret account book. "He has embezzled your money and wasted it on whoring and gambling. Your accountant has failed to detect this. You might want to hire another."

"How did you come by this evidence?" Jennings's eyes were darkening, a sign that anger was building up.

Lydia appeared to sense the approaching storm. Nonetheless she spoke calmly. "Wilson's behavior troubled me. So I asked Mrs. Thompson to investigate. She discovered that Wilson leads a double life: At Broadmore he is seemingly a meticulous manager of your money and supervisor of the staff. In New York he frequents expensive brothels and gambling dens. His losses and other expenses are far greater than his income." She deferred to Prescott with a gesture.

He explained, "At your wife's request, and aided by Mrs. Thompson, I secured Wilson's secret account book—we knew that he must have had one hidden away in his office. A brief comparison with the official audit revealed large discrepancies."

Lydia then remarked to her husband, "I'm sure you are disappointed that Wilson betrayed you, but you should be grateful that Mrs. Thompson and Mr. Prescott have brought you the evidence to deal severely with him. He returned to Broadmore late yesterday and may not yet realize that he has been exposed."

Jennings glowered at the three persons facing him and addressed his wife. "You could have come to me first, before ordering these private detectives to break into my steward's office. I had not given my consent."

"When the issue came up, Henry, you weren't here. So I acted on my own. After all, Wilson's criminal behavior is my concern as well as yours."

His face grew pinched. "Lydia, you have deliberately set out to humiliate me. I promise that you'll regret it. Now leave me. I'll deal with Wilson first thing tomorrow."

That evening, Lydia summoned Wilson to her study. She had also asked Pamela to be present for safety's sake.

As he entered, he appeared confident and calm, unaware of the storm he was soon to face. He noticed Pamela and nodded politely. He had probably grown accustomed to her presence at Mrs. Jennings's side.

She left him standing and questioned him concerning his trip to New York. With an expression of self-satisfaction, he described the errands he had run.

"Thank you, Wilson. Mr. Jennings will probably want to hear your report. Now I'll address an issue that's been on my mind for weeks." She paused for a moment to gain his attention, then asked, "Would you please explain what you meant by this note?" She handed him the one that said she was being betrayed.

Wilson scanned the note with mounting disbelief. Finally, he stammered, "I'm dumbstruck, madam. What must you think? While trying to disguise my identity, I didn't express myself correctly. I meant well."

Lydia nodded for him to continue.

"I wanted to warn you that Mr. Jennings and Mrs. Allen were having an affair that could lead to disaster for all involved, including Broadmore Hall itself."

"Unfortunately, Wilson, your note has troubled me. I grant that the scandal may be as threatening as you claim. A month ago, I sensed as much. Consequently, I engaged Mrs. Thompson to investigate. Unfortunately for you, the cat is out of the bag, as they say. Your secret life in New York's brothels and gambling dens is exposed. Mr. Jennings has also learned that your account books are out of order. You will soon hear from him."

By this time, the steward was gasping for breath and swaying dangerously on his feet. Lydia nodded to Pamela. She rushed up to him, sat him in a chair, and patted perspiration from his brow.

When he had sufficiently recovered, Lydia told Pamela to take him to his rooms. When she returned, Lydia said, "Wilson's character is weak, but he doesn't seem malicious."

Pamela hesitated to agree. "He appears well intentioned toward you. But I suspect that Mr. Jennings will be harsh and pitiless. That could inspire very hostile feelings in Wilson. He may act on them."

Lydia looked doubtful. "His character is so weak. What serious harm can he do to as powerful a man as Henry?"

Pamela replied, "Wilson is cunning and angry. That's enough. He doesn't need much strength or courage to stab your husband in the back—in a manner of speaking."

Early the next morning, Pamela drove Prescott to the station. He would return to New York for a few days to look after his business, consult with Harry Miller, and be back before the Fourth of July.

She reported on Lydia's conversation with Mr. Wilson. "I pity him."

Prescott nodded. "When Jennings finishes with him, he'll be a desperate man. Keep watch on him."

At breakfast, Pamela learned that Jennings had just called Wilson into his office. She hurried down the hallway to the room next to Jennings's study. She couldn't hear what was said between the two men, but she could imagine that Jennings accused the steward of betraying his trust and threatened to dismiss him. She opened the door a crack to observe the hallway.

When Wilson left the study ten minutes later, he seemed crestfallen. He glanced about and, seeing no one, began to weep. A few moments later, he dabbed the tears from his cheeks, straightened up, and tried unsuccessfully to regain his usual dignified expression.

Unobserved, Pamela followed him outside into the garden. He began to sob again.

She approached him, showing concern. "How are you, Wilson? You appear distressed."

He looked up, sad faced. "Since you know so much of my story, I may as well tell you that Mr. Jennings has ordered me to train my clerk to serve as a temporary steward. At the same time, I'll have to continue preparations for the festive celebration of the Fourth of July. Mr. Jennings said if I cooperated fully, he might be lenient."

"Well, isn't that encouraging?"

"Not really." Wilson was now dry-eyed, his expression bitter. "Mr. Jennings is a heartless liar. He will wring a few more days of hard work out of me and then destroy me."

The next afternoon, Jennings's accountant, a Mr. Carter, arrived by train from New York and was brought immediately to Broadmore. Standing in for Lydia, Pamela received him at the door. A small, thin, sallow-faced man in a dark suit, Carter looked anxious and grim. Pamela imagined the message that

Jennings must have telegraphed to him: "Fool! I've been embezzled. Drop everything; come immediately."

Pamela showed the accountant into Jennings's study. She lingered outside the door and heard Jennings at the top of his voice berate the man for failing to detect Wilson's fraud. Carter could not leave the cottage until he had produced a complete and accurate audit.

When he emerged, shaken, she took him to Wilson's office. The disgraced steward surrendered the keys to him and retreated to his private room. Carter was to live in the office. The housekeeper had arranged for a cot and other basic conveniences. His meals would be brought in.

"This is like being in prison," the accountant muttered. But he had no choice. If he didn't comply, Jennings would put him out of business.

For the next three days, the accountant remained hidden away in Wilson's office, occasionally meeting with the clerk, who guided him through the estate's records. At noon on Saturday, Carter told Pamela that he would be leaving. He had finished the final draft of his report and had given a clean copy to Mr. Jennings. She passed the information on to Lydia. Upset, she hurried to the office with Pamela in tow and demanded to see the results of the investigation. Pamela stayed in the background, observing.

Carter balked. "Mr. Jennings would prefer to keep that information between him and me."

Lydia bristled. "I'm not surprised. If this scandal got out, it could damage his reputation for business skill. But I own this house. Anything that's likely to hurt it concerns me."

Her outburst had its intended effect. The accountant gave her a copy of the audit and explained how Wilson had embezzled over a thousand dollars and lost it all in gambling. Mr. Jennings intended to fire him after the Fourth of July festivities and eject him from Broadmore without pension or recommendation. Wilson would be kept in the dark until then.

After Carter left, Pamela reported on her garden conversation with Wilson. "He realizes that Mr. Jennings intends to ruin him."

Lydia nodded. "Perhaps Henry is tempting fate. His crimes and weaknesses are familiar to Wilson and offer many opportunities for revenge."

CHAPTER 23

Wounded Warrior

2–3 July

The next evening, Pamela drove one of the estate's light, open coaches to the railroad station. Prescott was supposed to return to Lenox. She needed to tell him about Carter's audit of Broadmore's books, the financial scandal he had uncovered, and Wilson's dire prospects. The train arrived on schedule, and Prescott waved from a window. But he descended painfully to the platform.

Pamela was struck by his haggard appearance. "You look ill. What's happened?"

He replied in a weak, halting voice. "Young men at the club celebrated the thirtieth anniversary of the battle of Gettysburg. They had no idea of the slaughter—they were infants at the time. They drank and sang as if our side had won a football match. That distressed me. I called them insensitive clods. They called me weak-kneed and gutless. While we argued, images from the battle surged into my mind. I tried to describe how dreadful it was, and I worked myself into frenzy. By the time I went to bed, the anguish was almost unbearable. A glass of whiskey at the club had made matters worse. During the night, the most ghastly experiences of the war crowded into my mind. I hardly slept a wink.

"Today, I went to my office, couldn't concentrate on work, just sat at the desk all morning, my heart pounding, my head throbbing. Things just got worse on the train. That's my story."

By the time they reached his cabin, he could barely sit up. She helped him from the coach. He leaned on her as they made their way into the cabin. They staggered to the sleeping alcove, and he collapsed on the bed.

"Shall I call a doctor?" she asked anxiously.

He shook his head. "These spells happen occasionally. There's nothing doctors can do. They claim I lack moral fiber. 'Be a man,' they say. 'Thousands of other soldiers came out of the shock of battle mentally sound.' "

Pamela sat by his side. "Your doctors should learn from my mother, a wise and compassionate woman. During the war, she nursed hundreds of wounded soldiers, read and wrote letters for them, listened to their stories. Often as badly wounded in mind as in body, they confided things to her that they couldn't tell to another man."

"Did she share her views with doctors?"

"She tried, but they refused to take her seriously, because she was a civilian and a woman. She suspected that some of the doctors really didn't want to know the truth. It was more convenient and patriotic to blame the victim's character."

His expression remained skeptical. "What do you recommend for me that doctors haven't already tried?"

"Compassionate, careful listening and a serious, open-minded effort to understand. Speaking about wartime experiences might work like a catharsis and expel them from your mind, or at least bring them to the surface, where you could confront them. I'm willing to listen. You won't shock me after the horrors I've witnessed in the tenements of New York."

He had begun to sweat profusely. His breathing was labored. But his eyes expressed interest and a ray of hope.

She fetched towels from a chest of drawers and patted the sweat away.

"May I take off your boots and brew you an infusion?"

He gave her a weak smile of assent and let her loosen his collar as well.

When she returned with the tea, he was under the covers, his clothes piled onto a chair. She propped him up with pillows and served the tea. He sipped it thoughtfully, then said, "Many dreadful scenes of battle have haunted me, but I'll tell you about one that comes back frequently. It actually happened at Antietam in September of '62, the year before Gettysburg. A little after dawn, we were advancing in close formation on the Confederates. The fighting became intense. Cannon balls came at us thick as a hailstorm. The screams of wounded and dying men filled the air. Suddenly, a ball smashed my comrade's head. He fell against me and almost knocked me over. His blood soaked my uniform; his brains spattered me from top to toe. I laid him down and joined the others. The battle raged through the day, but I felt numb, as if my mind had left my body. That night, still covered with my comrade's blood, I had my first spell. His image came back more hideous than ever. My heart began to race. Soon I was weeping out of control. I hid from the others. They'd have thought I was a coward. I forced myself to go back into battle, then and many times thereafter. I've occasionally suffered similar attacks ever since."

"Think of your ailment this way," Pamela began. "It has nothing to do with your character—you're as courageous, as morally upright as any man I know. We don't understand exactly how mind and body affect each other. But common sense tells us they are closely connected. In that battle, your brain received a powerful blow. It still makes your heart palpitate and causes other symptoms. Think of it as an honorable wound, as worthy of respect as losing an arm or a leg in battle."

He gazed at her for a long moment. "Thank you, Pamela. Now I must try to rest. Tomorrow, I should feel better." He took her hand and kissed it and slid back beneath the covers. She continued to towel beads of perspiration from his forehead. In a few minutes he was asleep. She tiptoed from the room and returned to Broadmore.

Pamela awoke from a troubled sleep. In her dreams Prescott had lain feverish in bed. She had watched helplessly as he turned from side to side, seeking relief. She shook the dream from her mind, wondering if she should visit the cabin later in the morning. He might need medical attention. But she was loath to invade his privacy. Unless he was desperately ill, he would prefer to take care of himself.

Pamela finished breakfast in her room and walked out onto a porch. She sensed nervous excitement in the air. The final, hectic preparations for the next day's festival had begun already at dawn. The resources of this huge estate would be stretched to their limits.

When she returned to her room, Brenda was dressed, lines of anxiety on her brow. "Do you think tomorrow will be a disaster? There's so much to do."

"Don't worry. We'll be ready. For ten years, Wilson has arranged this event, and it has always run like clockwork. It'll be a great birthday party for our nation."

Brenda looked skeptical. "The Jenningses have invited more than a hundred guests, plus servants and children. How will they get here and where will they stay?"

"Many will come by train. Mr. Jennings has rented parlor coaches for them. A bus will ferry them from the train to the Curtis Hotel in the village. A large block of rooms is set aside for them. Cabs will move them to and from Broadmore. A select few will come directly to Broadmore and settle in the guest rooms on the first and second floors. Their servants will stay in the attic or the basement or above the stables. Tents have been erected for children and young college men. Many neighbors will come in just for the day. We must find space to park their coaches."

A bell rang in their room. "That's Lydia," Pamela said. "I'll see what she wants."

As Pamela entered the room, the remains of breakfast lay on the table by the window. Lydia seemed indisposed and irritated. "Neither Wilson nor my husband will keep me informed. 'Everything is going as planned,' they say. I realize they are very busy, and I'm not fit to run around the estate. So I'd like you to observe the preparations and occasionally give me a report."

Pamela agreed and was about to leave the room when Lydia called her back.

"What's wrong with Mr. Prescott?" she asked. "Last night, one of my guests from New York saw him on the train. He appeared to be ill. I was counting on him."

"I met him at the station," Pamela replied. "A wound from the war is afflicting him. He should be better today."

"I hope so," said Lydia. She hesitated slightly, then asked, "Would you go to his cabin? If he's well, tell him to watch out for tramps, confidence men, and other troublemakers today during the preparation and tomorrow during the celebration. The estate is going to be crowded and hectic, ripe for serious mischief. Think of what happened to you a month ago in the woods. Tramps are becoming increasingly insolent and violent."

"I'll go immediately," Pamela promised.

* * *

She found him outside the cabin, stripped to the waist, chopping wood and sweating profusely. As she approached, he looked up. "Excuse my appearance. I wasn't expecting visitors." He laid down the ax and put on an old shirt.

He looked fit, though the pain from his illness seemed to linger in his eyes.

"You appear better today," Pamela began. "I've come on an errand from Mrs. Jennings. She wants your help today and tomorrow and will pay an appropriate stipend, I'm sure. You're invited to lodge at Broadmore." She described Lydia's fears and the vigilance she hoped from him.

He thought for a moment. "Her concerns are reasonable. Tell her that I'll assume my duties in an hour. At that time, you can give me the details I need to know."

As she was about to leave, he gazed at her. The hurt in his eyes seemed to give way to a look of fondness.

"Thank you again, Pamela, for the care you gave me last night."

She nodded. "I pray that one day you will enjoy peace of mind." She lingered for a moment, meeting his gaze. "And now I must return to the cottage."

Pamela found Lydia sitting on a porch in a light pink frock, observing the activity on the garden terrace below. A wide-brimmed straw hat protected her face from the midmorning sun. A glass of fruit juice was on the table at her side.

Pamela joined her. Lawn furniture had been brought out of storage or borrowed or rented and was being set up all over the estate. Men were putting up tents to cover the serving and dining areas, ensuring that the celebration would go on regardless of the weather. Inside the tents, men were hanging colorful Oriental lanterns.

"What do you have to report?" Lydia asked.

"Prescott seems to have recovered his health and should be here any minute."

"And the preparations?"

"Moving ahead like clockwork, as Wilson repeatedly says. An orchestra from New York will arrive early this afternoon by rail and lodge at the Curtis. Later in the afternoon, they will practice in a special shed built for them. The chef and his staff came from New York a few days ago and have prepared a small mountain of food: meat for roasting, potatoes and various salads, fresh vegetables, and loaves of bread. Work has begun on the ice cream."

Lydia took a sip of the fruit juice. "At breakfast, my maid said that a huge 'birthday' cake will come from New York this evening. Its appearance is shrouded in secrecy, but I've been told that it will be spectacular."

Pamela described a litany of preparations. "Crates of beer and ale and wine—enough for a small army—are stored in a cool basement room. Gallons of coffee and tea are ready to be served, either iced or hot. Ice is being cut in the icehouse and put into coolers. Serving tables have been cleaned and will soon be placed in the tents. The fireworks for tomorrow night are being set up on a large raft in Lily Pond."

Pamela added that fresh sand had been hauled onto the pond's small beach for visitors who wished to bathe. The bathhouse there had been spruced up. The firing range, the tennis and croquet courts, and the exercise track had also been groomed.

Lydia seemed reassured that the celebration would be a success. She smiled wryly. "My husband lacks many of the attributes of a Christian and a gentleman. But he excels in organizing an enterprise, whether a copper company or a patriotic celebration. This event is the biggest and best of the Berkshire social season. It's the high point of his stay here and a thumb in the eyes of his critics in the social elite."

"Who are his critics?" Pamela asked. "And why should they object?"

"Mrs. Astor and her select Four Hundred," Lydia replied. "Henry resents their exclusiveness and mocks their pseudo pedigrees and their aping of British aristocratic customs and manners. He's an original American, a kind of simple democrat who believes that enterprise, hard work, and achievement should determine a person's social standing. It's an attitude that I've always appreciated."

Pamela detected feelings in Lydia akin to affection for her husband, feelings still alive—barely—after ten years of marriage.

Lydia allowed herself a few moments of nostalgia. Then her lips tightened and her eyes darkened, revealing deep hatred for the man. "Pamela," she said, "I would like you and Mr. Prescott to observe Henry and tell me what he's up to. I'm particularly curious about how he behaves toward Mrs. Allen."

At midmorning, Prescott arrived at Broadmore, his usual confident self. Pamela met him in her parlor and passed on Lydia's request that he investigate her husband's affair with Helen Allen.

He chuckled. "George Allen has charged me with the same task. Let's look for Jennings."

He was easily found. From the porches of the cottage, he was surveying the preparations. Puffing out his chest, his diamond lapel pin glittering in the sunlight, he struck the pose of a proud, confident potentate. He rarely smiled. From time to time he would give a curt order to Wilson. The steward would convey it to the gardener, the stable master, the cook, the housekeeper, or one of the other principal servants in the household staff. Jennings created the impression that his eye was on everyone. They should give their best effort and make no mistakes. Helen Allen wasn't in the picture—yet.

Pamela and Prescott took a walk through the cottage and its grounds. As she gazed at the men clearing vegetation from the pond and the others cleaning the bathhouse, she remarked, "I don't know half of the men and women working here today. That makes me uneasy."

Prescott shrugged. "Wilson or one of his men should have investigated the new, temporary staff before hiring them."

"Still, I'm concerned," Pamela persisted. "Wilson could have been extra careful in hiring because he would want to please Jennings, hoping to receive a generous pension and to retire with dignity. Or he's probably—and rightly—convinced that Jennings will show him no mercy or respect, regardless of how well he prepares the celebration. In that case, he could hire tramps, clean them up to look like decent, temporary workers, and pay them to beat and rob Jennings."

"You may be on to something, Pamela. The celebration will offer Wilson opportunities for revenge."

CHAPTER 24

Independence Day

4 July

At dawn Pamela rose from bed, still half asleep. The songs, loud shouts, and bursts of laughter from young people tenting on the lawn had kept her awake until near midnight. She threw on a robe and shuffled out onto a porch facing west. The sky was cloudless. In the distance Lake Mahkeenac lay still, its surface a smooth, glassy mirror. The air was sweet and fresh. Pearls of morning dew sparkled on the grass. She drew deep breaths and stretched out her arms toward the mountains. Nature promised a glorious day.

She performed her morning toilette and stepped out into the hall. Visitors who had arrived yesterday and spent the night in the guest rooms were still asleep. But their servants in the attic had begun to stir.

Led by the steward and the housekeeper, the staff was preparing breakfast for early risers, raising more tents, and making other last-minute arrangements. Pamela breakfasted with Lydia on a porch that gave a view of guests coming from the Curtis or the neighborhood. Lydia smiled or frowned, depending on whether they suited her. She turned livid when Helen Allen came into view together with her husband, George. He had forced a smile onto his face.

This was Pamela's first opportunity to see him undisguised. Today, he was clean-shaven, though a thief nonetheless. The beard he had worn that evening in Macy's jewelry department probably still lay in his closet at home on Gramercy Park. The thought of meeting him again this day caused her a frisson of fear.

Pamela shifted her eyes from Allen to study her mistress's reaction. Lydia seemed fatigued and tense.

"Did you sleep well last night?" Pamela asked.

"Frankly, no," Lydia replied. "Mr. Jennings and I had a sharp, very unpleasant disagreement in his study. He refused to be civil with his son, John. When I pressed him, he became rude, threatened me with divorce, and ordered me out. Then for hours, I lay fully awake. A sense of dread gripped me. Finally, I took a dose of laudanum and went to sleep." She sighed.

Pamela gave her a sympathetic smile. "It should be a bright and happy day. That also might calm your nerves."

Lydia nodded mechanically. "The animosity between my stepson and my husband tortures my soul. I fear it can only get worse." She shook herself. "Let's talk about business. Do we have sufficient cash on hand for the musicians and other providers?" She gave Pamela a key to the cash drawer in the desk.

Pamela opened the drawer and counted over a hundred dollars. "There's enough here," she replied.

"And there's more in the safe," Lydia added. "My husband claims that I keep too much cash at home. But I say that bankers cannot be trusted. Just look at the hundreds of bank failures in this country since January. Thousands of people have lost their life savings. I haven't lost a cent."

She had confided to Pamela that most of her money and personal financial papers were in locked boxes in a secret room off her bedroom, hidden behind a full-length mirror. "You should know just in case something happens to me," she said. Even her husband probably didn't know exactly how much she had or where she kept it. Pamela, however, had apparently won her trust.

As the sun climbed above the hills into a cloudless, azure sky, guests crowded onto the broad, grassy terrace in front of the cottage. Musicians installed themselves in the shaded bandstand and were soon filling the air with John Philip Sousa's rousing, patriotic marches. Children played games of chance with toys for prizes, crowded around booths dispensing ice cream and lemonade, and took pony rides. After breakfast some men had gone to the Lenox Club's nine-hole golf course for a leisurely round. Others joined the ladies in games of croquet.

Late in the morning, the band sounded a fanfare, announcing the track and field events. Guests gathered at the equestrian exercise track near the stables.

"Now the celebration becomes serious," said Lydia, sitting at Pamela's side in the shade of a parasol. "Every year for a decade my husband has challenged the neighboring great houses to send their best athletes to compete in track and field events as well as swimming and shooting. They are mostly young college men from Harvard, Yale, Princeton, and Columbia."

She waved to one of the athletes walking by.

"He's a neighbor attending Yale," she explained. "Throughout the past decade, our own son, John, has dominated the competition and was often crowned by his father with the prize, a laurel wreath. Since their falling-out this year, however, the competition was in doubt. Fearing that John might win the crown again, his father was reluctant to stage the contest. His neighbors shamed him into agreeing to continue."

Pamela watched John Jennings nearby, limbering up. He appeared to be in superb condition, though several years older than his competitors.

In the races that followed, he easily bested them on the track and in throwing the javelin. From there they went down to Lily Pond, changed to light, tight-fitting swimming clothes, dove off the pier, and swam across and back.

His body glistening in the sun, John Jennings emerged from the water again the clear winner. He and the other contestants changed to dry clothes and gathered in front of the bandstand for the laying of the laurel wreath on this summer's champion. Lydia and Pamela took front-row seats.

The band again played a fanfare, and a crowd assembled. But Henry Jennings was nowhere to be seen. After an awkward moment, a neighboring gentleman stepped forward and laid the wreath on John's still-damp head. The defeated young men shook his hand and congratulated him. He acknowledged them graciously, but Pamela could read the hurt in his eyes. She glanced at Lydia. Struggling to smile, she approached her stepson with outstretched arms.

"He's an extraordinary athlete," whispered Prescott, who had sidled over to Pamela. He had been checking temporary workers in the kitchen. "There's talk of reviving the ancient Olympic Games in Greece. I would choose John Jennings to represent our country."

"What do you make of his father's absence?"

Prescott frowned. "There's bad blood between them. Henry Jennings has always looked upon this patriotic celebration as an opportunity to proclaim his convictions. If he worships anything, it's the self-made man, fit and free, the product of unbridled competition especially in business—himself, in other words. John has angered his father by refusing to marry and have a son and by rejecting his mad pursuit of wealth."

Pamela asked, "Isn't John Jennings 'fit and free and competitive'?"

"In athletics certainly, but not in business." Prescott continued in a whisper, "Unfortunately, in his father's eyes he's also not a man, if you perceive my meaning."

She sighed. "It's tragic. The hatred of each for the other is mutual."

A bustle of activity interrupted their conversation. As guests continued to arrive, a troop of servants set up more tables and chairs. Large trays of food soon followed. Prescott asked Pamela, "Can we talk somewhere privately?"

"Come to my parlor in fifteen minutes," she replied.

They sat on the porch off Pamela's parlor and exchanged notes on the festivities. "Thus far, there's no sign of an impending disaster," Prescott remarked, then added, "And I haven't seen Helen Allen and Henry Jennings together."

"There they are," Pamela exclaimed, pointing toward the two lovers below, apparently engaged in an intimate conversation. "She's insisting about something."

"They may be arranging a rendezvous. I had better follow them." He started to leave.

She cautioned, "They're separating. You follow him; I'll follow her."

Helen Allen glanced furtively over her shoulder. Fortunately, Pamela was keeping a safe distance and had ducked behind a great oak tree. Helen walked slowly toward the greenhouse in the garden behind the cottage. The low rectangular building was deserted. The gardener and his assistants were working at the festive dinner. After looking in vain for her lover, Helen let herself in.

Pamela hurried around to the backside of the greenhouse and into a patch of tall, thick raspberry bushes. She drew her gown tightly to her body to avoid the thorns and edged through narrow, irregular paths between the bushes up to the greenhouse. All the windows were wide open to allow the summer's heat to escape.

She placed herself at a window opposite the entrance. A southerly breeze blew through the building and might carry snatches of conversation to her ears. A screen of ferns planted inside along the greenhouse wall concealed her.

A single, narrow aisle extended the length of the long, east-west axis. The only place for a conversation was the small entrance foyer by the door. It was hardly a suitable site for love-making. For a minute or two, Helen paced the aisle, too preoccupied to notice the hidden Pamela. Then Jennings entered and embraced his lover—coolly, tentatively, thought Pamela.

Helen spoke first. "Your wife seems aware of our relationship. Have you talked to her about it?"

He nodded. "I told her last night that I might want a divorce. She shouted, 'Over my dead body.' I wasn't surprised. Lydia is religious and convinced that the Bible forbids divorce. This is also her way to punish what she calls my infidelity."

Helen stared at him for several moments and said in cautiously measured words, "She has offered a plausible alternative to divorce."

He shrugged. "That's risky. Lydia must feel threatened. That's why she has hired the woman Thompson as her companion and has invited the detective Prescott to this celebration."

Helen appeared to grow exasperated. "You're clever and ruthless, good at taking risks. That's how you've gotten to where you are now, one of the wealthiest and most powerful men in the country. Lydia is a weak, dull, ugly old woman, of no use to anyone, a parasite who hasn't earned the wealth she hoards. She's leeching off you, Henry. Forget about divorce. Figure out a way to get rid of her that wouldn't look suspicious."

Jennings tilted his head in a skeptical gesture. "What about George, your husband? Has he agreed to a divorce?"

"Not yet. But he has the backbone of a jellyfish and is almost bankrupt. He can be bought off with enough money to pay his debts and a little extra."

"I like your mettle, Helen. You let nothing stand in your way. Still, I'll have to think about your suggestion."

"Don't take too long. I might lose interest." She untied her blouse at the throat in a teasing gesture, then drew him into a passionate embrace. He yielded, slightly hesitant.

They left the greenhouse separately. Pamela waited a minute, then set out for the cottage. From a toolshed Prescott called out to her. He had concealed himself there at a short distance from the greenhouse and was eager to find out what she had learned, if anything.

In the shed she told him, "Helen Allen and Henry Jennings want to get married, she perhaps more than he. Lydia Jennings stands in the way and must be removed. Helen told Jennings to find a method that wouldn't draw suspicion. But he didn't say he would do it."

"Now I understand," said Prescott. "As Jennings walked past this shed, he seemed unusually preoccupied. We should warn Mrs. Jennings of this threat. She should be careful on the stairs and any other place where a fatal accident could occur."

Pamela cautioned, "If exposed, the conspirators would deny everything. It's too early to bring in the police. Still, Mrs. Jennings might be safer back in New York."

Prescott agreed. "You should suggest that to her."

At one o'clock, Pamela and Prescott joined the picnic in progress on the front terrace. They filled their plates at the buffet table and sat with Lydia in the shade near the band. The scent of roasted meat surrounded them. The babble of over a hundred men, women, and children enjoying a glorious festive day in the country made any serious conversation impossible. Her eyes darting about, Lydia was sharply observing her guests, even while she made conversation.

Near the dinner's conclusion, the band played a fanfare for the dessert, concealed under a low tent in the middle of the terrace. A hush of anticipation came over the crowd.

Henry Jennings now mounted the bandstand and faced the crowd. "Fellow Americans," he began, "today we celebrate not only our nation's independence from Britain, but also our personal freedom. Everywhere in the world, a man's social class or religion, the accidents of his birth or family, determine and limit his achievement in life. Only in this country, I insist, can a strong, resolute, visionary man break through those bonds and fulfill a heroic destiny."

For a brief moment the crowd was still, taking in this stirring profession of faith, uttered with passionate conviction. Then they burst out in boisterous applause. Many of these wealthy, privileged cottagers apparently shared Jennings's sentiments.

At a signal from Jennings, his servants drew the tent away and revealed a giant rectangular cake. The crowd gasped. The frosting on top depicted in high relief an American flag of 1893 with forty-four stars. On the sides were inscribed E PLURIBUS UNUM and THE UNION FOREVER.

Jennings gave the band a vigorous signal. They struck up "The Star-Spangled Banner," and the crowd joined in full-throated voice. Pamela sang along with the others. But out of the corner of her eye she noticed that Prescott was tight-lipped. When they reached the phrases, "And the rocket's red glare, the bombs bursting in air," he seemed to struggle for a moment. But he kept his feelings under control.

As the song ended and the babble resumed, he whispered to

Pamela, "Thirty years ago, half a million men suffered dreadful deaths and many more were crippled for life. Why? For the Union or the flag? To free the slaves? More likely because the nation lacked the wisdom and the will to resolve its differences as civilized Christians." He sighed and shook his head. "Sorry, Pamela, you'd think I'd get over it."

CHAPTER 25

A Wife in Peril

4 July

For an hour after dinner, guests rested in hammocks and lawn chairs, or walked about the estate, enjoying the warm, fresh air and the charming vistas, or viewed Mrs. Jennings's collection of French and British silverware and Sèvres porcelain. The children also had more games, including an egg-and-spoon race.

Meanwhile, Pamela accompanied Lydia to her rooms for a rest, intending to inform her of the threat to her life. Prescott was to go to Mr. Jennings's study, where he would proudly display his weapons and hunting trophies to the male visitors.

Lydia took a seat by the window and motioned for Pamela to join her. "You look as if you have something to tell me."

"I didn't realize my expression was so transparent. Yes, I must report what I heard in the greenhouse." She described the conversation between Henry Jennings and Helen Allen but spared Lydia the latter's insulting remarks.

Lydia showed no emotion throughout this recital. "I'm not surprised that she would want me dead. I'm the chief obstacle to her lust for my husband's wealth and power. Nor am I surprised that he would entertain her suggestion—he must want to get me out of the way. But with you and Jeremiah Prescott looking after me, I feel perfectly safe. Henry Jennings is too practical to do Helen Allen's bidding. Eventually, he'll tire of her and look for another young, beautiful, but less demanding and greedy lover, perhaps the recent opera singer."

"Forgive me for asking, Lydia, but why do you continue to live with this man?"

For a moment, Lydia gazed indulgently at Pamela. "He was a much better man when I married him. Wealth and power have brought out his worst instincts. Society understands my situation and thinks none the worse of me. Many prominent women are no more happily married than I. A legal separation is possible. But our property is already separated, so why bother. Henry doesn't beat me. His abuse is merely verbal, and I can respond in kind. Finally, I must admit that I enjoy matching wits with his mistresses. Mrs. Allen has been my most serious challenge thus far, but I'm sure that I'll prevail." She paused on this note of stoic patience. "And now I should rest before tea. The evening will be strenuous."

As Pamela quietly retreated to her own rooms, she pondered Lydia's failure to mention that without her husband's good will and financial support she would probably lose Broadmore Hall.

Late in the afternoon, Henry Jennings ordered another fanfare from the band and announced the shooting and archery contests in the firing range behind the cottage. Pamela joined a group of women who were to participate with pistols. Some brought their own, packed in highly burnished mahogany cases. Others, like Pamela, used pistols from Jennings's arsenal.

He had built the firing range on the far edge of the property, where a steep slope of thickly wooded land provided a safe background. Nearby was a similar arrangement for archery, a. sport that had recently become popular. Pamela was pleased to see that he was concerned about safety. Only trained shooters and archers were allowed to compete. Jennings appeared to know them all.

First among the shooters was Helen Allen. As she entered the range, she gave her lover only a flicker of recognition. She had the air of an experienced amateur. With a two-handed grip, she raised her pistol, one of Jennings's Colt revolvers, and aimed at the target. At various distances all her shots hit the bull's-eye.

Thanks to Harry Miller's instruction, Pamela achieved a respectable score if not perfection. When the contest ended and Helen was crowned, Pamela approached her with congratulations. As she recognized Pamela, a wall of suspicion rose in her eyes. Pamela pretended not to notice and asked how she had become so proficient with the weapon.

"My father was a lieutenant in the Union army during the Great Southern Rebellion, as he called it. He had no sons, so he told me his war stories and taught me how to use firearms." She gazed at Pamela. "And who taught you?"

"A friend in New York. He said it might prove useful."

"As a companion to Mrs. Jennings?" Helen smiled wryly. "Or, should I have said, as her armed guard? Really, is Broadmore such a dangerous place?"

"I don't expect to use a pistol here. Still, any place is dangerous where people prey upon each other."

While the women were shooting, a small group of men had gathered at the range. Prescott had come to watch Pamela. Another observer was George Allen, whose eyes seemed fixed on his wife. His expression was inscrutable. Prescott approached him.

Allen remarked, "Henry Jennings's fascination with weapons is remarkable, wouldn't you say."

"Yes, indeed," Prescott replied. "He collects them more for their monetary and artistic value than for self-defense. Did you notice the British flintlock dueling pistols mounted on the wall in his study?"

Allen nodded. "Beautiful weapons, the work of a master gunmaker." His gaze shifted to his wife, who had just taken a shooting position in the pistol range. She fired six shots from the Colt revolver and every one hit the mark. "I suppose I should be careful not to antagonize a wife who has mastered a firearm. An argument with her could turn lethal." He smiled sardonically.

"Does she own a pistol?" This newly discovered side of Helen Allen's character intrigued Prescott.

"Yes," Allen replied. "She belongs to a women's pistol club that meets once a month to practice and to exchange information."

It was now Pamela Thompson's turn. She performed to Prescott's satisfaction. For a moment Allen's eyes fixed on Pamela with a mixture of anxiety and dislike. Then he seemed to notice Prescott's interest in her.

"An acquaintance?" he asked.

"She's a widow from New York and a former client in a legal matter. She now works as one of my agents and as a companion to Mrs. Jennings."

Allen was silent for a few moments, apparently fitting these pieces of information together.

"She's coming toward us," said Prescott. "I'll introduce you."

Allen stiffened and took a step back, as if about to withdraw.

Prescott guided him forward by the elbow. "Mrs. Thompson, this is Mr. George Allen, an expert tennis player from the University Athletic Club."

Pamela smiled politely. "I'm pleased to make your acquaintance, Mr. Allen—though I believe we met in Macy's jewelry department back in April. As I recall, you were wearing a luxurious beard at the time. The next night, we also passed each other on Fourteenth Street."

He blinked. Then he rallied. "You must be mistaken, madam. I would surely remember a lady as attractive as you."

"Thank you for the compliment," Pamela murmured. She excused herself and left the men.

Allen's gaze followed her for a moment, then he turned to Prescott. "Shall we find a more private place?"

Prescott gestured toward the garden. When they were out of earshot, Allen asked, "Have you uncovered yet the liaison between my wife and Henry Jennings?"

"As you already know, they appear attracted to each other. I haven't discovered any scandalous behavior, but I'll continue to observe them."

Allen and Prescott walked back toward the cottage. Near the building, Allen said he had to speak to someone on the front terrace.

Prescott turned back. Pamela intercepted him near the stables.

"So now George Allen knows that we know that he's a thief," said Prescott.

"And he also knows that we can't prove it," added Pamela. "But presumably Wilson has proof and is using it to extort money from Allen. How long will that last?"

At sundown Oriental lanterns were lighted over the terrace in front of the cottage. The band played another fanfare. Guests who still had energy assembled for square dancing, some in costumes of the Revolutionary period. Many went to their rooms to rest. Others stayed to watch. A member of the band would call the steps while his comrades provided lively dance tunes.

Pamela sat on a lawn chair next to Lydia. As men and women chose partners and formed squares, she leaned over to Pamela. "Would you join my stepson, John, in one of the squares? He'd like to ask, but he thinks that you want to keep me company."

"I'd be delighted. It's been a long time since I've square danced, but I'm willing to try." She beckoned the young man. He brightened, took her hand, and led her to a group of three couples. The music began, the caller shouted a command, and the dancers swung into action. John was nimble on his feet and quick to catch on to the moves. Pamela enjoyed the dance more than she had expected. The oppressive concerns of the past few years washed away. She felt young again.

During a brief intermission, Pamela asked her partner, "What do you hope to do with the rest of your life?"

For a moment the question bemused him, then he replied, "Sing and dance, swim, eat well until the money runs out."

"That will be forever—considering the size of your family's fortune."

He smiled dryly. "It won't be as long as you think. I expect my father to write a new will when he returns to New York sometime tomorrow. He will leave his entire estate to a very remote cousin—a laughing heir, they say—rather than to his wife. Broadmore Hall will eat up her money. She will have little left over for me."

Pamela tried to appear sympathetic, but financial conflicts, especially among rich families, left her cold. She tried to plant a seed. "Have you ever thought of sharing your talents with others?"

He looked at her quizzically. "And how would I do that?"

"Teach music and sports to children or young adults."

"I think not—I'd starve. Somehow, money will come my way." The light irony, so characteristic of him, had given way to a determined expression. Moments later, his carefree smile reappeared.

"The final set is forming," he said. "Shall we dance?"

As the groups began to form, Pamela noticed that George Allen paired up with Clara Brown. They had been seen together off and on during the day—proper and discreet under the vigilant eye of the stout chaperone. But now their relationship seemed more intimate, especially from his side. His eyes were unusually bright. She was flush in the face from the music and dance and perhaps from secretly drinking lemonade laced with gin. The chaperone was now sitting to one side, slumped over, an empty glass on the table in front of her.

When the dance ended, Allen and Clara slipped away, arm in arm. Pamela exchanged glances with John. He winked and murmured, "When the cat's in dreamland, the mice will play."

An evening meal of smoked ham, a large variety of cheeses, potato salad, and wine and beer was served under Oriental lanterns on the front lawn. Meanwhile, the band accompanied Helen Allen in popular tunes of the day. Her dark, sensuous beauty and her rich, clear alto voice thrilled the audience.

She acknowledged their applause with a deep bow and a winning smile, then announced, "Here's a special song from Lottie Collins in London. Everybody knows it. Join me in the refrain, "Ta-ra-ra-boom-de-ay."

In the first verse her voice was small and soft, her expression coy.

> "I'm not too young, I'm not too old
> Not too timid, not too bold
> Just the kind you'd like to hold
> Just the kind for sport I'm told."

Then she beckoned the audience and launched boldly into the refrain: Ta-ra-ra-boom-de-ay! Her body swayed sensually to the rousing beat of the music and the audience's full-throated, eightfold repetition of the refrain.

At a table off to one side, Pamela was tempted to join in. But she held back when she noticed that Lydia sat stiff and tight-lipped. Meanwhile, a servant came with food for each of them. Lydia seemed weary and ate little, but she focused intently on the singer. "She sings well. That I must grant."

Pamela added, "I've heard that she has had professional voice training, and she has sung at Carnegie Hall."

Lydia grimaced. "Helen has a siren's power over men. My husband lacked the prudence of Ulysses and failed to tie himself to the ship's mast when she began her seductive songs."

As Helen's performance drew to an end amid lively applause, Henry Jennings approached Lydia. His dark, menacing expression foretold pressing, nasty business. He spoke directly to his wife. "Lydia, we must talk. Now. Alone in my study." He glowered at Pamela.

"Couldn't this wait until tomorrow? As hosts, we shouldn't rush away from our guests."

"I'll be brief. Our guests won't miss us. Tomorrow, I must take the early train to New York, where I have important business."

For a moment, Lydia sat still, gazing at her husband. "I agree to this conversation if Pamela can help me get to the study. She will wait outside."

Momentarily, Jennings seemed overcome by anger and bared his teeth. But he quickly recovered, apparently aware that guests sitting nearby had begun to take notice. In a measured, soft voice, he said, "Have it your way. I'll expect you in ten minutes." He threw an unfriendly glance at Pamela and left.

Lydia and Pamela continued to sit at the table as if nothing had happened. With the rest of the audience they applauded Helen Allen's final song. She bowed and announced a popular encore. Lydia leaned over and whispered to Pamela, "Let's go. I've dreaded this moment for months. Please stand by me."

Pamela stood in the hallway outside Jennings's study. With Lydia beside her, she knocked, heard Jennings's sharp command to enter, and opened the door. Lydia gripped Pamela's hand as she passed by into the room. Pamela closed the door and said a silent prayer.

A few minutes later, Lydia emerged from the room, pale-faced but erect. Pamela stayed close by her as they walked down the hall. Suddenly, Lydia began to tremble and missed a step. Pamela held her under the arm and led her into an empty parlor. "Are you all right?" she asked and sat her in a chair. Lydia was breathless and grimaced with pain in her chest. Pamela gave her a dose of laudanum from a vial she carried for such emergencies. When Lydia recovered, Pamela asked, "Do you want to tell me what happened?"

"I may as well tell the whole world. They will soon know. Jennings will file for divorce out of state, in Connecticut, I believe he said. He wants to be free to marry again."

"And what will he do about his will?"

"Tomorrow, he's going to change it in favor of a distant relative. I'll no longer be his heir. I'm frankly surprised. I thought the new beneficiary would be Mrs. Allen, who would also divorce out of state, and they would marry."

Pamela thought again of the encounter between Helen Allen and Jennings that she had witnessed in the greenhouse. Their sexual attraction was still alive. But Jennings had appeared to put some emotional distance between them. Her suggestion that he murder his wife hadn't seemed to please him. Perhaps he had tired of Helen sooner than anyone had thought possible.

He might also have realized that he would surely lose much of his freedom if he were to marry her. And he probably had the young opera singer in his sights.

"The worst news," Lydia continued, "is that he will no longer support Broadmore and will build his own cottage on the western shore of Lake Mahkeenac. It will be the largest and most costly in the Berkshires. He can afford it. He has come into a great deal of money in the last few years."

"How will you maintain Broadmore? Would you consider putting it up for sale?"

"Losing this place is inconceivable. It's too much a part of me." For a moment she was deeply silent. When she spoke, her voice was shrill. "I'd rather die."

CHAPTER 26

Fireworks

4 July

A servant walked through the building ringing a bell. "The fireworks will begin in ten minutes," said Pamela. She had taken Lydia to her apartment and served her an infusion with a little honey. In a few minutes, Lydia recovered her composure, though she looked hollow-eyed and haggard.

"I'll watch from a porch," she said. Then, noticing Pamela's concern, she added, "I'll be all right. I want you to mingle with the guests and keep an eye especially on Helen Allen. She seems to have murder in her heart. If she learns of Henry's new will, she might take aim at him rather than me. Alert Mr. Prescott as well."

Pamela moved quickly through the building. Most of the servants appeared to have left with the steward and the housekeeper to take the view from the hillside behind the cottage. However, Maggie the pantry maid was still in the kitchen with her back to the door.

"Good evening," said Pamela. "Aren't you going to watch the fireworks?"

The woman jumped, then wheeled around, an anxious, distressed expression on her face. She shoved something into the pocket of her apron.

"I didn't mean to startle you," Pamela said. "Would you mind showing me the thing you put into your pocket?"

The maid's face turned beet red with embarrassment. "It's just the key to the kitchen door. I'm supposed to lock up until the fireworks are over." She showed Pamela the large, old-fashioned iron key. "In a minute, I'll join the others outside. It should be a great spectacle."

Pamela felt uneasy about the maid, but she left her there and went out by the back door. Something moved in the nearby shrubbery, and she started. It was too dark to tell whether it was man or beast—or wind. A breeze was blowing around her, catching her gown. She walked to the farthest edge of the garden terrace, where the lawn began to drop down to Lily Pond. Most of the spectators were seated on the slope, and their excited chatter rose in waves to Pamela's ears.

Prescott sauntered across the terrace toward her. "I haven't seen Jennings or Mrs. Allen yet. They might be up to mischief. The gardener and his men are in charge of the event. Jennings is only a spectator. Nonetheless, I'd expect him to make an appearance."

Lanterns still illuminated the garden terrace. In their light Prescott's face seemed thin and ghostly pale. Pamela grew concerned. "Are you well, Prescott?"

"I'm tired, but my spirit is good."

"How will you cope with the fireworks? Could they trigger another spell?"

"Festive noise, even fireworks aren't like the sounds and smells of battle. The atmosphere tonight is joyful. Bursts of laughter, little shrieks of pleasure, and the hum of friendly conversation fill the air. At Antietam and Gettysburg I could smell fear and dread in the men around me. The rattle of musket fire and the cannons' blasts were sounds of anger and hate. Wounded men screamed out of desperation and pain."

He took her hand and pressed it. "Your support is helpful, Pamela. Warn me if you see a relapse coming on."

She gently withdrew her hand. "Of course, but you now seem strong enough to cope. You should know that Henry Jennings is going to write a new will tomorrow, disinheriting Lydia and ignoring Helen Allen. With a stroke of his pen he'll create two mortal enemies. Now I'll take another tour through the cottage and look for Jennings." She hurried to the front door. Brenda Reilly opened it for her.

"Have you seen Mr. Jennings?" Pamela asked. At that moment, the opening volley of rockets went off with high-pitched, ear-piercing whistles. Explosions brightened the sky and shook the house.

"Not recently," Brenda replied. "He must be out on the lawn with the crowd."

Inside the house, the only light came from a few gas lamps and from the colorful bursts of rockets and flares outside. Pamela walked quickly through the entrance hall and peeked into the drawing room and the parlor. In the library, she glanced out a window just as a large rocket exploded, illuminating the room as if it were day. Dazed for a moment, she paused briefly to collect her wits, then checked the remaining ground-floor rooms. Nothing was out of the ordinary.

She climbed the stairs to the next floor. The rockets were now going up in rapid succession, causing deafening explosions and throwing a garish light into the cottage. Jennings had spared no expense for this spectacular display. With simmering anxiety, Pamela hurried down the hallway toward his apartment.

At the door she couldn't hear anything. So she went into an adjacent empty room. A window near Jennings's porch was open.

She could indistinctly hear Jennings and Helen Allen speaking to each other. Then suddenly Helen's voice grew loud and shrill, clearly angry. He raised his voice as well. They seemed to be having a serious quarrel.

The voices became faint and then disappeared. They must have gone inside. Pamela hurried to the door to the hallway and opened it an inch to give her a view of the exit from Jennings's apartment. Within minutes Helen stalked out and slammed the door behind her. As she walked by, her face appeared contorted with anger and grief. She began to sob convulsively into a handkerchief and was soon out of sight.

When the way seemed clear, Pamela continued her search of the upper floors of the building. A few guests were watching the fireworks from porches facing Lily Pond. Nothing seemed out of order. Recalling Maggie with the large iron key, Pamela hastened downstairs to the basement. As she neared the kitchen door, she treaded lightly. Voices were coming from inside. Through a window in the door she could see a large man in a gardener's outfit. Pamela didn't recognize him at first. His mop of gray curly hair had been trimmed, and his beard was gone. He was the tramp Ben, speaking earnestly to another man in a servant's uniform with his back to Pamela. He held a large knife in his right hand but didn't appear to be threatening the tramp.

Finally, he turned so that Pamela could see his face in profile. It was Tom the tramp. Pamela guessed that a theft might be under way. But she glanced at the tramp's knife. This wasn't the time to confront him. She quickly left the basement in search of Prescott.

The fireworks ended with a final blast. Bursts of color filled the sky. In their light Pamela sighted Prescott. She hurried up to him and reported the suspicious men in the kitchen. He instantly patted the pistol in his coat pocket and followed her into the house. The kitchen was empty. No sign of the tramps. After the house had been searched, there still was no sign of them. The housekeeper would check if anything was missing.

Pamela and Prescott retreated to the darkened library. Elsewhere, houseguests were going to their rooms. The steward and the housekeeper were looking after them. Neither Mr. nor Mrs. Jennings were to be seen.

Prescott began. "George Allen is fretting about his wife—and apparently for good reason. She disappeared at the same time as Jennings."

"I wonder how seriously George is concerned," Pamela mused. "Through most of the day, Clara Brown has consoled him. They wandered off together after the dance. As for Helen Allen, I think she and Jennings have had a falling-out." She related what she had heard of their quarrel in Jennings's apartment.

"Perhaps she will now turn against Jennings," conjectured Prescott. "It's said there's no fury like that of a woman scorned."

Pamela agreed. "His reckless behavior astounds me. He's also going to repudiate his wife and leave her cottage without resources while he builds a new and grander cottage for himself on Lake Mahkeenac in Stockbridge."

Prescott grimaced. "I can imagine that Lydia will take the threat to Broadmore very hard. A short while ago, he summoned Wilson to his study, fired him, and ordered him off the property by morning. O'Boyle has taken pity on him and is moving his things to a boardinghouse in the village. His clerk, Brewer, is temporarily taking his place."

"In a few words, Jennings is tempting fate." Pamela felt a tremor in her heart.

Prescott nodded gravely, then glanced at his watch. "It's nearly midnight. I should return to my cabin."

"It's too late," said Pamela. "Let me ask the housekeeper. There should be an empty guest room for you. I'm sure Mrs. Jennings would want you to stay. We'll all feel safer with you in the house."

He gazed gently at her and smiled. "Then I'll be your guest."

CHAPTER 27

Murder

5 July

The next morning Pamela joined Lydia downstairs in the breakfast room. A few houseguests were also there. Conversation was sparse and subdued though good-humored. Yesterday's celebration had pleasantly exhausted nearly everyone. Still, they all agreed that they had had a good time. The fireworks display had been a glorious finale. Henry Jennings had lived up to their expectations.

When Prescott arrived, Lydia welcomed him with a smile of surprise.

"Did you guard us last night? Had I known, I would have slept better. The fireworks jangled my nerves."

As they were about to leave the table, Jennings's servant appeared, white in the face. In a trembling voice, he announced to Lydia, "Madam, I took breakfast to Mr. Jennings a few minutes ago. He was lying on the floor of his study and didn't appear well." The servant bit his lip, then stammered, "In fact, he's dead."

At first, Lydia seemed shocked into silence. Finally, she

asked distractedly, "Where's John? He must go to his father."
She glanced at the servant.

"He left the house, madam, early this morning. Said he was
going to the lake to swim."

She turned to Pamela. "Would you please look into this
dreadful matter? I feel too weak to move."

Pamela nodded to Prescott, and they hastened to Jennings's
apartment, together with the servant. He had left the door ajar.
The study appeared undisturbed. The door to the porch overlooking the garden was open. Jennings was lying face down on
the floor next to his desk, crumpled like a rag doll. Pamela
stared for a moment, shivering. Unbidden, she recalled Jennings
in his prime—a powerful, commanding presence—now suddenly reduced to this grotesque, inert object. What had happened to him?

Prescott knelt down and studied the body. "He's been struck
at least twice with a blunt object, once on the right temple, then
again on the back of the head."

He felt the victim's jaw and determined that it was fixed.
"Rigor has begun. I'd guess that he died between twelve and one."

"Caught by surprise and from behind," added Pamela.
"There's no sign of forced entry or struggle. He must have
known the killer, probably a right-handed person. And there's
the lethal weapon." She pointed to the mace lying on the floor,
the one she had noticed on her first visit to Jennings. Hair and
blood were visible even to the naked eye.

"It was conveniently placed on the wall," Prescott remarked. "The killer might not have intended to kill, came here
unarmed, and acted on impulse."

With help from Jennings's servant, they searched the room
but found no more clues.

When the servant was at a distance, Pamela whispered,
"What do we do now? We couldn't conceal this crime even if

Mrs. Jennings so wished. The servant who discovered the body must have told other servants. Within an hour the entire town will know."

"We must call the local police," Prescott replied. "Unfortunately, their detective is new, a former NYPD patrolman with much less experience than he claims. The local Lenox authorities hired him because his rough tactics would scare tramps away from the town and especially from the great cottages."

"Is he at all qualified to investigate Jennings's murder?" Pamela asked.

"He is quite sure of himself, but he has never investigated a murder and has few resources."

As they were about to leave the room, Pamela asked, "Who do you think killed him?"

"That's a hard question," Prescott replied. "I have several potential suspects in mind."

Before he could name them, the servant rushed to the desk and exclaimed, "Mr. Jennings's lapel pin is gone."

Pamela and Prescott exchanged glances and said in unison, "Tom the tramp."

While waiting for the police, Pamela met Mrs. Blake in the housekeeper's room. She gave Pamela a list of a dozen silver spoons, forks, and knives, as well as several small silver platters, missing since yesterday.

"Have you talked to Maggie, the pantry maid?" Pamela asked.

"Yes. She claims to have seen no suspicious persons and had locked the back door when she left to watch the fireworks. I couldn't find the missing items in her room."

"Did any of the guests act suspiciously?" Pamela recalled her experience at Macy's. "Rich, respectable people will sometimes steal as well as the poor."

The housekeeper shrugged helplessly. "We had about a hundred visitors running in and out of this building. I couldn't begin to keep track of them all."

"Did you notice any strangers among the servants?"

"Yes, there were many faces I didn't recognize. Both the steward and the gardener hired extra help for the occasion."

Pamela added, "I recognized one of them, Tom the tramp. He was in the kitchen with another stranger, also a tramp, named Ben."

The housekeeper nodded vigorously. "There you have a pair of likely suspects."

Late in the morning, the detective and a constable arrived. A medical examiner from Pittsfield would come in a few hours. Mr. Brady, the detective, was a short, burly man, a few years past forty. He had a pug nose, deep brown beady eyes, and a square face. His movements were quick and aggressive; his scowl, intimidating.

Pamela and Prescott led the police to Jennings's study. The detective studied the body and the scene of the crime—rather too quickly and inattentively, as if he had already determined the killer. He declared that the case's resolution came down to the killer's motive and his or her opportunity. The potential suspects seemed limited to the houseguests and the members of the household, plus the tramps.

The detective called the guests and the household together in the great entrance hall and warned them to remain available in the cottage until he could interview them individually. Lydia requested that Pamela and Prescott be with her for support at the interviews. Brady seemed surprised but didn't object. He was known to defer to the rich and respectable.

He moved to a table in the adjacent library. The constable called everyone in, one by one. The detective began by questioning the servant who had discovered the body and quickly moved on to Mrs. Jennings. Prescott and Pamela sat by her side.

"We had our differences," she granted. "Mr. Jennings was often rough in his ways. But we all understood that he meant well, and we respected him for his success in business. I can't imagine that any of us would have done this terrible thing to him."

The detective nodded and smiled, appearing to share her sentiments. He moved on to John, who had returned by this time. He largely echoed his stepmother's testimony. The detective then briefly questioned the rest of the household and the visitors, none of whom could offer any clues.

After they had dispersed, the detective turned aside to Pamela and Prescott and asked if they had anything to add. They avoided conjecture and gave a factual report. But when they mentioned the bad feeling between Jennings and his son and Jennings's intention to divorce and change his will, the detective shook his head.

"You find similar discord in every family," he said. "It seldom leads to murder. I'll begin this investigation with the most likely culprits, the tramps Tom and Ben." He directed the constable to organize a search.

Pamela went upstairs to check on Lydia. A maid opened the door. Lydia was at the piano playing Chopin's funeral march. She acknowledged Pamela with a wan smile. John lounged in a seat by an open window and waved a welcoming hand. But his mind seemed elsewhere. Pamela quietly sat off to a side, listening, watching. Lydia went on playing. As if not fully engaged in the music, she often looked up from the instrument and gazed inwardly. Finally, she broke off in midcourse with a sigh and turned to Pamela. "What can I say? Even great music fails me. I hated him; still, I miss him."

"Do you wish to view your husband's body? It's kept in a basement room. I could bring you there."

"No, my dear. He's gone—God knows where. The rotting corpse he left behind is repugnant to me. I want my last impression of him to be at his best—yesterday, standing tall on one of our porches, looking proud and in command."

Pamela sensed that this tribute didn't come from the heart. Lydia's tone was matter-of-fact, and her eyes were dry. She must also be keenly aware that she would be a very wealthy woman when his will was probated.

Pamela glanced at John questioningly.

He shook his head. His expression was inscrutable.

Early in the afternoon, the medical examiner, a bright young doctor, came from Pittsfield. Detective Brady was away, hunting for the two suspects. So, Prescott met the doctor at the station and briefed him during the ride to Broadmore.

"Mrs. Jennings has hired me to watch over the estate," Prescott explained. "Her husband was struck twice on the head from behind by a heavy mace. I first thought that the blows were forceful enough to kill him instantly. With hindsight I'm not so sure."

"We'll soon see," said the doctor. "I'm open to whatever the facts tell us."

The study was empty, except for Pamela. Prescott had asked the others to allow the doctor to work alone. Now Prescott led him through the study, showed him the mace, and pointed to a chalk outline of the body's original position.

Then he told the doctor, "We've moved the body to a cool room in the basement. I'll take you there. I'd like my assistant, Mrs. Thompson, to attend the examination. For her benefit, would you explain the process as you go along?"

"Gladly." The doctor looked surprised, but not opposed. "Women are often more observant than men."

In the basement room the body was on a table, covered with a cloth. Prescott removed the cloth, and the doctor went to work. After a few minutes, he beckoned Prescott and Pamela to the table.

"The assailant's blows didn't cause death." He glanced from Prescott to Pamela. "My preliminary verdict is that Jennings was suffocated early in the morning. Look." He pointed to a slight bluish tinge on the lips. "The eyes are bloodshot and bulging. In the autopsy, I'll find burst capillaries and blood in the lungs."

Prescott seemed embarrassed. "The study was dimly lighted when I examined the body. Still, I should have noticed the symptoms of suffocation."

"No one else noticed them, either," remarked Pamela.

The doctor went on. "The most likely scenario is that the assailant realized that the blows were insufficient. For whatever reason, he finished Jennings off by suffocation. However, it's possible that the assailant mistakenly believed the blows were sufficient. If he left in haste, he might not have taken the victim's pulse. But if he did, it might have been so weak that he didn't detect it. Later, someone else could have suffocated Jennings."

For a few moments, the room was silent with reflection. Then Prescott asked the examiner, "Could you delay your official verdict until I test these ideas? If there were two assailants, they may not be aware of each other. That ignorance could be exploited during interrogation."

"I see your point, sir," replied the examiner. "I'll do as you wish."

Prescott turned to Pamela. "We should return to Jennings's study and search again for the weapon that killed him. Since we thought that the bloody mace was obviously the murder weapon, we may not have searched the room carefully enough to find the real one."

* * *

Back in the study, Pamela checked the drapes over the windows. They were intact and showed no sign of blood. The divan's cushions were also clean. Finally she said, "I can't find any bloodstained fabric in the room."

"Is anything missing?" Prescott asked.

Her eyes fixed on Jennings's chair. "Where's his white linen pillow with the red rose? It's soft enough to have been used for the crime and would be bloodstained. Brenda and I will look for it."

Prescott added, "Jennings's killer must have also smeared blood on his clothes. Search for them too."

"*His* clothes?" she asked. "The killer might have been a woman."

CHAPTER 28

Pursuit of a Tramp

Lenox and New York, 6 July

At midmorning the next day, Lydia told Pamela to go to the town jail, a few dingy rooms in the town hall. The police had rounded up several tramps and needed someone to identify the suspects, Tom and Ben. Neither the table silver nor the lapel pin had been recovered. The pillow was still missing.

"It wasn't easy to find these men," said the constable to Pamela. "Camped in the woods, dirty and desperate, they claimed to be ignorant of the murder at Jennings's cottage. They were just waiting for a freight train to New York City. A few more hours and they'd have been safely on their way."

He took her through a hallway to a barred room, where seven thin, shabby men stood in a line. They glared at the constable and stared curiously at Pamela. She felt very uncomfortable in this role.

"Pick out the culprits, ma'am," ordered the constable.

Reluctantly, she studied each of the men. Their faces were bruised, and perhaps other parts of their bodies as well. The sight angered her. "Have they been in a fight?" She hoped to shame the constable.

"No, ma'am." Her irony went over his head. "Detective Brady and I had to rough them up. It's the only language they understand. Still, we couldn't get the truth out of them. Hardened liars, they claimed to know nothing about Tom or Ben or the missing items or the murder. Now I need you to pick out Tom."

"He's not here, constable. He probably got away hours ago, perhaps with the lapel pin. It's hard to imagine that he would have taken the silver—too heavy and bulky. His companion Ben isn't here, either. He might have taken the silver and hidden it." She glanced at the men. "They were probably telling you the truth, at least about Tom. Your rough efforts were in vain."

Late in the morning, when Pamela returned from her visit to the jail, Prescott was waiting for her in Broadmore's library. They had the room to themselves. Most of the houseguests had left in a parlor car on the morning train.

"What have you learned?" he asked, a doubtful tone in his voice.

"Neither Tom nor Ben were among the tramps picked up by the police."

Prescott stroked his chin for a moment. "My best guess is that the two rogues have split. Ben took the silver, buried it somewhere in the neighborhood, and is hiding at a safe distance from the police investigation."

"And where is Tom?"

"He's probably in New York City, trying to sell the lapel pin at a small fraction of its true value. The Lenox detective will surely give Tom's description to the NYPD. They'll put spies outside every crooked jewelry dealer in the city. And the newspapers will describe Jennings's death in lurid detail and alert the public to watch out for his murderer."

Pamela grew agitated. "We must find him before the NYPD does. They would make mincemeat out of him and force him to confess. He would be quickly convicted and hanged. We have to bring him—and the lapel pin—back to the Berkshires. He's more likely to get a fair trial here than in New York."

"There you may have a point. You also know Tom much better than I. So what's your plan?"

"I'll speak to Maggie the pantry maid again. She might give me a contact for Tom in the city. Then I'll go and look for him."

"I must go with you," insisted Prescott. "My knowledge of the city could be helpful. I'm also familiar with the NYPD's detectives and could find out how their investigation is going."

Pamela pretended to be miffed. "Do you think that I can't manage on my own?"

"I'm sure you can," he replied gallantly.

"Then I'll tell Mrs. Jennings that I need to go to New York for up to a week. Despite her bias against tramps, she's fair-minded and should agree that Tom be brought back to the Berkshires for trial. She feels safe at Broadmore, now that the tramps are either in jail or have fled from Lenox. And Helen Allen is no longer a threat to her."

Pamela hurried to the kitchen. Maggie was helping the cook prepare lunch for Lydia, her stepson John, and a few guests. In an hour Maggie was free but reluctant to talk to Pamela. Nonetheless, she drew her into the pantry and shut the door.

"So what do you want?" asked Maggie through tight lips.

"I want you to listen to me with an open mind." Pamela went on to describe the risks that Tom would encounter in New York. "The police would almost certainly find him and beat him brutally. I want to bring him back, safe and sound, to Berkshire County. Can you tell me where he's hiding?"

Maggie listened stone-faced. "I haven't seen him since I brought you to his shed by the tracks. So I couldn't help you even if I wanted to."

Pamela was convinced that Maggie was lying. She had likely continued to feed Tom and probably knew that he had been hiding in Broadmore on the night of Jennings's murder. Still Pamela persisted. "In New York, Tom will be a hunted animal. If I told you that I have his best interest at heart, would you believe me?"

For a long moment Maggie stared at the floor. Finally, she nodded and said in a low, hesitant voice, "Back at the shed you didn't call the police when you could have. You gave Tom a good piece of advice. Maybe you could do the same in New York."

"Let's hope he cooperates," said Pamela. "You might recall somebody he knows in New York and a place where he'd be likely to hide?"

Maggie seemed to struggle with the question. Finally, she replied, "Tom has mentioned a saloon on the Lower East Side. One of the bartenders, an Irishman called Mark, is his friend. I don't know the address, but it's across the street from a church. If he's hiding in the saloon, you could try to talk sense to him. I doubt that he would listen."

Pamela found Prescott pacing back and forth in the library. She told him what she had learned from Maggie. "For a start," she said, "both the church and the saloon are most likely Irish and Catholic."

Prescott smiled wryly. "That narrows our search only slightly. But we also know that they are on the city's Lower East Side. Get ready. We should catch the afternoon train."

On arrival in New York, they took a cab to her boardinghouse. She kept an apartment there with a private entrance for occasional visits. As Prescott left her off, he said, "I'll speak to Harry Miller. He might be familiar with the saloon. Regardless, I'll pick you up in the morning, and I trust we'll find our tramp."

CHAPTER 29

Captured

New York, 7 July

A pall of humid summer heat already lay over the city when Prescott knocked on Pamela's door. He had left his coach, a nondescript vehicle, out on the street. Pamela was ready and waiting for him. There was a whiff of danger in the air. They hastened to the coach. "It's unwise to leave any vehicle unattended," she warned and glanced toward nearby clusters of agitated, angry men in the street. "They were laid off early this morning without warning and have nowhere to turn."

"Where we're going is no better." He helped her into the coach. "Our captains of industry have made bad investments in banks and railroads and caused this depression. Now they blame the law of supply and demand as if it were Holy Scripture and carved in stone."

They drove slowly through the city's hot, noisy, congested streets into a teeming urban jungle on the Lower East Side. For comfort's sake and to appear less conspicuous Pamela had dressed simply and chosen a pale blue light cotton dress. A straw hat protected her face from the sun. Prescott wore a lightweight, inexpensive tan suit and cap.

"Last night," Prescott began, "Harry Miller told me that Tom's friend might be working at McKenna's saloon. Across the street is St. Mary's Church. We need to be careful. The saloon has a reputation for vice and violence. But at this time of the day, it's as peaceful as it ever gets."

They left the coach in a livery stable and walked a block to the saloon.

"I've an idea," said Prescott. "Let's go to the church first and speak to the pastor."

Reverend Michael Moriarity was in a cramped sacristy at work on his books. "What can I do for you?" he asked in a lilting Irish accent. He was a middle-aged man with piercing blue eyes. A smile came easily to his broad face as the strangers approached.

Prescott spoke in a friendly way. "We're looking for Tom, a young man in need of help. He's a good lad, but he may have strayed a bit to the wrong side of the law."

The smile left the priest's face. "In other words," he said warily, "the police are looking for him, and you think he might be hiding across the street." His voice dropped to a cautious whisper. "Might you be one of Mr. Byrnes's plainclothesmen?" He threw a puzzled glance at Pamela.

"This is Mrs. Thompson, my assistant. She knows Tom. I'm Jeremiah Prescott, a lawyer and private investigator." He showed the priest his papers. "We want to talk with Tom. How shall we best do that?"

"I must be careful what I say about McKenna's saloon. He has a loyal following in this neighborhood. The police have been prominent among his supporters, but they've become skittish since Reverend Parkhurst and his reformers aroused the public against the saloons."

The priest stared at Prescott, then at Pamela, taking their measure. Finally, he said, "Some good men work at McKenna's because they can't find jobs elsewhere. I recommend Barney

Gough. This morning you'll find him cleaning up the place. Say that Father Moriarity sent you and give him this." He pulled out a card depicting Saint Mary. On the back side he wrote "from Father Mike."

Mr. Gough, a short, wiry man, looked up from sweeping the public room floor. Several men sat at tables clasping glasses of beer. They glanced curiously at the strangers, then returned to their drinks. As Pamela and Prescott approached Barney, fear came instantly to his eyes.

Prescott drew back; Pamela took the lead. "We're from the Berkshires in Massachusetts and have come to New York looking for an acquaintance. Father Moriarity sent us to you." She handed him the card.

He took it tentatively and studied it front and back, upside down at first. Then with a finger he traced the priest's greeting. Slowly he relaxed and smiled shyly. He had no teeth.

"Is the young man known as Tom?"

"Yes." Pamela's heart began to pound. "May we speak to him?"

"I trust Father Mike, but our bouncers won't allow your gentleman to come in. He might be a detective from the vice squad or a reformer or one of Parkhurst's spies."

Pamela flashed a questioning look to Prescott, then said to Gough, "The bouncers have no reason to fear me. I'll go with you alone."

Prescott blinked but didn't object. "I'll wait here for you." His voice sounded strained.

"As you wish, ma'am," said Barney. "Follow me."

He led her out of the barroom and up a flight of stairs to a table where three rough-looking men—bouncers, Pamela assumed—stopped them. The men studied her for a moment from head to toe. Pamela's throat tightened. Then their leader asked, "What's your business here?"

"I want to talk to Tom," she croaked.

"I'd better search her," chortled the leader. "She might be carrying a knife or a small pistol."

He approached her with a leering grin on his face. His comrades pinned Pamela's arms behind her back. She struggled in vain.

Barney had disappeared at the first sign of danger. Now he reappeared with a tall, robust, silver-haired gentleman wearing a black silk top hat and carrying an elegant walking stick. "What kind of mischief are you three idiots up to?" he thundered. He brought his stick down hard on their leader. The ruffians slunk back behind the table.

"Mr. McKenna himself," whispered Barney to Pamela.

"We thought she might be a spy," the leader stammered.

McKenna tipped his hat to Pamela. "I see that you are a lady. How can I help you?"

"I'm Pamela Thompson, and I want to speak to Tom and take him back to the Berkshires if I may."

The gentleman's eyes twinkled with pleasure. "You may have him, madam. Suspect in a murder, he's a plague on this fine house. I don't want the vice squad to find him here this evening, or ever." He paused for a moment, head tilted in curiosity. "May I ask if you came alone?"

"No, Mr. Jeremiah Prescott brought me. He's waiting in the public room."

"You keep good company, madam. He's a gentleman and the cleverest lawyer in New York. We've never met, but I've seen him in court. If I were ever arrested—Heaven forbid—I would want him to defend me. Now let's fetch Tom." He turned to the three ruffians. "Boys, I've a job for you. There's a police spy standing across the street. Remove him for about a half hour while this good lady escorts Tom from our premises. And be gentle. No broken bones, deep cuts, or ugly bruises. Okay?"

They nodded, exchanged eager smiles, and hurried downstairs.

"I'll take you to Tom, madam." He gallantly offered her his arm and led her through the mezzanine of a spacious auditorium. Musicians and young male and female singers were rehearsing on the stage below. McKenna pointed to them with pride. "They're preparing a program of popular music for tonight. We want to be at our best when the vice squad comes."

Finally, they arrived at a door at the end of a long hallway. "Tom's friend, one of our bartenders, hid him here last night. I objected as soon as I heard of it." He opened the door without knocking. "Tom, Mrs. Thompson has come for you. Count your blessings. I would have put you out on the street. Then in five minutes the police would have nabbed you and dragged you kicking and screaming to the Tombs, the city's most dismal prison. Grab your bag and follow me."

Tom sat on his bed, mouth agape and eyes wide with terror. He glanced from McKenna to Pamela and back to McKenna again, then obediently picked up his bag and set off with them. He hadn't said a word yet.

As they walked back to the public room, Pamela took his arm and whispered, "I'll explain everything when we're in the coach."

In a minute, they reached the public room. Prescott rose from a table, visibly relieved. McKenna extended a hand. "Prescott, it's a pleasure to meet you. I've brought your friend back safely out of my den of iniquity. And I've handed Tom over to her. I'd invite you to tea, but I'm busy preparing for a visit from the vice squad. Some other time?"

"Yes, of course," said Prescott. "I'd be delighted. Now we must be going. My coach is waiting."

Once they were under way, Tom spoke for the first time. "What's to become of me? Even a brothel turns me out."

Pamela replied gently, "McKenna was concerned that the vice squad might close his saloon if they were to find you there. That's a risk that he didn't wish to take."

Prescott added, "Reverend Parkhurst's criticism has stirred up the police. They are angry, like a swarm of bees flushed out of their hives. They want to look busy protecting the public, so they've cast a dragnet for you. A suspected murderer, you're one of their prime targets."

"Then I should move on to Hartford or Boston or perhaps go back to Chicago."

"The Pinkertons will follow your tracks until they get you. You are accused of killing one of our best known businessmen. Citizens across the country, even tramps, are looking for you and would betray you for a reward."

Tom stared at the floor of the coach. Finally, he looked up and asked, "What do you think I should do?"

Prescott replied, "Go back to the Berkshires with us, surrender to the district court in Pittsfield, and return the diamond lapel pin. People will begin to believe your story. If you're innocent, a court of law will clear your name."

"First," Pamela cautioned, "you must tell us what really happened that night between the fourth and fifth of July at Broadmore and how you were involved."

Traffic had come to a halt in the street's congestion. The sun was beating down on the coach. The temperature became unbearably hot. Pamela and the two men patted their brows with handkerchiefs.

Tom raised his head and began to speak, at first haltingly. "As the fireworks began, while Maggie was outside, Ben and I sneaked into the kitchen through an unlatched window. Ben wanted to steal silverware; I would take a knife, not to cut anyone but to carve my toys. Just before the fireworks ended, he left with the silver. I hid in a closet, thinking about Jennings. Should I strangle him while he slept? Or should I take something that was precious to him? When the house quieted down, I stole up the back stairs to his apartment, picked the lock, and went to his study. I had decided to hide his lapel pin where he would never find it."

"Why didn't you simply steal the pin?" Prescott asked.

"I knew I couldn't sell it." He hesitated and swallowed nervously. "Then I saw him, stretched out on the floor by his desk. I searched for a pulse. He was dead. I looked for his lapel pin. It was gone. So I left as quickly as I could. Everyone knows I'm a tramp and had threatened him. I would be the chief suspect and wouldn't have a fair trial. I caught the next freight train to New York and hid at McKenna's."

"Can you think of anyone who might have killed Jennings?"

He shook his head. "He had many enemies, some in his own household."

"Did Maggie help you?" Pamela asked.

"Not at all. I kept her out of it." Pamela wasn't fully convinced. Maggie could have unlatched the window for him. He also could have come upon an unconscious Jennings, suffocated him, and disposed of the pillow.

Traffic had begun to move again. Prescott said to Tom, "Your story sounds plausible. Unfortunately, the New York police detectives won't believe it. Nor will the magistrates. You should return to Berkshire County and allow me to help you. Since you are a tramp, the judge might not release you on bail. That means you will probably have to spend time in the Pittsfield jail. Your best defense is for us to find the true killer." He paused. "Will you accept our services?"

"Can you force me?"

"No, we aren't the police. We can only persuade."

He averted his eyes and appeared to sort out his options. Finally, he said softly, "I'll go with you. I really have no other choice."

Pamela asked Prescott, "How shall we get him past the police?"

Prescott turned to Tom. "We need to disguise you. The police are closely watching the train stations, looking for a bearded, shabbily dressed tramp. Unfortunately, my premises aren't suitable. Police spies keep an eye on my clients." He asked Pamela, "Could you change Tom's appearance—cut his beard and dress him in decent clothes—and hide him in your boardinghouse until the early train tomorrow morning? I'll change his name to Jimmy Barker and prepare documents to prove it. Then I'll buy the tickets and pick you up."

Pamela agreed reluctantly. Tom seemed to feel secure with her and was less likely to bolt. Still, she recalled him in Broadmore's kitchen with the knife in his hand. How well did she really know him?

By this time, the coach had come to within a block of the boardinghouse.

"We'll stop here," said Prescott. "Otherwise the neighborhood might wonder about a tramp riding in a coach."

Pamela and Tom left the coach and walked quickly to her boardinghouse. "Wash and shave yourself," she said to him, "while I go to a thrift shop for some clothes. When I come back, I'll cut your hair. Tonight, you can sleep on the sofa in my parlor."

By her return, he had shaved. She trimmed his hair. He put on the clothes she had bought: clean, worn, but decent. "You look like one of the 'deserving poor,' " she said approvingly. "Should anyone ask, tell them you are an honest, dependable woodworker. Until we get you safely out of New York, your name is Jimmy Barker. You've come east from Chicago to find a job. All of that is close to the truth."

At suppertime, she brought him into the dining room, where a dozen boarders waited for their food. She whispered to him, "This will help you get used to your disguise." The cook had been told to set two extra places for Pamela and a guest. As they sat down to a proper table, Pamela was pleased to see that Tom's manners had improved, and his surliness was gone. He fitted easily into the boarders' casual conversation. But her satisfaction was dampened by the sobering thought that she could be charged with aiding a fugitive criminal suspect.

After supper, she showed him to her parlor. They would rise early, eat something, and be waiting for Prescott's coach. Tom appeared to agree. But, as she lay in bed, she wondered if he might reconsider the plan, slip out during the night, and go back to the life of a tramp.

No sound came from the parlor. After a restless half hour, she rose and quietly opened the door. He was now snoring softly. Reassured, she went back to bed and fell asleep.

CHAPTER 30

Back in the Berkshires

New York and Lenox, 8 July

The next morning, to Pamela's great relief, Tom was dressed and ready for breakfast. Bright eyed and smiling, he seemed pleased with his new identity. After a light meal of bread, preserves, and tea, they waited at the front door for Prescott. Promptly at seven, his agent Harry Miller drove up to the house. From inside the coach, Prescott pushed open the door. Pamela and Tom scrambled in, and the coach set off for the train station.

"So far so good," remarked Prescott. He appeared tenser than Pamela had ever seen him. At dinner last night with a well-connected officer in the NYPD's detective department, he had learned that Superintendent Byrnes had ordered an all-out search for the killer of Henry Jennings. His murder by a tramp had aroused fear among the city's wealthy elite, already on edge because of social discontent rumbling through the country. A year ago, workers had fought a pitched battle with strikebreakers and their Pinkerton guards at the Carnegie Steel Company's plant at Homestead near Pittsburgh. A young anarchist had tried to assassinate Henry Frick, the president of the company.

Prescott glanced at Tom's knotted brow. "You needn't worry. The police are looking for Tom Parker, a bearded, shaggy-haired, shabbily dressed tramp, hiding in New York, just waiting for an opportunity to strike down another captain of industry. Fortunately, Mrs. Thompson has transformed you into Jimmy Barker, a poor but respectable woodworker. I'm confident that we'll bring you safely to the Berkshires."

When the coach arrived at the train station, patrolmen were standing at the entrance. Pamela's heart began to race. But they took no notice of the three travelers. Inside the station, Prescott stiffened momentarily. With his eyes he pointed to two men scrutinizing the crowd.

He whispered to Pamela, "Plainclothes detectives. I recognize the older man, Murphy. We've crossed swords before."

Then, to Pamela's dismay, Murphy sauntered over to Prescott.

"Where are you going, my friend?" Murphy didn't smile. His eyes were a cold, icy blue.

"I'm traveling to Lenox with my assistant, Mrs. Pamela Thompson, and Jimmy Barker, an artisan I've hired to work on my cabin. Here are the tickets."

The detective glanced at them. "Lenox isn't as safe as it used to be. Did you know that a tramp killed one of the rich summer residents?"

"So I've heard."

Murphy then asked for identification. Prescott showed him a business card. Pamela gave him a letter of recommendation from Mrs. Jennings. And Parker handed him a contract with Prescott.

The detective's eyes fixed on Parker. "Show me your hands." Parker held them up. The detective examined them closely.

"The hands of an honest woodworker." He gave the tickets back to Prescott. "Have a pleasant trip." He tipped his hat to Pamela and returned to his companion. Pamela released a quiet sigh of relief.

*   *   *

The travelers arrived in Lenox at noon. Pamela got off the train while Prescott and Parker continued on for a few miles to Pittsfield. Prescott had telegraphed to Charles Garner, Berkshire County's district attorney, requesting a meeting in his office.

Garner was waiting for them at his desk. Prescott introduced Parker and added, "The Lenox detective and the New York police regard him as the chief suspect in Henry Jennings's murder. He has returned from New York to clear his name. Will you give him a hearing?"

The district attorney glanced, puzzled, at Parker. "You are said to be a tramp, though you don't look like one."

"Whether I'm a tramp or a robber baron doesn't matter in the eyes of the law. I want a fair hearing. The Lenox detective has wrongly accused me of the crime."

"Tell me briefly what happened."

Parker recounted his earlier quarrel with Jennings, his years as a tramp, and his attempt to punish Jennings on the night of the Fourth.

The district attorney looked skeptical. "Why did you run away?"

"In Lenox a tramp couldn't get a fair hearing."

Garner leaned forward, fixing the tramp in a cool gaze. "There are reasonable grounds to treat you as a suspect." He turned to Prescott. "What do you say?"

"Keep an open mind. The case against Parker is circumstantial. Other suspects had equal or greater opportunity and motive for the crime." He briefly explained Henry Jennings's problematic relationships with his family and other persons close to him.

"I agree with you, Prescott, on the need for further investigation. The Lenox detective was badly trained in New York and is out of his depth in this case. We need a more competent man." He met Prescott's eye. "You and your assistant know the family intimately and are professionally qualified. May I hire both of you as special investigators?"

"Yes, you may. We'll work for the usual compensation and expenses."

"Good. I'll do the paperwork immediately."

"In the meantime," Prescott continued, "Parker needs a place to stay."

"That can be arranged," Garner replied. "A local police officer and his wife run a boardinghouse in Pittsfield. Parker can stay there for a few days until the judge schedules a hearing."

Prescott turned to the tramp. "Do you accept these arrangements?"

Tom replied glumly, "They're the best I can expect."

Prescott suspected that flight was still an option.

Back in Lenox, Pamela telephoned Lydia from the railroad station and learned that the police had found a tramp with the stolen silverware.

Lydia's voice was excited. "They think he's Ben, Tom's partner, and they want you to identify him. Afterward, come to my apartment and report on your visit to New York."

Pamela went directly to the jail. The constable on duty brought out the prisoner. "Is this the tramp they call Ben?"

"Yes," she replied without hesitation. "I'd like permission to speak to him."

Her request seemed to surprise the constable. "He admitted his guilt and led us to the silver." The constable took her to a small waiting room. A minute later, the tramp arrived, his feet and wrists shackled. The constable attached Ben's chains to rings in the floor. "That should hold him, ma'am. I'll wait outside." The constable left the room.

Pamela asked, "Did Tom, your partner, help you steal the silverware?"

"No, he said it was too difficult to turn into cash."

"Then why was he in the cottage? I saw the two of you in the kitchen."

"We got in through a window. Tom told me he wanted to play a trick on old Jennings. He would steal his famous lapel pin. I said that was as foolish as stealing the silverware. How could he ever sell it? He said he didn't expect to. He just wanted to hurt Jennings in return for the trouble Jennings had caused him."

"When did you part?"

"I left just before the fireworks ended. He said he would hide in the house until it quieted down, early in the morning, then sneak into Jennings's study, where he kept the pin."

"Did he ever say that he would kill Jennings that night?"

"He said he had thought about it but had given up the idea. Too risky."

"But if he surprised Jennings in the study, he might have killed him, right?"

Ben pursed his lips and glanced toward the door. "I don't know," he replied. Pamela understood that the constable was listening.

At midafternoon, Pamela arrived at Broadmore. Lydia seemed eager for news. She wore black, but that was her only sign of grief. Pamela couldn't blame her.

"The tramp Tom Parker has returned from New York," Pamela began. "But we haven't recovered your husband's lapel pin. Parker insists that he didn't steal it and also denies killing Mr. Jennings."

Lydia frowned. "I recall his fight with my husband. I'm glad he's in custody, but I wish he had confessed. Then he'd be quickly convicted and punished, and we could turn the page on this sad chapter." She paused. "Did he implicate the maid Maggie?"

"No," Pamela replied.

"Then you should speak to her. I'm upset and can't decide what to do. She has apparently abetted the theft of silver from the pantry. I may need to dismiss her, unless the police arrest her first."

Pamela couldn't find the maid. Other servants said she had gone into the village to shop. When Maggie finally returned to the cottage, she grew wary as she saw Pamela approach. They sat at a small table in the pantry with the door closed.

"Tom Parker is in police custody in Pittsfield," said Pamela.

"I'm not surprised," the maid said. "He was foolish to run away to New York. But he didn't kill old man Jennings."

"How do you know?"

"I just know. Tom's desperate and talks tough, but he wouldn't hurt a fly."

"And Ben?"

"I don't know him well like I know Tom."

"Did you help them get into the cottage?"

"No, they didn't need help. They must have sneaked in through a window and got out the same way."

After this conversation, Pamela took a walk in the garden to enjoy the flowers and to reflect on the maid's story. Maggie wasn't a good liar. She might have unlatched the window for the tramps and hidden Tom in the closet. She could even have suffocated Jennings. Pamela was in a quandary. If she shared her suspicion with Lydia, Lydia would fire the maid. But that seemed rash. Pamela paced the garden back and forth, arguing quietly with herself. Finally, she decided to hide her suspicion and give Lydia only the facts. She hoped no harm would come of that.

As Pamela was about to leave the garden, Prescott appeared. She pointed to a bench, and they sat next to each other. Pamela reported on her conversation with Maggie. "She refused to implicate either Tom Parker or Ben. I learned nothing useful from her—except perhaps that she might not trust me."

"That's predictable," Prescott remarked. "We've just brought her friend Tom back to face an uncertain future. But let's talk about the Lenox detective. He's here questioning the servants, and I've spoken briefly with him. He wants to charge Tom for the murder of Jennings. He would be tried and convicted in about a month and hanged shortly afterward in a state prison far from the Berkshires."

"What a travesty of justice!" Pamela exclaimed.

"I agree," Prescott said. "The local authorities in Lenox desperately want to put this incident behind them as quickly as possible. Rich summer residents must be assured that they are safe here, or they might leave and take their money with them. Hanging is unsightly and should be kept at a suitable distance."

"What did the district attorney tell you?" asked Pamela.

"He wants a thorough investigation of several suspects and wants me to lead it rather than Mr. Brady, the Lenox detective. Brady must be told of the new situation as kindly as possible to avoid making an enemy of him."

"That will be difficult," Pamela pointed out. "He's stubborn and aggressive. Won't his investigation collide with ours and cause delays and other complications? How will the local authorities and the cottagers react to that?"

"With dismay and impatience," Prescott replied. "Most of them agree with the detective that the tramp killed Jennings. If the truth be told, they would have Parker hanged tomorrow in a distant place so that their social life could return to normal."

"Their attitude is self-serving," she said. "No one actually saw the tramp kill Jennings. Other potential suspects had sufficient motive and opportunity. Mrs. Allen, for example. Jennings apparently had promised her marriage and money, then rejected her. Or, George Allen, her husband. Jennings had cuckolded him. Or, John Jennings. His father had abused him for years."

Prescott waved a warning hand. "You had better stop listing possible suspects. You will soon reach Maggie the maid, or even Lydia Jennings, her husband's heir. Her motive is as strong as any of the others."

Pamela gazed at him with reproach. "That would be totally out of character and very hard for me to accept. We have become friends."

"Sorry, Pamela, the investigation has to include her, as well as those you mentioned, plus Wilson the steward—my favorite. They will all be irate that we suspect them."

"So what should we do?" asked Pamela. "We have no authority here. These suspects can refuse to talk to us."

"Don't worry. The district attorney in Pittsfield has given us all the written authority we need." He reached into his pocket. "Here are our official papers from the district attorney, authorizing us to assist him. We must use our authority carefully so as not to make the suspects skittish."

As they rose from the bench, Prescott said, "Now let's break the news to the Lenox detective."

They found the detective at a table in a lounge of the Curtis Hotel, drinking coffee and smoking a cigar. He had completed his investigation at Broadmore and seemed overjoyed to have resolved the case so quickly.

"Sit down," he said cheerfully. "Tomorrow, I'm going to Pittsfield to lay out the case for the county's district attorney. I phoned him an hour ago and gave him the gist of it. He told me to meet him first thing in the morning."

"Well, I'm glad we caught you in time," said Prescott. "We have some thoughts to share."

Prescott's remark seemed to confuse the detective. He also glanced doubtfully at Pamela.

"Mrs. Thompson is Mrs. Jennings's companion and is also working as my assistant. She needs to hear what we say." Prescott went on to argue for a wider investigation. "Unfortunately, we lack proof that Parker committed the crime. He also claims to be innocent. Others had as much motive and opportunity as he."

While Prescott spoke, the detective forgot his coffee and put his cigar aside.

"But," Brady insisted, "the fact that he's a tramp should go a long way to prove his guilt. The other 'suspects,' as you call them, are primarily wealthy, well-bred gentlemen and ladies, concerned about their reputations. They might quarrel with the victim, even hate him, but they wouldn't kill him."

Prescott acknowledged the detective's point with a deferential nod. "Your belief in the distinction between tramps and respectable people is widely held in this country. But you won't find it in the law. There, all men are equal and entitled to the same due process with a presumption of innocence."

The detective glared at Prescott. "Don't lecture me. I happen to know the law, thank you. Inspector Williams of the NYPD taught me police investigation. Does your tramp refuse to confess? I'll beat the truth out of him."

Prescott stared incredulously at the detective. "You are new here, sir. We do justice differently in Berkshire County. I'll have a word about this conversation with Charles Garner, our district attorney, and with the judge, an experienced jurist and a fair-minded man. If you have any sense, you will yield this case to a more experienced investigator. Otherwise, you will play the fool."

Prescott signaled Pamela, and they left the room. At the door, she cast a sidelong glance at the detective, who looked very glum. He called the waiter, paid for his drink, and walked outside to a cab.

"He's full of frustrated bravado," Prescott remarked. "But

the district attorney will bring him to his senses. He might act more prudently in the future."

Pamela shook her head. "He feels humiliated. He will appear to cooperate but secretly he will try to make you stumble and fall flat on your face."

Prescott and Pamela sat on the veranda and watched people come and go. As Pamela mulled over the investigation, she grew uneasy.

Prescott asked, "Do you have something on your mind?"

She nodded. "My part in the investigation makes me uncomfortable. As Mrs. Jennings's companion, how shall I investigate her without betraying a trust? There could be other complications. Should I resign?"

"No, don't resign. Simply follow the evidence wherever it leads. Otherwise, an innocent person might be convicted and a guilty person might remain free to do further harm."

They left the veranda. "By the way," Pamela said, "neither Brenda nor I have found the missing pillow or any blood-stained clothes."

"Keep looking for them. We'll investigate the Allens now. They are both strong suspects. You take Helen, and I'll take George. Afterward, we'll arrange a meeting place."

CHAPTER 31

A Tricky Suspect

8 July

Late in the afternoon, Pamela found Helen Allen in the Curtis Hotel lounge, alone and unhappy. During the evening fireworks four days ago, she and George had quarreled, and he had moved to one of the hotel's modest, furnished houses nearby. Their separation was grist for the rumor mill. She was said to have been Jennings's kept woman, unfaithful to her husband.

"Would you like company?" Pamela asked.

"Yes, indeed," Helen replied. "I'm treated here like a leper."

Pamela inclined her head in a gesture of surprise. "Let's find a quiet corner and order tea."

When the tea was poured, Pamela asked, "How are you taking Henry Jennings's violent death? You were counted among his friends."

"I admired his vigor, self-confidence, and bold pursuit of wealth. If he wished, he could also charm birds out of trees. I miss him greatly."

In Helen's expression there was sorrow and a feeling of loss but nothing resembling heartfelt grief. She might indeed regret that he hadn't written a new will in her favor.

Her tone grew bitter. "Word has gotten out that I was Henry Jennings's rejected, angry mistress and may have done him in."

"Is there any truth in that?"

She shrugged. "Late that evening we met in his study. He had told his wife that he would divorce her. I said then we could marry. He claimed he wasn't ready. I said, that means no to me, and I walked out. I should add that I was upset but I didn't kill him."

"Malicious gossip can be contagious and should be stopped before it spreads. What are you going to do about it?"

"I'll return to New York on Wednesday and leave the gossip behind."

Pamela feigned ignorance. "Will your husband be going with you?"

Helen's cheeks lightly flushed. "We've separated. He's renting a house in the town. I don't know how long he'll stay there. He has accused me of having an affair with Henry and said that he wanted a divorce. I told him, good riddance. But I won't make it easy for him. He's a poor excuse for a husband, secretive and seldom at home. He may have concocted that rumor about me killing Henry."

"If I may ask, where *were* you at the time he was killed?"

Irritation flashed in her eyes, but she kept her temper. "I was in my room at the Curtis. After meeting Henry, I left Broadmore by cab and arrived at the hotel shortly before midnight. The desk clerk at the Curtis will remember me. I hammered on the counter and woke him up."

"Do you have any reason to believe that George killed Henry Jennings? If he thought himself a cuckolded husband— as you've indicated—he could have been angry enough."

Helen grimaced. "I honestly don't know how much he really cared. Perhaps he raised the issue to extort money from Henry. Or, he may have wanted to divert attention away from his own frequent infidelity. If sufficiently provoked, however, he could react violently. I've seen him severely beat an opponent who cheated at tennis. Still, I think the tramp killed Henry."

Meanwhile, Prescott learned that George Allen could be found at the Lenox Club on Walker Street. The barroom was dimly lighted and empty, except for Allen, his hands clasping a brandy glass. He appeared to be feeling sorry for himself.

Prescott and Allen greeted each other with conventional smiles.

Allen squinted at Prescott. "Where's your woman, the bold one I met at the pistol range?" His speech was slurred.

Prescott put ice into his reply. "Drink seems to have muddled your wits, George. The lady you met is Mrs. Thompson. She works for me, and she's also Mrs. Jennings's companion."

Allen flinched. "Sorry. I was less than a gentleman."

Prescott pulled up a chair facing Allen. "I'm helping the district attorney gather information concerning the death of Henry Jennings. I have a few questions for you."

Suddenly, Allen appeared more sober. "I thought the case was solved. The tramp did it."

"He's a suspect, of course. But the D.A. wants to cast a wider net. The victim was too important for a hasty investigation."

"You know I resented the attention that he paid to my wife. But I didn't kill him."

"Where were you in the hour after midnight on the fifth of July?"

"I was at home in bed with a woman."

"Shortly after the square dances, you were seen leaving the festivities together with Miss Clara Brown." Prescott paused and met Allen's eye. "Did you spend the night with her?"

Allen glared at Prescott. "Do you have to know? I'm honor-bound to protect her reputation. She comes from a highly respected banking family. Her parents are religious and very strict with her."

"Your honor be damned, George! You're a cuckolded husband, a prime suspect in Jennings's murder. If you claim a certain young lady as your alibi, I have to know her name and question her. I'm not a gossipmonger. I'll be as discreet as the investigation allows."

Allen's voice dropped to a whisper, as if he were afraid that the barman was eavesdropping. "It was Miss Clara Brown. Please don't go to her home. The servants spy for her father. He would erupt if she were involved in a scandal. I fear for her safety."

"Where can I meet her?"

"She will be at the Lake Mahkeenac boathouse early this evening under the supervision of a guardian who tipples and dozes off. Clara can evade her. Could Mrs. Thompson join Clara in the boathouse and take her testimony?"

"That could be arranged. She would attract less attention than I. Besides, they seem to be friends of a sort."

"Thanks," George murmured. He emptied his glass in a single gulp and signaled the barman for another.

Prescott waved the man away and turned to George. "You've probably had enough to drink. I'll take you home." He drove Allen to his rented house. Allen was nearly asleep when they arrived, his head lolling to one side. Prescott summoned the manservant, and the two of them hauled him to bed.

Pamela joined Prescott at a table on the veranda of the Lake Mahkeenac boathouse for a picnic supper outdoors. The weather was still warm and sunny, though clouds were gathering in the west. Neither of them had eaten since breakfast. She brought bread, cheese, and fruit from the kitchen at Broadmore Hall; he served pear tarts from the pastry shop in the village. Over the meal, they discussed the Allens.

Prescott asked, "Can we believe Helen's claim that she checked into the hotel before midnight?"

Pamela laid cheese on her bread. "At the time, I wondered if she had deliberately staged that noisy encounter with the desk clerk for the sake of an alibi. She could have slipped out the back door, returned to Broadmore Hall, and then killed Jennings."

"That's possible," Prescott agreed. "She could have walked the half mile from the Curtis to Broadmore Hall under cover of darkness and entered through Jennings's private entrance without being observed."

"Did you find evidence against George?"

"Not enough to convict him of Jennings's murder. I'd like you to check his alibi. Meet Clara Brown here and ask for a ride in her boat. When you're far enough from shore, ask whether George was with her that night. After leaving Allen, I spoke with his manservant and with Clara Brown's guardian. Their stories appear to confirm Allen's alibi and compromise Clara. She has much to explain."

Pamela grimaced. "Sailing with her is the easy part. Probing into the intimate details of her relationship with George Allen is a challenge. Still, I'm willing to try."

"Good. I'll wait for you out of sight near the boathouse."

At that moment a loud clap of thunder shook the air. A sudden burst of wind came with scattered drops of rain.

Prescott glanced up at rapidly approaching dark clouds. "We must carry our food inside."

They had scarcely closed the door when the sky released a torrent. "It will soon be over," he reassured her.

They continued their meal at a rough wooden table.

Their conversation dwindled as they finished the food. They were alone. The room fell into a deep silence, broken only by the drumroll of rain on the roof. He gazed at her with an expression of tenderness and longing. She felt wanted and, at the same time, honored.

"Sorry," he said wryly. "For a moment, a tender emotion got the better of me."

She smiled kindly. "You needn't apologize. I felt touched and blessed." She tilted her head and hearkened. The rain had diminished to a light patter. "The storm has moved on," she said. "Miss Brown will soon launch her boat into the lake."

Ten minutes later, Clara arrived, surprised to see Pamela waiting for her. "May I ride with you in the sailboat?" Pamela asked.

"I'd be delighted," Clara replied, smiling generously. "I thought I'd have to sail alone. My guardian is indisposed."

"I'd like to help you with the boat." Pamela followed Clara downstairs to the lakeside area. They slid the boat into the water, raised the sail, and set out. The breeze was light and the air still smelled of rain. When they reached the middle of the lake, Clara lowered the sail and let the boat slowly drift back toward the boathouse.

"I believe you have something on your mind, Pamela."

"I do. May I first ask an impertinent question?"

Clara nodded noncommittally.

"How well acquainted are you with George Allen?"

"He's my father's friend and tennis partner. They go together to the Jekyll Island Club in Georgia—he's Father's guest. I call him Uncle George. He's much older than I. Still, he's good-looking, amusing, and clever. He's teaching me how to play tennis."

"As you must know, Mr. Jennings was murdered early Wednesday morning." Pamela paused momentarily, allowing the young woman to recall the ghastly event.

"Yes, of course," she exclaimed. "How can anyone feel safe here?"

Pamela pressed on. "George Allen is one of several suspects. When questioned, he claimed that he was with you during the early hours of that morning. Is that true?"

"Of course not! I'm outraged that he would say such a thing!"

"A short while ago, Mr. Prescott spoke to your guardian. She said that you didn't return home from Broadmore until dawn. As a consequence, you and she had a mighty row in the morning."

Clara looked stupefied. For a few moments, she stammered nonsense. Then she became angry and reproached Pamela. "How dare you snoop into my business? That old drunken witch hates me and has made up that story to make me look bad."

Pamela continued. "George Allen's manservant admitted picking up you and George after the fireworks at Broadmore, taking you to George's house in the village, and bringing you home at dawn." Pamela spoke in a soft but insistent voice. "This is very serious, Clara. A man's life could depend on whether you tell the truth."

"The manservant was supposed to keep the secret." Clara began to sob, like a much younger girl in trouble.

Pamela fixed a severe gaze on her. "Can you honestly say that George Allen was with you from about eleven until dawn?"

"Yes," she said almost inaudibly. "I was very tired. We had a drink and went to bed. I slept through to dawn."

"Would you have noticed if he got out of bed while you were asleep and made his way to Broadmore Hall alone, killed Jennings, and returned to your bed?"

Clara's expression slowly hardened. "In view of George's treachery, I don't want to give him an alibi. Nor for that matter do I ever want to see him again." A sly look came over her face. "Yes, he could have drugged me. The drink tasted odd. I almost never sleep straight through the night."

"You may have learned a painful lesson."

"Could we keep it from the public's eye? If my father were to find out, he would be very angry."

"Mr. Prescott and I don't wish to embarrass you. However, if George Allen were to go on trial, he would claim you as his alibi. His defense attorney would summon you to the court as a witness and would ask you bluntly: Were you in bed with Allen, yes or no? If you were to say no, you would perjure yourself and face criminal charges. As for your father, I fear that your guardian will certainly inform him. She's quite wrathful." Pamela gazed at the stricken young woman. "In a word, Clara, I can offer you little comfort."

Clara turned away and looked out over the water. "If what you've just predicted comes to pass, I'll throw myself into the lake and end it all."

"Don't give up, Clara. There's a saying, when one door closes, another opens. Your prospects for a brilliant role in high society may have dimmed. But how much does that really matter? You still have remarkable beauty, health, and intelligence. Other opportunities will open up that are far more fulfilling than what you may have lost."

Clara faced Pamela, her eyes skeptical and unfriendly. "Thank you for the advice, Mrs. Thompson. You speak from experience. We'll sail back to the boathouse now."

Pamela waited outside the boathouse and gazed at the lake. A light haze hovered over the water and filtered the fading sunlight. A contemplative mood overtook her. A few minutes earlier, Clara had said a curt good-bye and left on her horse. Pamela's thoughts followed the young woman. She was at a crossroads in life. What would become of her? Had she, Pamela, done enough to help her?

Then Prescott appeared, holding a military telescope.

"Through the haze I watched the two of you and wished I were with you in that boat. Miss Brown appeared disturbed. Tell me about it."

"She's angry that George Allen exposed her, so she gave him an ambiguous alibi. Yes, they went to bed together. But he could have drugged her and stolen away while she was asleep."

"Then, he remains a suspect in Jennings's death."

CHAPTER 32

A Tragedy Revisited

9 July

The next morning Pamela awoke early, yesterday's supper with Prescott still on her mind. She had dreamed during the night of the rain beating on the boathouse roof and the fond expression on his face as he gazed at her. Now a warm feeling began to stir in her heart. She abruptly rose from the bed and threw open a window. The view of Lake Mahkeenac turned her thoughts to willful Clara Brown, staring dejected out over the water. Was there still hope for her?

A note had been slipped under the door, inviting Pamela to Sunday breakfast downstairs. Lydia wanted to hear how the investigation into her husband's death was proceeding. When they were alone at the table, Pamela spoke briefly of Tom Parker's judicial proceedings in Pittsfield. "He will face a hearing in the district court tomorrow to determine if he should be held for trial."

Lydia frowned. "Might he be set free and other suspects investigated?"

"That's possible," replied Pamela. "No one actually saw him kill Mr. Jennings, and he denies doing it. But even if the judge releases him tomorrow, he will remain a suspect while the investigation is widened. Yesterday, we questioned George and Helen Allen. Others will follow."

Lydia appeared distressed. "The district judge absolutely shouldn't release Parker. He fled to New York. Isn't that a sufficient confession of guilt?"

"Perhaps not." Pamela cautiously played the devil's advocate. "At the time, he believed he couldn't receive a fair trial in the Berkshires. A typical jury would be biased against him. Since then, Prescott and I have persuaded him to trust the court."

Lydia vigorously shook her head. "Who else could conceivably have killed Henry? The cottagers can't be suspect. Even those whom I don't like are too concerned about their reputations to have committed such a crime." She hesitated. "Of course, I can't vouch for the Allens, neither of whom are truly respectable. Among our servants, Mr. Wilson has a bad character and a strong motive to take revenge on Henry. And then there's Maggie, a good servant up to recently. I was thinking of promoting her to housekeeper. But to judge from her familiarity with the tramp, she might be his secret accomplice. I would like you to investigate her background."

Pamela agreed, but she reminded herself to keep an open mind.

As breakfast was ending, Lydia asked Pamela, "Will you join me for church this morning? My stepson, John, has excused himself. He claims that a long swim in Lake Mahkeenac would cleanse his soul better than an hour at Trinity."

"I'll go with you, Lydia," Pamela replied. "Would you mind if Prescott accompanied us?"

"Not at all. It might do him good." She met Pamela's eye. "After church, you could have a chat with Maggie. I've asked her to go with us."

* * *

The weather was mild and calm, so they left Broadmore in an open coach. Maggie was reluctant to ride with them. "A servant should know her place," she said.

"Nonsense," insisted Lydia. "In the eyes of the Lord we are all on the same level. That should be especially true on the way to church." She introduced Maggie to Prescott.

He tipped his hat to her. "We've seen each other from a distance, Maggie. I'm pleased to meet you." For the rest of the short ride, he entertained the women with amusing small talk. By the time they arrived at Trinity, Maggie appeared at ease with the others. Prescott had a way with women, Pamela thought wryly.

During the service Maggie was seated between Pamela and Prescott. "I'm a heathen," he whispered to the maid with a twinkle in his eye. "You must help me through the service so that I don't make a fool of myself or distract others."

She smiled and said softly, "You're teasing me."

Prescott winked to Pamela. She understood. As Maggie gave up her habitual reserve, it would be easier to probe into her secrets.

After the service Pamela and Maggie went by coach to a rustic hilltop gazebo overlooking Lake Mahkeenac. Prescott and Lydia had excused themselves. The air had grown warmer, and the sky was cloudless. The lake shimmered in a light breeze. From Broadmore, Pamela had brought along a fine white wine. Maggie supplied bread, cheese, and fruit.

During the meal Pamela led the conversation toward Henry Jennings. The minister at Trinity had announced a memorial service for him. Maggie had frowned.

Now Pamela remarked, "At the church door on the way out, I inquired about the Jennings memorial. The minister told me that he didn't have the details yet. Mrs. Jennings was making the arrangements."

Suddenly, Maggie began to tremble. Her jaw became rigid with rage. "Jennings! That monster! How can the church dare to honor him? His widow knew him as a base rogue. She's a hypocrite to pretend he was a good and great man." The maid began to sob.

Pamela laid a comforting hand on her shoulder. "I share your view of Jennings. How has he hurt you?"

Maggie shook her head, at first unable to reply. Pamela remained still for a moment, then gave Maggie a handkerchief. The maid dabbed away the tears from her face and met Pamela's eye. "I'll tell you about Jennings."

Her story began in Michigan's Upper Peninsula on Christmas Eve, 1887, during a bitter labor dispute at Jennings's copper mine in Calumet. She had just returned home from her first semester at college in Chicago and was going to the striking miners' party in the social hall above a tavern.

"On my way I passed the company office, its rooms ablaze with light. I imagined Mr. Jennings in there, scheming to break the strike. A few days earlier, he had arrived from New York in a private railroad car. Since then, violent clashes between his scabs and the strikers had taken place daily.

"As I approached the tavern, a man stood near the door, thickly wrapped in fur. I couldn't make out his features. He shifted his weight from one foot to the other, fighting off the bitter cold. Was he expecting someone? I wondered.

"I lowered the scarf from my face and walked up to him to offer help. He leaped back to prevent me from looking closely at him. I grew suspicious. Should I challenge him? Just then, someone opened the door and music drifted out, distracting me. So I left the stranger and climbed up the long, steep stairway."

Maggie now seemed engrossed in the story and seemed to be reliving every detail. "At the far end of the crowded hall two fiddlers were playing a jig. To their right was a large buffet table. Father was slicing ham, and Mother was pouring punch."

"Were your parents involved in the strike?"

"No, they were sympathetic to the workers but didn't speak out. The company school had only recently hired them. If they supported the strike, the company would fire them and close the school. The children would suffer."

"Why were the workers on strike?" Pamela asked. "They must have been desperate to take on a powerful company."

Maggie explained that several accidents in the mine had angered them. A recent cave-in that killed seven men had been the last straw. The workers demanded more pay, greater safety, and a union. The company wouldn't even talk to them. Most of the workers voted to strike. The company locked them out and hired scabs to take their place.

At that point Maggie paused, staring into her glass. She seemed to shiver, her eyes focused on an inner, dreadful vision.

"Please continue," said Pamela softly.

Her face drawn with sorrow, Maggie drew a deep breath. "I was searching in the crowd for friends when suddenly I heard a cry, 'Fire! Fire!' Men, women, and children rushed screaming to the stairway. I struggled to a niche in the wall, and the crowd surged past me. People fell and were trampled.

"I edged along the wall to the stairway. . . ." She stopped, overcome by the horror she was reliving.

Pamela leaned forward and touched her hand. "Rest for a moment, Maggie. Continue when you can."

Maggie took a bite of the bread and a sip of the wine. "I must go on," she said. "The stairway was filled to the top with writhing, moaning, and screaming men, women, and children. I felt sick—my parents might be in that carnage. Then I realized that there was no smoke—and no fire! Someone had provoked the panic, perhaps the stranger I had met at the door. The next day I learned that at least seventy persons had died, including my parents."

"Did an official investigation find the man who called out 'Fire'?"

"No. Jennings's lawyers persuaded the state's investigators to blame a nameless anti-union worker. But I blame Mr. Jennings himself or someone he hired."

"How would you know?" Pamela's mind balked at the conjecture. "Was there any proof?"

"None that a court of law could use. Like a puppet master, Jennings remained out of sight in his private railway car or his office and worked through trusted henchmen. Still I grew convinced of his guilt. Back in college, I kept in touch with a committee of concerned citizens who carried out a private investigation. In the end the committee was convinced that none of the miners, including the few who didn't support the strike, could or would have committed the crime. By a process of elimination the committee settled on Jennings, who had been near the scene and was known to be hateful and ruthless. Of course, he would have ordered someone else to actually cry 'Fire.' "

Still skeptical, Pamela poured more wine into the maid's glass. "Jennings might be as guilty as you believe. But why did you decide to pursue him to the Berkshires? It doesn't seem practical."

Maggie took a thoughtful sip. "I got the idea from Tom Parker in Chicago. On Christmas Eve, 1888, I was sitting in a church brooding on my parents' dreadful fate. Tom came and sat next to me. We had become friends, so he invited me to Ahern's Irish restaurant near the Water Tower. I told him what had happened to my parents. He declared that Jennings was the same rich man, 'the Copper King,' for whom he had once worked in Massachusetts. When Tom had protested against poor pay and conditions, Jennings had called him an anarchist, ordered him off the property, and poisoned his reputation. He had moved to Chicago, but he hadn't forgotten or forgiven Jennings.

"A plan for revenge began to grow in my mind. Tom told me all he knew about the man. For a few weeks in the summer, he vacationed in a great cottage, Broadmore Hall, in the Berkshires at Lenox. Tom had worked there. Jennings's wife Lydia, a decent, capable woman, had built Broadmore Hall. She and her husband were now virtually separated. He was a bully, but she stood up to him. I thought if I could work for her as a maid, I might find opportunities to punish him."

Pamela couldn't conceal her doubts. "Why would Mrs. Jennings hire a perfect stranger?"

"My parents were from this area. I had relatives here who could recommend me. Tom also said the pay was poor, so there was frequent turnover among the servants. I would persuade her to hire me on a trial basis."

Pamela still wasn't convinced and said so.

Maggie persisted. "The way to expose Jennings was probably through his wife. She disliked him, probably knew his secrets, and might want to bring him down."

"What did Tom think of your plan?"

For a moment Maggie chewed on her lower lip. "He thought it was a fool's errand and said he would miss me. It was hard to leave him. But punishing Jennings was something I had to do. Whenever I grew discouraged, I thought of my parents and carried on."

"Then I must ask. Did you kill Mr. Jennings?"

"No. I wanted to, but someone else did it before I could. I also have no alibi. After the fireworks I went to bed and slept through the night. That's all I want to say."

Her face had taken on a defiant expression. Their conversation at an end, the two women packed the remnants of the picnic into baskets.

As they left the gazebo, Pamela asked, "By the way, have you figured out who hollered 'Fire'?"

"I thought you had forgotten to ask," Maggie replied. "The

workers' own investigation pointed to a clerk in Jennings's office. But he disappeared before the investigators could question him. Four months later, a decomposed body was found in Portage Lake and identified as the suspect.

"Since then, I've come to believe that the dead man was a vagrant who resembled the clerk. The clerk most likely changed his name and his appearance and moved to another part of the country." She paused; her eyes seemed to narrow and darken. "I've found him. Here in Lenox—Mr. Wilson." Her voice dropped to a throaty whisper. "He killed more than seventy innocent men, women, and children. Sometimes in the middle of the night, I hear them cry out for justice."

Pamela left Maggie at Broadmore Hall and drove to Prescott's cabin. He was sitting outside with a pot of tea reading a New York newspaper. Declining his offer of tea, she reported on her troubling conversation with Maggie. "Her desire to punish Jennings seems passionate, bordering on fanatic. It led her to Broadmore Hall, bent on justice. Nonetheless, she denies killing him and claims no alibi for July fourth and fifth. I'd like to believe her."

Prescott shook his head. "Maggie sounds to me like an avenging angel. Your sympathy for her may have clouded your judgment. Her version of events in the night of July fourth and fifth is incredible. During the fireworks display, she must have hidden Tom in the kitchen closet. Late that night, he could have assaulted Jennings in a botched robbery attempt, perhaps confessed to Maggie, then fled in panic to New York. Unbeknown to Tom, Maggie might have gone to Jennings's study, discovered him still alive, and smothered him. And what shall we make of her charge against Wilson in the death of her parents?"

"It's plausible," Pamela replied. "I don't know his background, except that he worked a long time for Jennings and had to carry out his master's orders to the letter, and without blinking. He would yell 'Fire!' in a crowded building if Jennings said he should."

Prescott agreed that Maggie's accusation seemed plausible, but evidence was lacking. "I'll dig into his past when I visit him later in the afternoon. His future is likely to be brief and end violently. Maggie isn't the only one who hates him. The thieves, George Allen and Sarah Evans, surely resent his extortion and will go to great lengths to end it."

CHAPTER 33

A Disgruntled Servant

9 July

Pamela's cautionary words were in Prescott's mind as he approached Wilson's boardinghouse in the village late in the afternoon. Maggie Rice was convinced of the former steward's role in her parents' death and was seeking justice. Wilson might be unaware of this threat. Or, oddly enough, he might already know Maggie's background. His investigative skills—and his cunning—were sufficient to the task.

Alone on the veranda, he recognized Prescott with a friendly smile. He probably recalled their cordial meeting on the train from New York back in June.

"How are you getting on?" Prescott asked. The former steward's face was flushed, more likely from alcohol than from the sun. "Do you mind if I keep you company for a few minutes? I'd like to ask a question or two."

"I'm happy to have someone to talk to," Wilson replied. "I've nothing to do and am bored silly. I can't imagine living like this for the rest of my days."

"Could you move to the city and work in a hotel or one of the mansions on Fifth Avenue?"

Wilson grimaced. "I've thought of that. But I lack the money and the recommendations I'd need."

Prescott feigned surprise. "You've worked for Henry Jennings for over twenty years. He should have remembered you generously in his will and given you a substantial pension. He also owed you a sterling recommendation."

"Though he was one of the richest men in America, he wasn't generous to me." Wilson reached for his glass and found it empty, as was a nearby whiskey bottle. He glanced expectantly at his visitor.

"Allow me." Prescott brought out his silver flask and filled Wilson's glass almost to the brim. He poured a little for himself into the cap that served as a cup.

The two men toasted each other. Wilson took a swallow and exhaled with pleasure. "Jennings gave me only ten dollars and no pension. That's an insult. He said that the irregularities in my accounts kept him from writing a positive recommendation."

Prescott remarked sympathetically, "That's not fair, considering how long and faithfully you worked for him. Were you always his steward?"

"No," he replied. "At the beginning, back in Michigan, I was a kind of clerk and managed the Calumet office of Jennings's copper mines, the biggest and most profitable in the Upper Peninsula. When he came from New York on a visit, he'd ask me what the miners were up to, and which supervisors were cheating him. I'd report what I'd learned. He'd say that I was his Michigan eyes and ears. I've done the same kind of work for him in New York City and at Broadmore."

Wilson drank from his glass. Prescott filled it again. His speech was now slurred, but his mind still seemed reasonably clear.

"Then you probably know a lot about that stampede six years ago in the Calumet social hall. What was Jennings's role?"

Wilson glanced over his shoulder and lowered his voice to a whisper. "It was Jennings's idea from the start. The strike had made him very angry. He came from New York especially to fight it. 'This is war,' he said, again and again."

"That sounds like Jennings," murmured Prescott. "Sorry to interrupt. Please continue."

Wilson nodded, took a sip from his glass and carefully set it down. "Christmas Eve, the entire strike committee and the most committed strikers were to meet upstairs in that hall. A man sympathetic to the strikers owned the building. Everything else in the town belonged to the company.

"Jennings wanted to break up the meeting and make it look as if workers opposed to the strike had done it. That would sow anger and dissension among the miners. The company was tough and unwilling to compromise. The miners would soon realize the strike was futile, and they would go back to work."

"How did Jennings propose to break up the meeting?"

"Someone should secretly go to the foot of the stairs and yell 'Fire!' The strikers would panic and rush from the building."

"Wouldn't they get hurt?"

"A few broken bones were part of the scheme. The strikers weren't angels. They had badly beaten many scabs and destroyed company property."

"Whom did Jennings order to yell 'Fire'? That could be very risky."

Wilson whispered again. "He said I was the only man he could trust. If I did it, he would take me to New York and make me a rich man. I thought about it quickly—he was impatient and didn't give me much time. I agreed. On the spot, he handed me a hundred-dollar bill. 'That's just a down payment,' he said.

"So I put on a false beard and a wig, dressed in workers' clothes, and pulled a cap down to my eyes. I waited near the hall for a moment when no one was coming or going. Then I hurried to the foot of the stairs and called out 'Fire' a couple of times. I could hear the stampede as I ran away." He paused, and his gaze turned inward. For a moment, he seemed to live the experience again. Then he met Prescott's eye. "I was scared to death. A young woman had seemed suspicious of me. I nearly panicked. If I had been caught, the strikers would have killed me."

"Did you know that the hall would be packed with women and children?"

"I knew there would be some," he admitted. "During the afternoon, the strikers had been encouraged to bring their families and turn the event into a Christmas party. I told Jennings. He said, 'Go ahead. It'll make an even greater impression on the bastards.' I felt uneasy that so many women and children would be in the room. Still, I never imagined that anyone would get killed."

"What happened next?"

"When Jennings learned the following day that seventy men, women, and children had died, he realized that the state would be forced to investigate. He publicly expressed his regret at the loss of life and put the blame on dissident miners who opposed the strike committee. He doled out a little money to survivors and to families of the deceased. Then he left for New York and took me along. His lawyers had to deal with the investigation. The strike soon ended."

"Six years have passed. How do you feel now?"

"I often think about all those people, most of them young, piled on top of each other, crushed to death. What a terrible way to die."

"Do you think Jennings had any regrets?"

"None that I could notice. He was bent on becoming the richest man in America. Nothing else mattered." He paused and stared into his glass. "In hindsight, I rue the day that I began to work for him and became his slave. In New York he treated me with contempt and paid me poorly. After a couple of years, I complained. He said that if I didn't like my situation, he could put me in a Michigan prison for years. He had only to declare that I had acted contrary to his orders."

"Have you kept a diary?"

Wilson smiled wryly. "You know me better than I thought. Of course, I've written a full account of the Calumet incident. Over the years, I've also gathered evidence of his fraud and other illegal business practices. One day I thought I'd have enough evidence to turn over to the state and bring him crashing down. Unfortunately, someone killed him before I was ready."

"Would you show me what you have?" Prescott struggled to tamp down his eagerness. "The state or his enemies might be interested, and you could earn some money."

Even half-drunk, Wilson still had the good sense to say, "Let me think it over. In the meantime, don't go to the police with my tale. At a hearing I could simply deny everything I've told you."

"I understand perfectly. In a manner of speaking, we're both professional private investigators. Have you also gathered information on my client George Allen that you'd care to share? He appears to have developed a risky taste for jewelry."

A wry smile appeared on Wilson's lips. "I'll consider your request when my head is clear. But for now, remember, if I disappear mysteriously or die in the near future, you will receive a message from me."

The two men exchanged knowing looks. Wilson lapsed into reverie. Prescott said good-bye and left. When he was out of sight, he turned into an alley and sneaked back to a point where he could watch Wilson unobserved. For several minutes, Wilson continued to sit on the veranda looking pensive. Then he weaved his way into the house. He was probably in no condition to go out. Prescott waited for a few more minutes, cautiously entered the house, and showed his papers to the landlady. For a modest sum she agreed to keep an eye on Wilson.

Early that evening, Pamela met Prescott alone in a parlor in Broadmore Hall. She asked, "What did you learn from Wilson?"

"He actually confessed with remorse to yelling 'Fire!' at the social hall six years ago, but he would deny it in court. He also gave hints that could tie him to Jennings's death. Wilson must have doubted years ago that Jennings would willingly give him a decent pension. On the night of July fourth, he might have tried to extort it from him, threatening to reveal evidence of his financial crimes. Jennings would have dismissed the extortion with contempt and promised to have Wilson arrested. Wilson then might have attacked Jennings. What did you learn from Maggie?"

"She had a powerful motive to kill Jennings, going back to that tragic incident in Michigan. She holds Wilson and Jennings personally responsible for the Christmas Eve panic in the social hall. I feel that she didn't kill Jennings, but it's unwise to count on feelings."

Prescott nodded. "Now we should find out who has Jennings's diamond lapel pin. He or she would most likely be the murderer. Let's start with Wilson."

Pamela and Prescott went to Wilson's former office, together with the temporary steward, Brewer. He had cleaned out Wilson's things from the obvious places but hadn't found the lapel pin. The three of them searched the walls, floors, and ceilings of Wilson's private rooms and his office and found nothing of interest.

Brewer remarked, "You might look in Wilson's hidden room in the attic. He swore me to secrecy. No one knew about it. He could rest there without fear of being disturbed." The steward gave Prescott the key.

He and Pamela hurried to the room. They were surprised to find a large storage area. The low ceiling and the walls were unfinished. The floor was covered with rough wooden planks. Evening sunlight slanted through two dormer windows. Against the wall at the highest point of the room were a bed, chair, and table. A worn rug lay on the floor.

They searched in vain for the missing bloodstained pillow or other evidence implicating Wilson in Jennings's murder.

"Do you know where we are?" asked Prescott.

"We're directly above Henry Jennings's apartment," Pamela replied. "This must be where Wilson spied on his master. Let's search for peepholes."

In an hour they had found several. They also found a grille that vented warm air from Jennings's study. Pamela descended to the study. Prescott could hear her speaking in a normal voice. Prescott joined her there. Standing in the middle of the room, they looked up at the ceiling and couldn't see anything unusual. The peepholes were cleverly hidden in the decorative plasterwork. The grille was painted in the wall's color and hardly noticeable.

Prescott shook his head in amazement. "Wilson could have easily discovered where Jennings hid his papers, money, and precious objects such as the lapel pin."

"If he didn't kill Jennings himself, he could have observed someone else doing it," Pamela remarked.

"And taking the lapel pin as well," added Prescott.

"Assuming that Wilson observed the murder, he should have reported it to the police, but he kept it to himself. What can we make of that?"

"Given Wilson's venal character, I would expect him to try to extort money from the killer."

"That might be risky," Pamela warned.

"He's aware of that. He hinted that his secrets would come to us if something should happen to him. Tomorrow, I must attend Tom Parker's hearing in the Pittsfield courthouse. In the meantime, go to Wilson's boardinghouse and try to search his room."

CHAPTER 34

A Missing Man

10 July

The next morning, Pamela borrowed a one-horse coach and drove Prescott to the station. On the way, he remarked, "I had hoped to post bail for Parker and keep him out of jail. Over the weekend, however, I've noticed strong public sentiment in the newspaper against tramps in general. About Parker they write that he has blood on his hands and shouldn't be allowed out into the community. What do you think I should do?"

This public outcry against Parker distressed Pamela. She began to regret that she had persuaded him to return to the Berkshires for a possibly unfair trial. He must be strongly tempted to flee again.

"Forget about bail," she replied. "Parker will be very unhappy in jail, but safer there than outside, until we find Henry Jennings's killer."

At the station she waved good-bye to Prescott, then drove off to Wilson's boardinghouse and parked out of sight. He might recognize the coach. She asked the landlady about him. At first she frowned, but Pamela added that she had also been a landlady in New York and understood the need for caution when dealing with strangers. She showed her papers from the D.A. and explained that this visit was part of an official investigation into the murder of Henry Jennings.

That made all the difference. The landlady invited Pamela into a parlor and described her boarder Wilson as a solitary man who asked for pen and ink and spent long hours writing in his room. When he went out, it was to mail letters or to buy strong spirits. By suppertime, he was usually glassy-eyed.

He had complained at breakfast of a splitting headache. "Too much sauce yesterday," said the landlady. "He looked preoccupied and has gone for a walk this morning to clear his head."

"Does he have visitors?"

"No, but he receives sealed messages."

"If you wouldn't mind, I'd like to search his room while he's gone."

"I dare not give you permission, but his door will be ajar for twenty minutes while I fetch fresh linen and other supplies. If he returns, I'll ring the bell."

"I understand," said Pamela evenly.

A minute later, when no one was watching, she slipped into the room and began hunting for Wilson's secret diary and hidden papers. The small room was furnished with a bed, a dresser, a table, and two plain chairs. On the floor in a corner was a pile of books. Where would he hide anything in such a place?

In vain she lifted the mattress, looked inside the dresser drawers, and searched his clothes hanging in a closet. On the floor was his black satchel. It was locked. Curious, she shook it but heard no recognizable sounds. She had to find the key, a thing that was easy to hide. Unfortunately, she was in a race against time. Ten of the twenty minutes had passed.

She drew a deep breath and calmed her nerves. Managing the

boardinghouse in New York had given her insights into the minds of her sometimes-thieving tenants. They would store stolen tableware in locked satchels like Wilson's and hide the key. She let her gaze drift slowly around the room. It stopped at the dresser. She pulled out the drawers one by one. Taped beneath the bottom drawer was the key.

She opened the satchel, and her hopes fell. Inside were neatly folded underwear, monogrammed handkerchiefs, and stockings. But she poked carefully through the clothing until her fingers touched a solid object. With a quick glance she saw that it was a small book wrapped in plain brown paper. That looked interesting! Perhaps a diary. A file box and a pistol lay beneath it.

There wasn't time to study her find. One of the books in the corner, Mark Twain's *The American Claimant,* resembled the diary in size and shape. She fanned the pages. In the margins were many marks, abbreviations, and brief comments. Passages were underlined.

She switched the brown paper to the Twain book and put it into the satchel. She began to finger through the file box, recognized the names of John Jennings and George Allen among others, but then broke off. Time was running out. She stuck the diary into her bag, locked the satchel, and returned the key to the dresser.

The landlady's bell rang, and seconds later a loud footfall sounded in the hall. In desperation Pamela threw herself under the bed and lay hidden by the overhanging bedspread. Wilson entered—she recognized him by his polished shoes. He walked directly to the dresser for the key, then to the closet, and drew out the satchel. Pamela lifted the bedspread a bit to watch him better. He thrust his hand into the satchel, seemed to feel the book and the file box but didn't inspect them. He put the pistol into his pocket, locked the satchel, and carried it out of the room.

As Pamela was crawling out from under the bed, the land-lady walked in. "My goodness!" she said. "That was a close call. He was in a great hurry."

"Fortunately for me!" Pamela said, brushing dust off her clothes. "But I found what I was looking for. Thank you." She paused. "Could you see where he was going?"

"No, I couldn't. But I'll ask the maid downstairs. She's cleaning the veranda."

The maid reported that a cab had been waiting for Wilson. "It set off in a great rush toward the Stockbridge Road."

Pamela hurried to her coach and drove on the Stockbridge Road in the direction of Broadmore Hall. What could Wilson intend to do there—with a pistol?

Pamela kept a safe distance from Wilson's cab. He could be watching out the rear window. Just short of Broadmore, he left the cab and disappeared into the dense woods between Broad-more and the neighboring estate. After tethering her horse, Pamela cautiously followed the narrow path that he appeared to have taken. She couldn't see him. So when the path forked, she couldn't decide which one to take. She retraced her steps to the coach and returned it to the stables.

No one there had seen Wilson, nor had the doorman or the maids in the cottage.

She went to her rooms, her curiosity growing by the step. She searched the rooms for intruders or spies and locked her-self in. Finally, feeling safe, she sat at her table and retrieved Wilson's diary. She groaned. It was written mostly in code that she couldn't decipher.

In the afternoon, Pamela borrowed the coach again and drove to the station to pick up Prescott returning from Parker's hearing in Pittsfield. She arrived a few minutes early and waited in the station. As the train approached, she remained inside. Trains sometimes spewed a dirty steam over the platform.

Her heart beat a little faster, as if she were about to meet a dear friend. That disturbed her at first. She told herself that she and Prescott had merely a business relationship. Then she admitted that they had indeed become friends and cared for each other. A romance, however, would be foolish. He might win her trust and love, then move on to another woman. How could she bear that? Her spirits sank.

The noisy arrival of the train distracted her. It pulled into the station and began to disgorge its passengers. As Prescott stepped out onto the platform, Pamela moved toward the station door. But she stopped when Prescott suddenly turned back toward the train and assisted Clara Brown down the steps. As he gazed at her, his arms reached out as if in humble supplication. Soon, her stout guardian and a maid rushed up and whisked her away.

A momentary mixture of jealousy and envy flashed unbeckoned through Pamela's mind. She was afraid that Prescott would notice her discomfort as he came through the door. But he merely looked surprised when he saw her, then said, "Thank you for coming."

At the coach outside, he sat next to her. "I had intended to hire a cab, but I'd rather watch you drive. When did you learn?"

She gave the horse a command and set off. "My parents gave me a small horse when I was still a young girl. I rode mostly on vacations at our Williamstown summer home. As I grew up, they also gave me a little coach. I used to drive children on country lanes near the village." She smiled at him. "But we have more important things to talk about. Tell me what happened at the hearing."

As they rode the short distance to the village, Prescott explained that the judge had found sufficient reason to hold Tom Parker in custody while the investigation into Jennings's murder continued.

"Poor Tom!" she exclaimed.

"Yes," Prescott agreed. "The judge's decision doesn't surprise me. The wealthy and respectable members of society must have strongly pressed him to make an example of the tramp and to do it quickly. In private he said that I should continue to investigate other suspects. And what do you have to report?"

"I've searched Wilson's room and discovered his diary. Many passages appear to be in code. How shall we read them?"

"I'll ask Harry Miller to translate. If he can't, I'll turn to an expert."

She went on. "I followed Wilson on the Stockbridge Road but eventually lost track of him near Broadmore. At the cottage, the servants haven't seen him. I should mention that he's carrying a pistol."

Prescott's brow creased with concern. "Drive to his boarding-house. Maybe he has returned."

Pamela turned onto Wilson's street and parked in front of the house. The landlady was sitting on the veranda.

"Are you looking for Wilson?" she asked. "Well, he's not here. Looks like he'll miss supper. I haven't seen him since this morning. According to my servants, he's not been in the village."

Prescott turned to Pamela. "Drive to the Curtis."

At the hotel, he was in and out in less than a minute. He climbed into the coach and said in a low voice, "I think we have a missing man."

It was soon too dark to search for Wilson. Pamela drove Prescott to his cabin. They sat outside and continued their conversation. Prescott asked, "Why would Wilson run off with a pistol, the supposed diary, and his secret papers?"

Pamela reflected for a few moments. "He was going to meet Jennings's killer, someone whom he feared and didn't trust, hence the pistol. But he also wanted to engage that person in a deal concerning the diary and the secret papers."

Prescott nodded. "Wilson might tell the killer that he had witnessed the crime and had recorded his observations. For a sum of money, he would sell them. The killer might have made a counteroffer. Bargaining ensued. At some point it broke down. The killer assaulted Wilson and seized his satchel and the key."

"How would the killer react when he discovered that the diary was missing?"

"He had to wonder where it was. I'd expect him to go to Wilson's boardinghouse and search his room."

"We must warn the landlady."

"I'll do it tonight without mentioning the diary. That must be kept a secret." He gazed at her kindly. "You should return to Broadmore. It's late."

"Thank you," she said. "I fear for Wilson."

At the door, the porter told Pamela that Mrs. Jennings wanted to speak to her. Pamela hurried upstairs. Lydia would still be waiting; she kept late hours.

As Pamela entered the parlor, Lydia was sitting in an upholstered chair, a book in her lap. She brightened when she recognized her companion. "Sit down, my dear. You must have had a busy day. You look worn out and hungry."

Pamela confessed that she hadn't eaten since breakfast.

Lydia called a maid and ordered a small cheese omelet for Pamela. "While we wait for the food, tell me what you've learned."

"Mr. Prescott and I have discovered that Wilson had a hiding place above your husband's study. From there he could have observed the murder or gone to the study and carried it out himself. This morning, in his boardinghouse room, I saw hidden documents that might yield clues."

Pamela had it on the tip of her tongue to mention the diary, but a tiny inner voice urged her to hold back. "Wilson's behavior this morning is mysterious. He set out from the boardinghouse toward Broadmore, where he disappeared into the woods. Prescott and I have searched for him in vain. Prescott continues to work on new clues. We may soon know the killer."

While Pamela was speaking, she noticed Lydia begin to frown and to wring her hands.

"How could a rogue like Wilson be a credible witness? He might accuse an innocent person in order to extort money. Even if the accusation were proved to be baseless, it could nonetheless taint the person's reputation."

"True," conceded Pamela. "That's why it's important to find Wilson and confront him. We should remind him that extortion and slander have legal consequences."

The reference to slander and its punishment seemed to mollify Lydia. "I'm grateful, Pamela, for your efforts to get to the bottom of this matter. Now I'll retire. The maid will bring the food to your room."

As Pamela ate her omelet, she imagined that Prescott was across the table sharing the food, exchanging opinions. She raised a glass of wine in a toast to his ghostly presence and turned her mind to Lydia. She seemed to insist too much that the murderer had to be a man from the lower class, either the tramp or the steward. Up to a point, Lydia simply shared the typical wealthy, privileged lady's fear of poor, discontented people. Or she might believe that the trail of evidence could lead to her stepson, John. Wilson could have observed him in

Jennings's study. Granted, Wilson was an extortionist. He might also be a credible witness.

The omelet finished, Pamela prepared for bed. As she lay down bone-tired, somewhere in the vast building a clock struck one, probably the hour when Henry Jennings had died violently six days ago. She carried that somber thought into her sleep.

CHAPTER 35

An Icy Grave

11 July

Pamela slept later than she had planned. Rays of sunlight were streaming into her room, and birds had ended their morning serenade. While waiting for breakfast, she dressed in a simple, white muslin summer frock. Brenda came with a tray of tea and toast, butter, and preserves, set it on a table by the window, and handed Pamela a message. "Mr. Prescott sent this a few minutes ago."

Pamela stopped eating in mid-bite as she read: "A fisherman has just found Wilson's satchel in Lily Pond. I'll meet you at the cottage entrance in fifteen minutes. Wear stout shoes. I'll give you the details while we walk to the pond."

The news came as a shock, though she had been expecting Wilson to meet a violent end. An extortionist, he had tried to outwit desperate, ruthless men and women. She put aside her tea, changed shoes, and rushed downstairs to the entrance. Prescott was waiting there.

As they hurried to the pond, he explained, "The fisherman snagged the satchel in ten feet of clear, calm water. Its shape was visible on the bottom. A young man dove down, attached a rope to it, and pulled it up. The fisherman, who had worked at Broadmore, recognized the satchel as Wilson's and informed me."

"Where is the satchel now?"

"It's in the icehouse. Let's look at its contents."

A small stone replica of a Greek temple, the icehouse stood in a shady grove near the pond. During winter, ice was cut from the pond, hauled up a narrow, smooth stone roadway, and stored under a thick layer of straw in a brick-lined storage pit.

Pamela lit a gas lamp in the antechamber. The wet leather satchel lay on a wooden table. Sawdust lightly covered the floor. A thick oak door to the ice room was closed. Still, even the antechamber was cool enough to make Pamela shiver. "Let's be quick about it, or I'll get a summer cold."

Prescott opened the satchel and asked Pamela, "Is it Wilson's?"

"Yes, I'll check the contents. A rough hand has been here." The sodden clothing was topsy-turvy. The file box had been opened, and its papers were scattered, ink-smeared, and illegible. She searched through to the bottom and reported that the pistol and the Twain book were gone.

Prescott nodded. "You said earlier that Wilson had marked and commented in the book's margins. The murderer may have kept the book, thinking that those observations are in a strange code. By the way, what's distinctive about this copy?"

"It's entitled *The American Claimant* and appeared last year. Wilson's name is written in ink on the flyleaf."

Prescott glanced around the room. "We're not likely to find Wilson alive. His body is probably in the pond. We'll engage divers to look for him."

"Wait. I'm curious," said Pamela, studying the floor. She gathered her dress, squatted, and rubbed her finger in a dark spot, then in another. She followed the thin trail of blood to the ice pit's door. "Shall we have a look inside?"

Prescott opened the door and peered into the dark, windowless chamber. Pamela handed him a gas lamp. He aimed a beam of light over the pile of straw on the ice.

Pamela seized a rake and began pulling the straw away. "I see the toe of a boot," she exclaimed. Then a booted foot appeared. The rest of Wilson's body lay partially hidden from view in a deep depression in the ice.

Two servants, charged with maintaining the icehouse, were summoned to crawl over the ice and retrieve the dead man. They found his pistol nearby. Frozen stiff, he was laid on the table and covered with a tarpaulin.

Prescott leaned over the table and lifted an edge of the cover. "He's been stabbed. If you're game for it, I'll show you."

"I've seen dead men—one of them was my husband. You were there."

"Sorry," he murmured. He pointed to frozen blood on the man's chest. "The wound is small, like a stiletto's."

One of the two servants spoke up. "Sir, an ice pick is missing. We'll search the pond."

"That must have been the murder weapon," observed Prescott. "The killer apparently came here unarmed without intending to kill Wilson."

"Did he die instantly?" asked Pamela. "Or was he placed still alive in the ice and froze to death?"

"I don't know," Prescott replied. "I'll call the medical examiner in Pittsfield today. He'll determine the cause and time of death. We'll keep the body in the icehouse."

Pamela examined the pistol. "It hasn't been fired." She handed it to Prescott.

He nodded. "Perhaps Wilson took it from his pocket but was struck before he could fire."

They left the building, locking it behind them. Pamela remarked, "We can't blame Tom Parker."

"True," Prescott agreed. "Any one of our other suspects in Henry Jennings's death might have killed Wilson."

While divers searched for the pick, Pamela and Prescott looked for clues at the edge of the pond. Unfortunately, the ground was trodden too much to yield any useful footprints.

As they walked back toward the cottage, Prescott said, "We must find out what John Jennings was doing last night and then question George and Helen Allen."

When Prescott left to telephone the medical examiner in Pittsfield, Pamela visited Lydia. She was in her apartment by the window reading a book. A tray with the remains of a late breakfast lay on a nearby table.

"Sit down, my dear," she said gently and set the book aside. "By the look on your face, you have something to tell me."

"Mr. Wilson is dead. His body was found in the icehouse near Lily Pond."

Lydia turned pale. "A suicide?"

"No, a murder. The Pittsfield medical examiner will determine the precise cause."

"How can you be sure?"

"Mr. Prescott and I observed a wound to the chest."

"What could possibly be the motive?"

"Wilson hinted that he had observed your husband's death. The killer might have decided to protect himself by eliminating the only witness to his crime. Other explanations are possible."

Lydia was now gasping and appeared about to faint. Pamela brought smelling salts from the medicine cabinet and a glass of water, then fanned her face. She regained a measure of calm and said, "The troubles of the past few days are too much for my heart. I need to rest. Please take away the breakfast tray."

Pamela carried the tray to the basement. Maggie and Patrick O'Boyle should be drinking midmorning tea in the servants' hall. Other servants might have given them useful information.

This morning Maggie and O'Boyle were alone and in an earnest discussion.

"May I join you?" Pamela asked.

"Of course you may," the coachman said in his rich, friendly Irish voice. He pulled out a chair for her. Maggie came with tea and offered sugar and milk.

"Is it true that old Wilson was drowned in the pond?" Maggie asked.

"Not exactly, Maggie," Pamela replied. "He died in the icehouse. We don't know how he came to be there or who killed him."

"We got the word at breakfast," volunteered O'Boyle. "One of the servants claimed to have seen Wilson near the icehouse late last night."

"I'd like to speak to that servant, if I may."

"He's a coach-boy. I'll fetch him."

A few minutes later, O'Boyle returned with a bright-looking, handsome young man, near twenty, and introduced him as Edgar Smith.

Pamela smiled. "Sit down, Edgar, and tell me what you saw." She spoke calmly to put the young man at ease.

He spoke haltingly at first. "It was a little past midnight. I was going for a swim from the pier near the icehouse. I had taken off my clothes when I heard someone approach. I was naked." He averted his gaze from Pamela. "So I hid behind a bush. Mr. Wilson walked by, carrying a small satchel. I recognized him in the light of his lantern. He seemed nervous, looked left and right, and went into the icehouse. A few minutes later, another person also came with a lantern and went inside. He was wearing a long, flowing cloak and a deerstalker hat that shaded his face. I can't tell you for sure whether it was a man or a woman."

"Describe his or her walk."

The young man thought for a moment. "I'd say that he strode like a man, but I've seen a few women do that."

"What did you do then?"

"I picked up my clothes and ran as fast as I could away from the icehouse. When I felt safe, I dressed and went to my room upstairs in the coach barn."

"By the way, did you see John Jennings last night?"

"No, ma'am." But he nervously averted his eyes from her.

Pamela thanked him and sent him back to the barn. Maggie came with a fresh pot of tea. As she filled their cups, she asked Pamela, "Will they now set Tom free? The person who killed Wilson must have earlier killed Henry Jennings."

"The authorities might come to the same conclusion," she replied. "But it's still uncertain until we catch Wilson's killer."

Pamela finished her tea, then hesitated and looked over her shoulder. "Have either of you seen John Jennings lately?"

O'Boyle and Maggie exchanged glances. "No," replied Maggie. "Do you suspect him?"

"But I saw him," interjected O'Boyle. "I was outside the stable in the dark, enjoying the cool, late night air when someone walked by in the direction of the coach barn. He stepped into a beam of light coming from inside, and I saw his face. It was John Jennings. Ordinarily, I'd have said a friendly word. But there was an intense look on his face that stopped my mouth."

"Tell me, is he a particular friend of young Edgar?" asked Pamela.

"I don't know what goes on between them," O'Boyle replied. "As long as Edgar is respectful and does his job, I don't pry into his personal affairs."

"They're friends," said Maggie, and added pointedly, "They often swim together in the pond."

* * *

From the servants' hall Pamela went up to her parlor. Prescott was waiting there. "I've contacted the medical examiner in Pittsfield. He'll be here this afternoon."

Pamela reported on what O'Boyle, Edgar, and Maggie had told her. "I believe that John Jennings spent the night in Edgar's room. If pressed, the young man would give Jennings an alibi. To probe any deeper might cause scandal and especially harm Edgar."

"Nonetheless, we should question Jennings. Let's find him."

He was alone in his room, having tea. His hair was damp. "I've been swimming in Lake Mahkeenac. The water's perfect. I recommend it."

"Another time," Prescott said. "Have you heard of Wilson's death?"

Jennings nodded. "The news is all over Broadmore. Dreadful thing!"

"I have to ask, were you in the icehouse with Wilson last night?"

"No. I was alone in my room."

"But late in the night you were seen outside walking near the coach barn."

Caught in a lie, Jennings flushed. "I'm ashamed that I tried to deceive you. In fact, I was in the coach barn visiting a friend, Edgar Smith."

"All night?"

"Until dawn." He hesitated. "I may as well explain. Early in the evening, Wilson sent a message, attempting to extort money from me in return for his silence and certain incriminating papers. I should meet him in the icehouse. He claimed to have observed me kill my father. I knew he had made up the story, so I refused to go."

"We have his diary written in code," Prescott said sharply.

Jennings's face filled with confusion. Prescott went on. "We should soon learn if it's authentic and trustworthy."

"I'll challenge the diary," Jennings sputtered. "It's a malicious work of fiction."

"That's for a court to decide," said Prescott. "In the meantime, you must remain in Lenox for further questioning." Prescott signaled Pamela that it was time to go.

As they left the room, Pamela glanced over her shoulder. Jennings had a troubled look on his face.

Pamela and Prescott returned to her rooms and discussed what they had heard from John Jennings. There was a knock on the door. Pamela opened it and an anxious Brenda Reilly slipped inside. Pamela had asked her friend to spy on John Jennings and, in particular, to search through his trash.

She acknowledged Prescott with a nod and said breathlessly, "Early this morning, I cleaned young Jennings's apartment and found something to show you." She handed Pamela an envelope. "He left in a hurry to go swimming. These papers were in his trash basket. I recognized your name and took the liberty to read on. What I found has troubled me."

Pamela sifted through the papers and passed them to Prescott. They were copies of John's notes to his stepmother and notes he had received from her. Two days ago, Jennings had written to Lydia: "Shouldn't you send Mrs. Thompson away? She's bent on saving the tramp, Tom Parker, and blaming me for my father's death."

Lydia had replied, "Calm down. I want to keep her. She has been helpful to me, and I'm fond of her. In any case, with her as my companion, I can reason with her that you are innocent. To send her away now would suggest that I have something to hide."

The exchange ended with John writing, "Perhaps you're right—for the time being."

When Pamela finished reading, her hands were trembling. She leaned back into her chair and breathed deeply.

"Are you ill, ma'am?" asked Brenda with concern. "You see how two-faced John Jennings is!"

"Thank you, I'm well, but, yes, I'm disappointed in him. Still, even an innocent man could be upset and lash out if suspected of a serious crime."

CHAPTER 36

A Prime Suspect

11 July

Late in the morning, Pamela and Prescott rode into the village to find out if either George or Helen Allen had Wilson's copy of the Twain book or had alibis for the time of Wilson's murder. The first stop was the Curtis Hotel.

Helen was sitting in the busy lounge by the door, dressed for a coach ride in the country.

Pamela stood to one side while Prescott approached Helen. "Excuse me, ma'am, I'd like to ask a few questions. Could we go to a more private place?"

She appeared surprised and irritated. "If you insist, we could sit in the breakfast room. It's nearly empty at this time."

They found a quiet, secluded corner, and she asked, "What's the matter now?"

Prescott replied evenly, "Wilson was murdered overnight. We found his body early this morning."

Her eyes widened; her hands flew to her lips. "How dreadful! I hadn't heard." For a moment she was silent, withdrawn perhaps in calculation or reflection. Finally, she glanced at

Pamela then at Prescott and asked, "Do you know who killed him? But of course, if you knew, you probably wouldn't be questioning me."

"So tell me what you were doing last night."

"Until ten, I sang a few songs and played cards with a dozen guests at Mr. John Parsons's home. Afterward, I returned to my room and went to bed at eleven. A dull evening, I must admit. Sorry to disappoint you."

"Has your husband lent you a book by Mark Twain?"

"No, he hasn't."

"Would you allow us to inspect your room?"

"Of course not! How rude of you to ask!"

"Would you rather that I speak to the manager?"

She grimaced. "Then come along with me if you must."

It was a spacious, tastefully furnished, and expensive room. Henry Jennings must have paid for it. Helen stood by the door while Prescott and Pamela opened drawers and looked under the sofas and the bed.

Helen shook her head. "If you want my opinion, you look ridiculous." Her voice was laden with acid. "Perhaps I should help you." She looked under a small pot of flowers.

Prescott ignored her taunts until finally he whispered to Pamela, "The Twain book isn't here—nor any evidence of either Jennings's or Wilson's murder." He motioned Helen to a chair and sat facing her.

"Madam, I understand that you and your husband live separately, but still see each other from time to time. Can you tell me what he was doing last night?"

"Yes," she replied. "He was playing poker at an acquaintance's house. He does that often. I don't know when he finished. This morning, we happened to meet on Walker Street after breakfast. He was on his way to a tennis match at the Lenox Club."

Prescott and Pamela seized this opportunity to search George's house while he was away. Since it belonged to the hotel, the manager could allow the search. Inside, it was as messy as George's quarters in New York. Nonetheless they soon found the deer-stalker hat and the cloak that Edgar had described, as well as the Twain book. In the fireplace were the charred remains of a shirt. "Most likely bloodstained," remarked Prescott.

"Here's a locked drawer," observed Pamela at a desk. "Should we take a look?"

"I'll try to pick the lock," replied Prescott. "I must ask Harry Miller to teach you how to do it."

In a few minutes the drawer yielded its secret: an artist's sketchbook. Among its recent entries were detailed floor plans of a large building with cryptic notes in the margins and the date 11/12 July.

"That's Ventfort Hall!" exclaimed Pamela. "The Morgans are gone for a few days with their personal servants. The rest of the household is much reduced. Would a jewelry thief like George Allen be interested?"

"That's an opportunity he couldn't resist."

Within an hour they found a kit for picking locks, a crowbar for prying open windows, and a saw for cutting through iron bars, as well as a mask, gloves, and dark clothing.

Prescott remarked, "Let's hear what George has to say."

They set out for the tennis court, accompanied by a consta-ble from the city jail.

George was in the middle of a match when they arrived. They waited in the shade of a great elm tree and watched George effortlessly outplay his opponent. When the match ended, the two men changed sides and prepared to start another.

Prescott approached the court and confronted George. "I need to speak to you."

"Can't it wait?"

"Wilson was killed last night. Where were you?" Pamela and the constable remained a few steps away.

George wiped beads of sweat from his brow, stared at the ground, and nervously twirled his racquet. "That's none of your business." He turned to leave.

"Stay, George. You're strongly suspected of killing Bernard Wilson. His body was found this morning."

George glared at Prescott. "Why on earth would I kill him? I hardly knew him."

"But he knew you very well. On Jennings's orders, Wilson followed your tracks around New York City, gathering evidence of marital infidelity that Jennings could use against you in divorce proceedings. In the course of his investigation, Wilson also discovered that you stole jewelry as a profitable pastime. He most likely tried to extort a share of your ill-gotten money. In sum, you had strong motives to kill him."

"That's just talk. You haven't any proof. I'm a rather clever lawyer. I'll destroy you in a court of law."

"Skip the bravado. Wilson's Twain book was hidden in your house. Your hat and cloak were seen on a man entering the icehouse shortly after Wilson. I also found evidence that you are planning to rob Ventfort."

George sputtered, "Your so-called evidence was mischievously planted in my house. I was home in bed last night. I don't need an alibi."

"Be sensible, George. You need a better defense than that. We know that Wilson was armed. You killed him with an ice pick that was at hand. What happened in the icehouse?"

Allen was silent for a long moment, chewing on his lower lip, eyes lowered. "Right, I'll plead self-defense. Wilson tried to extort money from me. Showed me a satchel. Claimed it was full of evidence that I was a jewel thief. That's false, of course, but the accusation could damage my reputation. He demanded five thousand dollars. On an impulse I tried to grab the satchel. He pulled a pistol from his pocket, cocked it and aimed at me. In the second before he could fire, I stabbed him with the pick. He fell dead. I dragged him into the ice pit and threw the pistol after him. From the satchel I took out a brown paper-covered book that I thought was his diary. I tossed the satchel in the pond. The water would destroy the papers inside. Then I hurried home. As you've seen, the book was merely a novel by Mark Twain. Wilson was intending to cheat me."

"Probably not," Pamela interjected. "He thought that book was his diary. Unbeknown to him, someone had switched them."

Baffled, George stammered, "I didn't know."

Prescott signaled the waiting constable to approach with handcuffs. "George, the officer will put you in the town jail for now. We'll turn our evidence over to the district attorney. He'll decide what to do with you."

As George was led away, Pamela remarked, "Perhaps now he'll be punished for trying to run me over."

"I dearly hope so," Prescott said. "He has richly earned it."

Late in the afternoon, Prescott and Pamela went to the servants' hall for tea, invited by Brewer, the temporary steward, who cryptically promised useful information. With a preoccupied expression on his face, he presided over the table, placing Prescott on his left. Pamela sat between Edgar and O'Boyle.

As the tea was being poured, Brewer leaned toward Prescott and whispered, "I've a message for you from the dead. Come to the office after the tea. Bring Mrs. Thompson."

Afterward, they followed Brewer in silence to the office. He shut the door, opened a safe, and drew out a sealed envelope. "Yesterday morning, Mr. Wilson secretly met me here and said you should have this if he were to die." Brewer's hand trembled as he gave the envelope to Prescott.

Prescott and Pamela hastened upstairs to the library and read the contents together. Wilson wrote that he had hidden file boxes in his basement rooms in the Jennings's New York mansion. He gave instructions how to find them and concluded, "Sir, I hope the evidence I've gathered will help bring George Allen and Henry Jennings to justice."

Wilson's envelope also enclosed a brief message for Maggie Rice:

> "When you came to Broadmore looking for a job, I recognized you almost immediately. You were that young lady who accosted me outside the social hall on that Christmas Eve in Calumet. I feared that you were seeking revenge, but I hired you anyway. It seemed safer to have you nearby and in the open rather than lurking in the dark behind my back. For a short while, I thought of killing Henry Jennings and shifting the blame onto you. But I gave up that idea—too risky—and decided instead to expose and ruin him. I knew and respected your parents and have regretted my part in their death. I'm sorry that I've lacked the courage to apologize to you personally and don't expect you to forgive me."

A deep silence followed the reading. "Shall I bring that message to Maggie?" Pamela asked.

"Do it now," Prescott replied. "Tomorrow, we must travel to New York, join Miller at the Jennings mansion, and look for Wilson's secret archive."

CHAPTER 37

Justice Done

Pittsfield, 11 July

That evening, Maggie sat in the train to Pittsfield with a basket of goods for Tom Parker. A riot of conflicting thoughts troubled her mind. Pamela had just shown her Wilson's posthumous message. It was unsettling to realize that he had known who she was, yet hadn't dismissed her. Part of her still hated the man—and for good reason. Nonetheless she believed his apology was sincere. Perhaps he was atoning for the wrong he had done.

Pamela had sent her on this trip, suggesting that Tom might need encouragement. "Take him fresh clothes," she had said, "and some of his favorite foods." She had given her a companion, the simple maid Agnes Jones, and money for expenses.

Out of the blue, Agnes asked Maggie, "Is Mr. Parker your friend?"

Taken by surprise, Maggie hesitated. She cared for him. Did he really care for her? She wasn't sure. Still, she replied, "I would say so, Agnes."

As the train rumbled through the Berkshire countryside, Maggie thought fondly of Tom and their Christmas Eve supper at Ahern's restaurant in Chicago, four and a half years ago. His kindness and consideration had lifted her out of the depression caused by her parents' tragic deaths. She had probably loved him at that point. Nonetheless, she had left him to bring Henry Jennings to justice in Lenox.

Since then, her affection for Tom had lain dormant. But a month ago it had revived when he had appeared as a tramp at Broadmore Hall. She had welcomed the opportunity to return his kindness and had fed him. Since then she had watched with helpless concern as he became entangled in the investigation of Jennings's murder. Had he done it? She didn't think so, but she wasn't quite sure.

At the Pittsfield jail, she presented Mr. Prescott's letter of introduction and requested a visit with the prisoner. Agnes waited in a parlor. Maggie followed an officer through barred doors into a small room. He examined her basket while a matron searched her clothes. The matron led her to a visitor's room. Tom came shortly, and they sat facing each other at a table. Maggie was pleased to see that he wasn't in irons, but he looked glum.

She put the basket on the table. "This might pick you up," she said hopefully.

He threw a quick, incurious glance at the gifts. "I should have taken my chances on the open road instead of coming here."

"How are they treating you?" His indifference hurt, but she tried to show compassion.

"I have my own cozy little cell. The roof doesn't leak on me. The food's not as good as I get from Broadmore's kitchen, but it's tolerable. Last night's supper was bread and boiled cabbage. The guards treat me fairly enough, like I'm not a criminal but neither am I a free man."

"It sounds like you're better off here than in a New York prison. What bothers you most?"

"That I'm destined to spend the rest of my life in prison. I feel helpless, like a man caught in quicksand. The more I struggle, the deeper I sink."

"Mrs. Thompson and Mr. Prescott are working hard on your behalf. They think they'll soon find old Jennings's killer, and then you'll be freed."

He shook his head. "The people in power want to prove to the public that tramps like me will be dealt with firmly. They are already convinced that they have the guilty man."

Defeated by his self-pity, Maggie was now at a loss for words. Her eyes filled with tears. She dabbed them away with a kerchief

Tom stared at her, perplexed. Then a light of understanding slowly dawned in his eyes. He said softly, "I'm sorry, Maggie. Forgive me. I've thought only of myself and ignored your kindness toward me." He gestured toward the basket. "I'm deeply grateful and encouraged."

He reached across the table and took her hand. "I feel fortunate to have you for a friend. From now on, I'll try to think of others and look at life from the bright side."

She patted his hand. "There's actually ground for hope. It sounds crass to mention this . . . but Mr. Wilson was found dead in the icehouse this morning."

"Murdered?" Tom asked, his eyes widening with astonishment.

She nodded. "The person who killed Henry Jennings might also have killed him."

"Well, it couldn't have been me. So who did it?"

"Mrs. Thompson told me that Mr. George Allen killed Wilson, but she doesn't know if he also killed Mr. Jennings."

They lapsed into a congenial silence. Tom inspected clothes from the basket, smiling his newfound gratitude. Maggie offered him a cheese sandwich.

As he ate, he gazed thoughtfully at her, then asked, "Do you realize, Maggie, that the two men most responsible for your parents' deaths have themselves died violently this week?"

She nodded. "In some strange way, justice was done. I should rejoice. Still the scene on that Christmas Eve comes back to haunt me. I feel so sad for my parents. What a dreadful way to die." She again dabbed tears from her eyes, then clasped his hand. "Tom, I feel so fortunate to have you share the burden of that memory. Help me overcome it."

He gently squeezed her hand. "I'll try. We'll help each other."

CHAPTER 38

Truth Emerges

New York, 12 July

With bells clanging and the engine puffing, the early morning train for New York pulled out of the Lenox station. Pamela and Prescott sat side by side in the parlor car. She studied him out of the corner of her eye. He had become unusually silent and unsmiling.

At the station he had bought a New York newspaper, *The Evening Telegraph*, and had begun to read it. Suddenly, he stiffened, softly swore an oath, and slapped the paper. Pamela was startled. He glanced at her. "Sorry I disturbed you. I suppose I should share this." He handed her the paper, opened to the society news.

> "According to recent rumors, Mr. Jeremiah
> Prescott, the noted criminal lawyer and man about
> town, is enjoying the company of Mrs. Pamela
> Thompson at his summer cabin in the Berkshires.
> Readers will recall her husband's suicide last year
> under a cloud of embezzlement. Prescott

successfully defended her from the accusation that
she was an accomplice in her husband's crime."

"The malice in this piece betrays my wife, Gloria. I sincerely
regret any distress it causes you." His words seemed heartfelt.

"Don't fret," she said, though the nasty innuendo stung.
"Reasonable people will recognize her spite and suspend judgment. You've always treated me fairly and with respect. That's
all that matters."

The train rattled on. A nagging anxiety troubled Pamela.
Was she fooling herself? She and Prescott seemed to be growing
closer. How would that end? For the rest of the journey she
wrestled fruitlessly with the question. Finally, she glanced out
the window. "We're approaching New York. There will be
much to do."

They arrived at Grand Central Station about noon and took
a cab to Jennings's mansion. Harry Miller was inside and
opened for them. In the entrance hall, the giant, stuffed brown
bear stood tall defending his lair. The heads of elk, bison, and
other hunting trophies still stared down from the walls, their
eyes rigid and glassy, unaware of their master's fate. Miller led
Pamela and Prescott through darkened rooms. Thick maroon
drapes were drawn over the windows. Linen sheets covered
chairs and tables. The city's noise was no more than a distant
rumble.

Jennings's office was in the back of the house. French doors
opened onto a neglected formal garden. A huge bearskin, the
head intact and flashing its fearsome teeth, lay spread out on
the floor. A long row of locked filing cabinets stood behind a
large brown mahogany desk. A giant map of Michigan's Upper
Peninsula, framed in copper, hung on the wall.

His main business office was downtown. The state's attorney would soon investigate its files. The mansion's private office was the more likely place to find personally sensitive or compromising documents. Prescott had had his agent search particularly for information concerning the tragic incident in Calumet six years ago. It should support Wilson's version.

As they sat around the desk, Harry laid out long memos that the Copper King had written to himself late at night. They revealed Jennings's conviction that he was indeed a captain of industry and at war with the labor movement. In his view, human progress depended on leadership from a superior class of men like himself, lions, kings of the jungle, visionary and ruthless. Without these natural masters, the workers were a headless monster, ignorant and primitive. With neither compunction nor regret, Jennings admitted having ordered Wilson to provoke the panic in Calumet that killed seventy people: workers and their families.

Harry next led them to Wilson's apartment in the basement. It was a rambling complex of rooms with a private exit. One sparsely furnished room served as a study. Its only luxury was a wall of books, mostly novels and biographies. With Wilson's instructions in hand, Prescott approached a bookcase built into a wall, removed a volume of General Grant's memoirs, and pressed a hidden lever. The case slid backward, exposing a small office. File boxes stood neatly in a row. Harry lifted a box labeled CALUMET FIRE onto a table, and they scanned Wilson's detailed, candid summary of the incident.

Prescott remarked, "We now have enough written evidence to force Michigan's authorities to open a new investigation into Henry Jennings's role. An official condemnation might deter other business leaders from following his example."

"And," Pamela added, "to the same end, we should share the

facts we've discovered with progressive journalists. They could write a powerful, dramatic story of this conflict."

Then Prescott moved on to a box labeled COPPER MOUNTAIN. After an hour's search, he waved a hand over the box and remarked, "This should convict Henry Jennings of monumental fraud in the sale of bogus shares to Jack Thompson and other investors."

He met Pamela's eye. "If you sued Jennings's estate, you could recover a sizeable sum, even after the lawyers have taken their share."

Pamela grimaced. "Jack's death has tainted that money. If any of it reaches me, I'll give it to a settlement house."

The next box of interest was called JEWELRY. Wilson had gathered evidence of several thefts involving George Allen, including the ring at the University Athletic Club. Sarah Evans had passed it on to George to sell to a fence.

"How had Wilson found so much detailed information?" asked Pamela.

Harry Miller replied, "Sarah Evans gave it to him—she had to. He had discovered a Chicago warrant for her arrest under her true name, Susan Eagan. He threatened to betray her to the NYPD unless she kept him informed of her thievery and gave him a cut of the profits."

"What will you do with this file?" Pamela asked Prescott.

"I'll bring it to Inspector Williams's attention. He'll probably recover much of the stolen property and arrest Eagan/Evans, George Allen, and their accomplices."

Pamela and Harry frowned in unison.

Prescott waved a dismissive hand. "It's really Williams's business. True, we can't expect him to be grateful. Still we might win a favor from him."

They left Jennings's mansion, and Harry returned to his office. Prescott then asked Pamela, "Could we have supper together this evening? It would also be a pleasant diversion from our nearly constant diet of crime."

"I'm intrigued," she replied. "What do you have in mind?" Pamela asked herself again, would dining and dancing with Prescott endanger her reputation? No, she argued. The question of her reputation seemed moot. She was the mature widow of a failed, disgraced businessman, a suicide. Her name was also associated with a boardinghouse in one of New York's worst slums. Finally, she now worked as a private detective in the pay of the notorious Prescott.

Any "reputation" she might have had in high society had long since evaporated. She now was far more concerned with keeping her self-respect—she must not be cheated, tricked, or betrayed. And she would do something useful with her life.

He replied hopefully, "I propose a modest Austrian music hall near my office. The food is excellent, the ambience is charming, and a violinist plays waltzes and selections from Viennese operettas. You might meet some of my friends there."

"That sounds enjoyable. I'll accept your invitation on the condition that I pay my own way."

For a moment he gazed at her with a bemused expression. "I accept your condition, though I might have to raise your salary in view of the outstanding work you've done at Broadmore."

True to Prescott's word, the Volksgarten Café was charming and friendly. They took a table in a mezzanine overlooking the dance floor. Several couples were moving to the violinist's "Blue Danube." One of the women, a young dark-haired beauty, was especially graceful. As the music ended, she glanced up at Prescott and winked. He gave her a nod and a smile. Turning to Pamela, he remarked, unembarrassed, "A winsome acquaintance, sharp as a tack. She dances like a professional, as you've just seen."

Pamela felt a stab of resentment mixed with envy. But she concluded that Prescott was simply being himself, a sophisticated gentleman, and wasn't trying to make her jealous. "You have good taste in women," she remarked with as much poise as she could muster.

He gazed at her. His eyes were friendly, even admiring. "Thank you. I admire female beauty when goodness and wit enhance it."

A waiter arrived, and Prescott ordered breaded veal cutlets and an Austrian white wine.

"A small portion of the veal for me," Pamela added, then turned to Prescott. "How did you acquire this taste for things Austrian?"

"In 1865, I traveled to Europe to get the bitter sights and sounds of war out of my head. I had a notion that Austrians loved sunny, melodic music like Mozart's operas and Schubert's symphonies. That should heal my troubled spirit, I thought. And I knew enough German. So I spent several enjoyable months, mostly in Vienna, and discovered the waltz."

Pamela glanced with anticipation at the men and women on the dance floor. The waiter returned with the meal. The veal was delicately breaded and tender. The wine was light and fruity. Conversation focused on food and drink. At a break in the meal, Pamela asked Prescott if he had gone back to Austria.

"Yes, many years later, when I became a private investigator, this time to Graz."

"Why Graz?"

"For criminology! The lectures of Professor Hans Gross introduced me to a scientific approach to investigating crime, my present passion. Eventually my German grew proficient enough that I could compress the essentials of his work into the readable handbook you're using. Professor Gross tells us to gather evidence systematically, then look into the criminal's mind and discover the patterns of thought that govern his actions. Unwittingly, the criminal leaves his signature at the scene of the crime."

"That sounds too easy. How can we recognize the signature?"

"By systematic recording of careful, detailed observations, followed by skillful application of psychology."

Pamela still was confused. "Haven't detectives always done that?"

"The best ones, surely, in many cases. The key difference that Gross brings to investigation is a system that could be taught even to the Lenox detective. Take Jennings's murder for a simplified example. In his study the pillow was missing. Why? If the tramp used it, he would have left it behind in the study since he couldn't use or sell it. So why did it disappear? If the killer were an enraged male servant or relative, he would have finished off Jennings with another blow from the mace. So the killer was probably a woman familiar with the victim, either Lydia, Maggie, or Helen."

"I see your point," Pamela granted, "but I could imagine a sly, calculating man, like Wilson, using the pillow to kill Jennings and hiding it to throw suspicion on one of the women. Still, I'll read your handbook with even greater appreciation." She folded her napkin. "Now, shall we dance?"

"With pleasure." He took her hand and led her to the dance floor. The violinist struck up another Strauss waltz, and they began to dance, tentatively at first. Then it went well. She hadn't forgotten the steps, and he was light on his feet. After an hour of dancing, she felt pleasantly tired and suggested that they leave. He walked her the short distance to her former rooms on East Fourteenth Street that she had reserved from Lenox. At the entrance, she thanked him for a delightful evening. He bowed, kissed her hand, and watched until she was safely inside. Then he strolled away with a jaunty air in the direction of his office.

In her bedroom Pamela gazed at herself in the mirror. Habitual lines of worry on her forehead had disappeared. She couldn't recall the last time she had enjoyed such agreeable company.

CHAPTER 39

A Tragic Reckoning

Lenox, 13–14 July; August

The next day in the afternoon, Prescott, Pamela, and Miller arrived in Lenox, encouraged by the revelations in Wilson's files and eager to confirm or put them to rest. At the post office Wilson's diary was waiting, having been deciphered by an expert. Retiring to Prescott's cabin, they studied its story of Henry Jennings's murder.

"The diary strongly implicates John Jennings," Prescott concluded. "Wilson claims to have seen him in his father's study at midnight, trying to persuade his father to give up his plans to divorce Lydia and write a new will. Jennings refused, called his son a sneaky sodomite, ordered him out of the room, and contemptuously turned away. Enraged, John hit him from behind with the mace. In haste he felt for his father's pulse. Apparently believing Henry was dead, John fled from the room. That's as far as the narrative goes."

Miller remarked, "Wilson might never have found out that someone later suffocated Jennings."

"Why didn't he go downstairs to the study to check if Henry might still be alive?" asked Pamela.

Prescott replied, "Perhaps he feared being noticed and then blamed for the crime."

"True," Pamela countered, "But on the other hand, he could have smothered old Jennings but simply didn't put it in his diary."

"That's entirely possible," Prescott granted. "Wilson could also have confronted Jennings in the study, struck him with the mace, and then have written a story in his diary that laid the blame on John Jennings."

"Unfortunately, the diary isn't as helpful as we had hoped." Pamela sighed. "From this speculation we can't accuse anyone of the murder. We need more evidence."

After supper, as Pamela approached Lydia's door, she could hear piano music. When she knocked, it stopped, and Lydia welcomed her in. "What did you do in New York?" she asked, her voice eager with curiosity.

"We searched Wilson's files. He recorded having seen John kill his father."

While Pamela spoke, Lydia grew pale and seemed to withdraw into herself. She shook her head. "I can't believe that John would kill his father. Wilson made up the story to extract money from John. Either Wilson himself or George Allen or the tramp must have done it."

"I suppose that's possible." Pamela didn't pursue the issue any further and excused herself as tired from the journey.

That evening, she resumed the hunt for the diamond lapel pin and the bloodstained clothing and pillow. Neither the maid in charge of Broadmore's laundry nor those who cleaned the building had seen any bloodstained items since Henry Jennings's murder. The rooms of other suspects had already been searched. Pamela's next step was to search the rooms of John and Lydia Jennings. The court in Pittsfield had given her and Prescott search warrants.

John was away for the evening. Pamela got his key from the housekeeper, who asked no questions. She knew that Pamela was one of Prescott's agents investigating Jennings's death. Though the apartment was vacant, Pamela still had to take care, since it was next door to Lydia's. Lydia would likely raise an alarm if she heard any suspicious noises.

It was nightfall now. Pamela had to pull the drapes in order to light a candle. She feared that someone would notice. After an hour, she gave up the search. Neither the bloodstained items nor the lapel pin were to be found in the closets or drawers or other likely places. He could have hidden them in the woods or disposed of them somehow in the village.

The next day, Pamela nervously watched Lydia's apartment for an opportunity to search it. At midmorning Lydia went to the garden with a book. Pamela again got a key from the housekeeper and sneaked into the apartment, feeling like a false friend.

The most likely hiding place was the walk-in safe hidden behind the full-length mirror in Lydia's bedroom. Pamela had devised a plan for getting inside. Lydia had recently installed a modern combination lock on the safe's door and kept the combination a deep secret. Anticipating this obstacle, Pamela had called Harry Miller from Prescott's cabin and placed him in her own parlor. "A cousin, in Lenox for the day," she told Lydia. Now she fetched him.

He arrived with a sack of tools, pulled the mirror aside, and studied the safe's door. "It's as thick as Tiffany's. The lock may be new but it's mediocre. Still I'll need at least ten minutes to open it. Do we have the time?"

"I think so," Pamela replied. "Mrs. Jennings will enjoy the garden for a while."

Miller set to work. As he leaned closely toward the lock, listening to its movements, his concentration grew intense. After nearly ten minutes, he announced, "It's ready now." With a creaking sound, he pulled the door open and turned on an electric light. They walked into a room with barely enough space for two adults. An empty counter faced the door. Locked metal boxes of various sizes rested on shelves on the sidewalls.

"This is fireproofed and organized like a bank vault," he said, glancing at the boxes. "What does she usually keep here?"

"Cash, jewelry, and financial records. Let's try opening the largest box."

Miller attacked it with a pair of tools from his sack. In a minute he announced, "Here's what you're looking for." Pamela peered over his shoulder at a pillow, a lady's gown, and a small jewelry box.

Brown smears and spots discolored the pillow. The same was true of the gown. Pamela opened the jewelry box and lifted out Jennings's diamond-studded lapel pin.

For several moments, Pamela gazed silently at this trove of evidence of a heinous crime. Then, suddenly, a great sadness came over her, and she began to weep. "I didn't want to find these things. Lydia Jennings has been good to me."

Harry gazed at her, the cynicism gone from his eyes. "It can't be helped, ma'am. You did what you had to. Under pressure, even good people like Mrs. Jennings do bad things."

At that moment the door to the bedroom opened. Lydia walked in and stared at the open safe, eyes wide with horror. "Oh no," she murmured, and collapsed on the floor.

Pamela and Miller carried Lydia to her bed, and he went to fetch Prescott. They returned shortly. Prescott directed Pamela to question Lydia. Miller would take down the interrogation in shorthand. In a few minutes, smelling salts revived Lydia. She sat up on her bed, eyes darting fearfully from one visitor to the other.

Pamela began gently with measured words. "Your husband's autopsy revealed that he was smothered to death by a pillow from his office. We've just now found that pillow in your safe, bloodstained. We've also found your bloodstained gown and the missing lapel pin. What's your explanation?"

Lydia remained silent for a moment, her eyes cast down, her lips pressed tightly together. Then she spoke softly. "Since Henry's death, I've dreaded the moment when I'd be forced to confess. But here it is." Her voice trailed off, as if she couldn't muster the will to continue.

Finally she said, "I'll start from the beginning. It was late that night. I was alone reading in my study. Suddenly John burst in. 'I think I killed Father,' he cried. He was in a terribly distracted frame of mind. He had quarreled with his father in the study and assaulted him and had fled immediately to me. I told him to stay in his apartment. I would go to the study and see what could be done. I found Henry barely breathing and unconscious. If he recovered, he would accuse John of attempted murder and put him in prison. And he would also go forward even more forcefully with his plan to divorce me and cut off all support for Broadmore."

"Was that sufficient reason to kill Henry, or anyone else for that matter?" Pamela asked.

"I wasn't thinking clearly. Given an opportunity to save the estate and my stepson, I took the pillow from Henry's chair and smothered him."

"Was that difficult to do?"

"Under ordinary circumstances, I could never have done it. At the time, it seemed right. I had no qualms. My sole concern was how to deflect suspicion from John. So, I took Henry's lapel pin, hoping to make the incident look like a robbery and thus turn suspicion toward a tramp like Tom Parker. At that moment I studied my hands—they were bloody from lifting Henry's head. Blood had also stained the pillow and my dress. In a panic I ran back to my apartment, hid the pillow, the garment, and the lapel pin. The hallway was dark and empty. I was sure no one had seen me."

Harry Miller asked, "Did you tell John what you had done? Or did you leave him thinking that he had killed his father?"

"I was torn, but I simply told John that his father was dead. That's what he had assumed, so he didn't question me."

"Was that fair or wise?" Pamela asked, disappointed in Lydia's breach of integrity.

Lydia blinked at the question. "In hindsight, I suppose it wasn't. I'm fond of John, but he's not entirely reliable. At the time, I didn't trust him to act with my interest in mind. So I withheld that part of the truth. Moreover, it seemed unlikely that he would be charged at all. There were other stronger suspects, especially the tramp, or perhaps the disgraced steward, Wilson, or the discarded mistress, Helen Allen."

"I appreciate your candor, madam," Prescott said to Lydia. "Mr. Miller will now transcribe his copy for you to sign."

Miller went to Pamela's room to work at her desk. Prescott pulled Pamela aside and nodded toward Lydia. "Watch her closely. She might try to kill herself before she's obliged to sign the confession."

Pamela looked doubtful.

Prescott added, "She would thus somehow aid John. Without the signature he could claim that the confession was fraudulent. I want to confront him with an authentic confession. If you need help, I'll be across the hall with Harry, checking her statement."

"I understand," said Pamela, and began to think of various poisons and sharp objects that must be kept away from Lydia.

Pamela took a seat near Lydia and tried to engage her in conversation about a book she was reading—something by Henry James, chief among her favorite authors. A few minutes passed in a desultory exchange while Lydia grew increasingly restless.

Her eyes darted nervously from window to door and around the room.

"Excuse me," she said. "I need to go to the bathroom." She rose from the bed.

"I'm sorry," Pamela said, putting as much sympathy in her voice as she could. "But I must go with you." She genuinely regretted what Lydia must regard as a humiliation.

"Really!" exclaimed Lydia. "How unfeeling of you."

Pamela held her ground. "I have no choice. I fear that you may harm yourself."

Lydia sniffed, thrust out her chin, and shuffled to the bathroom, Pamela following close behind. Lydia opened the door, then suddenly leaped forward and tried to shut it behind her. Pamela had anticipated that trick and shoved a foot into the opening. She threw her weight against the door to force it open, while Lydia pushed back to close it. Abruptly, Lydia released her pressure. The door swung suddenly inward, causing Pamela to stumble and nearly fall to the floor. Meanwhile Lydia dashed toward a pair of long, sharp scissors lying on a counter. As Pamela recovered her balance, Lydia raised the weapon and faced Pamela, as if about to strike her and then herself.

Pamela lunged forward and seized Lydia's upraised right arm. Lydia was a frail woman, but now—eyes wide and bright, teeth bared—she had the strength of a fury. The two women grappled, Lydia driving Pamela back against the counter and thrusting the scissors perilously close to Pamela's eyes.

Desperately, Pamela seized Lydia's right thumb, pressed against it, and forced the scissors from her hand. They fell clattering on the tile floor. Pamela then pinioned Lydia's right arm behind her back and pushed her into the bedroom. A few moments later, Prescott and Miller entered the room, mouths agape at the scene.

"Seize her!" Pamela cried out.

Miller drew handcuffs and fastened Lydia's arms behind her

back. By this time, her strength was utterly exhausted. She stared at the floor, softly sobbing. Finally, she looked up at Pamela. "I'm sorry, deeply sorry. I acted like a crazed woman in there." She glanced toward the bathroom. "Can you forgive me?" She didn't wait for a response, but lowered her gaze again to the floor.

Prescott followed Pamela to her parlor while Miller remained in the bedroom, guarding Lydia. He soon joined the other two. "Mrs. Jennings was having difficulty breathing. I gave her laudanum and called a doctor. The servants are caring for her."

He sat with Pamela and Prescott at a table, and she offered them brandy.

"What happened?" Prescott asked, casting a glance toward Lydia's apartment.

"As you feared," Pamela replied, "Lydia tried to kill herself—and me as well." She went on to describe the struggle in the bathroom.

Prescott blanched; Miller stared in disbelief.

She smiled sadly. "It was one of the worst moments of my life. I saved Lydia for the humiliation of a trial, conviction, and prison. For her that's a fate worse than death."

The two men nodded thoughtfully. Prescott remarked, "Nonetheless, you did the right thing. Otherwise, Tom Parker and others would still live under suspicion of murder. I'm proud of you! Lydia's fate now lies in the hands of a competent, fair-minded court."

A month later, Pamela was dressing herself for dinner with Prescott at the Volksgarten Café. He would arrive in an hour. That afternoon in the office he had told her of the death of Lydia Jennings. She had never signed her confession. Her heart had given out before she could be brought to trial. Unless a distant heir prevailed in a civil suit, Henry Jennings's wealth would go into Lydia's estate. Her will assigned it, together with Broadmore Hall, to various charities. John Jennings received a small trust fund from Lydia's personal account.

The district attorney had released Tom Parker. He and Maggie Rice would work on the estate for the time being.

As Pamela recalled Lydia, her eyes begin to tear. Scenes from Broadmore now raced before her mind's eye—like John Jennings at the piano with Lydia. He was facing trial for the unpremeditated assault on his father. Pamela had visited him in jail; no longer a playboy, he was a much-chastened man.

On the strength of Wilson's evidence, George Allen was arrested for jewelry theft. He also pleaded self-defense in Wilson's death. His wife, Helen, moved out of New York and began divorce proceedings.

Pamela sighed at this panorama of human misery and finished dressing. A letter from Brenda Reilly that had come in the morning mail now lifted her spirits. Brenda and Peter O'Boyle had gone off together to the state agricultural college in Amherst. Her father was securely in prison. The letter was full of excitement and joy at the prospect of higher learning and gratitude for Pamela's support.

The doorbell rang. Prescott had arrived. Pamela glanced in the mirror and pushed back an errant lock of hair. She had returned to New York with him and moved into decent rooms near his office. The work of a private detective appealed to her. Prescott had become her friend. Where that might lead she didn't know. Life was so uncertain. But for now she was content.

Author's Notes

Mark Twain coined the term "The Gilded Age" in his 1873 satirical novel, *The Gilded Age: A Tale of Today*. The application of a thin layer of gold to lead or other base metals is widely taken as an apt metaphor for the unbridled greed and other excesses of the decades following the Civil War. "Robber baron" is an old concept going back to medieval German knights who extorted money from travelers and merchants passing through their lands. In the late nineteenth century it was applied in the United States to rapacious, lawless, so-called captains of industry, like the railroad magnate Cornelius Vanderbilt or the real "Copper King," William A. Clark.

See H. Wayne Morgan, ed., *The Gilded Age: A Reappraisal* (Syracuse, 1963) for a variety of views. Barry Werth, *Banquet at Delmonico's: Great Minds, the Gilded Age, and the Triumph of Evolution in America* (New York, 2009) deals with the penetration of Charles Darwin's ideas of natural selection and survival of the fittest into late nineteenth-century American social thought. They profoundly influenced prominent business leaders, like Andrew Carnegie, as well as the fictitious Henry Jennings.

For a time in the late nineteenth century Michigan's Upper Peninsula produced not only more copper than any other region but also the highest quality. The industry was concentrated in Calumet and its vicinity. The story's Christmas Eve incident of 1887 is based on the Italian Hall Disaster of Christmas Eve, 1913, also in Calumet. Seventy-three persons died. The perpetrator has never been determined. Well-informed opinion leans toward the view that management's agents were responsible. See Steve Lehto, *Death's Door: The Truth Behind Michigan's Largest Mass Murder* (Troy, MI, 2006).

Broadmore Hall is a lightly edited version of Charles and Sarah Lanier's great cottage, Allen Winden, 1881. The main building was destroyed shortly after Charles's death in 1926. See *Houses of the Berkshires, 1870-1930,* by Richard S. Jackson and Cornelia Brooke Gilder (New York, 2006; 2nd edition, 2011), for excellent commentary, floor plans, and superb photographs of Allen Winden as well as thirty-four other "cottages," including the Morgans' Ventfort, 1893. At present, Ventfort is undergoing restoration while it serves appropriately as the Museum of the Gilded Age. See also Carole Owens, *Berkshire Cottages* (Englewood Cliffs, NJ, 1970, 1984) for informed comment on the cottagers' social lives. In the 1890s, their season in the Berkshire Hills extended from May into October. In 1893 Lake Mahkeenac was also known as the Stockbridge Bowl, the name commonly used today.

With the depression of 1893 many tramps drifted into Berkshire cities and towns in desperate pursuit of work. The rich and respectable found them dangerous. For an overview of the phenomenon, consult *Walking to Work: Tramps in America, 1790–1935,* a collection of eight essays edited by Eric H. Monkkonen (Lincoln, NE, 1984). For an analysis of social and economic conditions in the U.S., go to *Democracy in Desperation: the Depression of 1893,* by Douglas Steeples and David O. Whitten (Westport, CT, 1998).

Elaine S. Abelson's book, *When Ladies Go A-Thieving: Middle-Class Shoplifters in the Victorian Department Store* (New York, 1989), presents a social and psychological analysis of shoplifting. For a detailed view of the department store in

1893, see Ralph M. Hower's *History of Macy's of New York 1858–1919* (Cambridge, MA, 1943). Susan Porter Benson's *Counter Cultures: Saleswomen, Managers, and Customers in American Department Stores, 1890–1940* (Chicago, 1986) describes the challenges facing salesgirls.

Frank Morn's *"The Eye That Never Sleeps": A History of the Pinkerton National Detective Agency* (Bloomington, IN, 1982), offers a brief account of Kate Warne (1833–1868), the first female detective. In the late nineteenth century the Austrian magistrate and professor Hans Gross (1847–1915) developed a widely adopted scientific approach to criminal investigation. For "Clubber" Williams and policing in nineteenth-century New York City consult James F. Richardson's *The New York Police: Colonial Times to 1901* (New York, 1970).

Moses King, *King's Handbook of New York City 1893* (Boston, 1893; New York, 1972) and Karl Baedeker, *United States 1893* (New York, 1893, 1971) are detailed, accurate sources of information. For the value of money in 1893, consider the following examples: The price of a high-season night at the Curtis Hotel in Lenox in 1893 was four dollars. A cup of coffee cost ten cents. A domestic maid might earn one hundred dollars in a year. As chief of the New York Detective Bureau, Thomas Byrnes drew an annual salary of two thousand dollars, exclusive of "gifts" from wealthy patrons.